ALSO BY MELANIE GIDEON

Valley of the Moon

Wife 22

The Slippery Year: A Meditation on Happily Ever After

DID I SAY YOU COULD GO

MELANIE GIDEON

SIMON & SCHUSTER
New York   London   Toronto   Sydney   New Delhi

Simon & Schuster
1230 Avenue of the Americas
New York, NY 10020

First Simon & Schuster trade paperback edition August 2021

SIMON & SCHUSTER and colophon are registered trademarks of Simon & Schuster, Inc.

For information about special discounts for bulk purchases, please contact Simon & Schuster Special Sales at 1-866-506-1949 or business@simonandschuster.com.

The Simon & Schuster Speakers Bureau can bring authors to your live event. For more information or to book an event, contact the Simon & Schuster Speakers Bureau at 1-866-248-3049 or visit our website at www.simonspeakers.com.

Interior design by Carly Loman

Manufactured in the United States of America

10 9 8 7 6 5 4 3 2 1

Library of Congress Cataloging-in-Publication Data

Names: Gideon, Melanie, 1963- author.
Title: The invitation / Melanie Gideon.
Description: First Simon & Schuster hardcover edition. | New York : Simon & Schuster, 2021. | Summary: "A suspenseful novel about a friendship ruptured by obsession, secrets, and betrayal, with shocking twists that don't stop until the very end"—Provided by publisher.
Identifiers: LCCN 2020037335 | ISBN 9781982142124 (hardcover) | ISBN 9781982142179 (ebook)
Subjects: GSAFD: Suspense fiction.
Classification: LCC PS3557.I255 I59 2021 | DDC 813/.54—dc23
LC record available at https://lccn.loc.gov/2020037335

ISBN 978-1-9821-4212-4
ISBN 978-1-9821-4217-9 (ebook)

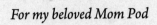

For my beloved Mom Pod

PART ONE

RUTH

Is that her ex? Over there by the apples? In the faded Red Sox baseball cap pulled down low over her eyes?

Ruth Thorne ducks behind a banana display. The last time she saw her BFF was over a year ago at Rite Aid. Ruth had run in to get some dental picks, and there was Gemma waiting in line at the pharmacy. Ruth hid that time, too, in the toothpaste aisle, hoping she'd overhear the pharmacist murmur the name of Gemma's medication. All she discovered was her co-pay was fifteen dollars.

A wave of déjà vu rolls over Ruth. Did she dream this moment into reality? She's thought of nothing but Gemma for the last week and now here she is, practically trembling with anxiety as her hand dips into the pile of Galas, searching for the unbruised gems.

Ruth gets out her phone and refreshes the *San Francisco Chronicle*'s home page. The article is still the number one most-read story and has 998 comments. With Gemma standing only twenty or so feet away from her, she reads it anew, as if through Gemma's eyes. Has she been obsessively refreshing the page for the last week like Ruth?

Study Right, Oakland and Test Prep Center, Involved in Cheating Scandal

Gemma Howard, the owner of Study Right, claims she had no idea that one of her most popular tutors, Julie Winters (Harvard,

BA English, 2017), had a profitable side business taking SAT and ACT tests for nine of her clients.

Gemma rolls her cart down the produce aisle and stops at the nectarines. Ruth knows her favorite variety are the Diamond Brights, but they've come and gone already; she'll have to settle for the Honey Blazes. Gemma tears a plastic bag off the roll and tries to open it, biting her lip in frustration. Finally, she licks her finger, and the edges of the bag separate. Gemma glances up, doing a quick check. *Has she been made?*

Ruth squats, her heart thumping wildly. Quads firing, she continues reading the article.

" 'Julie Winters was a sole operator. A bad actor,' said Howard. 'I was shocked to find out she'd been running this kind of scam.' "

Ruth mouths Gemma's words silently. *I was shocked.* Julie Winters had pled guilty. And even though Gemma had been cleared of all wrongdoing, attendance at her test prep center had declined by nearly 50 percent.

Ruth skims the latest comments.

What a disgusting little cheat. Of course she was in on it.

Lying scum. Burn the place down.

She's got a daughter. Whattya wanna bet her SAT scores are off the chart hahaha.

Bitch. She should be thrown in jail.

Jail? That's taking it a little too far. Still, Ruth can't help the smile that creeps across her face.

Comeuppance. She's always loved that word. Gemma Howard is finally feeling what it's like to be exiled from a community. To be publicly pilloried, just as she'd been, seven years ago, when Gemma and her daughter, Bee, turned their backs on Ruth and her daughter, Marley. Tossed them aside like they were strangers.

Like they hadn't been allied since that long-ago kindergarten meet and greet party that Ruth hosted at her house. Gemma was a widow and Ruth was divorced. They were the only single moms in the class and they'd bonded instantly. Within months, they were like family. They became each other's emergency contacts. They spent Thanksgivings and Christmases together. They were inseparable until the girls were in third grade, and then Ruth hooked up with Mr. Mann on Tinder.

Mr. Mann was irresistible. A Stanford linguistics professor. Erudite and incredibly fit. He told her he did the Bar Method three times a week; she liked his long, lean muscles. They'd slept together twice before Ruth discovered Mr. Mann's true identity: Barry Egan, father of Chance Egan, a boy in Marley's class, very much married with three children, a wealthy contractor with a thesaurus in his back pocket. His opening gambit? *Did she know the etymology of the word* obsequious? No, she had not.

At the same time Ruth had discovered Mr. Mann's identity, his wife, Sal, discovered hers. The news spread like a virus through the Momonymous pods. Momonymous was an anonymous app for mothers. In order to participate, you either had to start a mom pod (taking on the role of moderator) or be invited to join. The pods were similar to sororities, each with its own rituals and vetting processes. Members were rabid about hiding their true identities. The moderator knew who was in the group, but once the members chose a username, she was in the dark, just like everybody else. The anonymity allowed for uninhibited speech. That was the whole point of Momonymous.

In the best of cases, pods shared tips and complimented children, mothers, and teachers. In the worst of cases, the pods were cruel. They gossiped about the mothers who hadn't been invited to join (Ruth!). About the scapegoats, the mean girls, who got their period first. Many of the pods were basically cabals. Cabals that threw Ruth Thorne to the ground and ripped out her throat.

Ruth had begged Gemma to see her side of it. Mr. Mann had lied. He said he was single and did the Bar Method (in retrospect that was a glaring red flag—how had she missed that?). And what about his accountability? He pursued her. Why was she being slut shamed? Why did he get off scot-free?

Gemma didn't abandon them all at once. She and Bee pulled away slowly, which in the end was more painful.

Gemma leaves the produce aisle and disappears around the corner. A minute later, Ruth follows her. She's picked up her pace, trotting past the cereal, the cleaning supplies, the toilet paper, the soda. Ruth has to walk briskly to keep up with her. Finally, Gemma makes an abrupt turn into the wine and liquor aisle and puts four large bottles of Woodbridge sauvignon blanc into her cart.

Ruth refreshes the page again. Nine hundred and ninety-nine comments. One thousand. *Ding! Ding! Ding!* "Buy low" is Ruth's tenet. She sends Gemma a text.

Come to dinner Saturday night. xx

Ruth can hear Gemma's phone chime, even though it's buried in her bag. A clarion call straight from the *Hobbit* soundtrack; she's had the same text alert for years. Gemma doesn't pick up her phone but she startles at the sound of the notification. She hurriedly joins a line, readjusting her baseball hat so it covers her eyes completely.

I bet she wishes she could go back to the Shire, Ruth thinks.

GEMMA

Nearly an hour has passed since Gemma got home and put away the groceries, and her anxiety hasn't diminished, not one little bit. Adrenaline and cortisol continue to flood her nervous system; she's still in fight-or-flight mode. Thank goodness she didn't run into anybody she knew at Safeway. It just wasn't worth the risk, she decides. Next time, she'll use Instacart.

Gemma sits down at the table with her laptop, and just for fun googles "crisis managers" and reels at their exorbitant fees, which she never could afford, especially now that she's lost half her clients.

She'd let Bee call in sick for her shift at the Juicery.

"Mom, I simply cannot," said Bee when the news broke. "I. Can. Not."

Gemma Can. Not. either, but she must. Her mantra? "Cleared of all wrongdoing." She'd written that phrase on Post-it notes and put them all over the house. On the fridge, the bathroom mirror, and the TV. Bee thought they were ridiculous but Gemma didn't care. She needed reminders to keep her sane and prevent her from falling into an abyss of shame—shame that she didn't deserve. She didn't do anything wrong except open her heart to that con artist Julie Winters.

What *was* Gemma guilty of? Of being a bad judge of character. Of thinking the best of people. Of allowing herself to be manipulated and used.

Also, she'd been seduced, as had all the parents who had begged her to assign Julie to their children. Julie with her coveted Ivy

League degree and her sad, made-for-TV story. A foster child, shuttled from home to home. Barely making it in remedial classes. The kind teacher in high school who finally figured out she wasn't getting Cs in school because she was dumb; it was because she wasn't challenged. He helped her to apply to colleges. Paid her application fees. And finally, she got the Holy Grail—Harvard!

She wanted to give back now. That's what she had said, and Gemma had fallen for it.

It was all bunk. Julie came from a wealthy family in Connecticut. Her father was an insurance executive. He bought her way into Harvard, donating a cool two mil, over the table, not under. He knew how the game was played. $500K got you nothing.

Gemma gets her phone out of her bag and is shocked to see a text from Ruth Thorne. An invitation. Come to dinner Saturday night. xx

Now authentic shame, shame that she wholly deserves, engulfs her.

———

Ten years earlier, Ruth Thorne had hosted the Hillside Academy kindergarten meet and greet. When Gemma and Bee arrived at 626 Buttercup Drive there weren't any cars on the street. *Did she get the time wrong?* she wondered. Then a man in a black jacket ran down the stairs and waved at her. A valet.

The house was the most exquisite example of a Craftsman she'd ever seen. Perfectly restored. Intricate stonework, the arches and beams gleamed, newly varnished.

Parents and children milled about on the porch. Most of the girls were intentionally, charmingly mismatched. Striped leggings and polka-dot dresses.

Gemma glanced in the rearview mirror and thought, *Crap.* She'd let Bee choose her outfit. She was wearing her favorite Old Navy tracksuit. Bright red jacket and matching pants along with a pair of beat-up Pumas. Her hair was smashed down in the back.

Gemma had intended to wrangle it into braids, but detangling Bee's thick hair was always such a struggle. She didn't want to fight with her today.

Gemma didn't look much better. A faded denim skirt, an embroidered peasant shirt from her college days, and clogs. *Was it too late to go home and change?*

"Excuse me, ma'am," said the valet, standing at her window.

Gemma got out of the car and handed him the keys.

———

"Come in, come in," a woman cheerfully called out. She strode across the room to greet them.

"I'm the host, Ruth Thorne." She gazed down at Bee. "And who are you?"

"I'm Bee."

"*B-e-a*? Or the letter *B*?"

Bee made a face. "*B-e-e*, like the insect."

"All right, Bee like the insect. Why, aren't you the most adorable thing ever."

Bee shrank back, unsure of what to make of this elegant, impeccably groomed woman. She smelled like caramel.

Ruth wore a sleeveless black dress with espadrilles. Her arms were lightly muscled, like a dancer's. Her hair was daffodil yellow and cascaded in loose waves down her back. *That color can't be real*, thought Gemma.

She looked at Gemma. "And you must be Mommy."

Gemma hated it when adults referred to her as Mommy. "Gemma Howard."

"Ah, Gemma."

Ruth smiled openly at her, and Gemma had the sense she was being gathered up. It wasn't altogether unpleasant.

"You know you look exactly like Ali MacGraw in *Love Story*. It's remarkable. You're literally channeling her."

"Oh, thanks, I guess. It wasn't intentional." Despite thinking Ruth's compliment was disproportionate and not wholly believable, Gemma blushed. Maybe there was a grain of truth in there. She did wear her dark brown hair straight with a middle part. She did have a bit of a hippie preppie vibe.

Gemma scanned the room. The men wore tastefully distressed jeans and untucked button-up shirts—the ubiquitous private school Bay Area Dad look. The women were in sundresses and bejeweled sandals. "I'm afraid I'm a little underdressed. *We're* a little underdressed. We thought it was a picnic."

"Nonsense. You two are a breath of fresh air," said Ruth.

Did she know they were on full scholarship? Had they given themselves away? Gemma could never afford a school like Hillside on her own.

A waiter approached with a tray. "Truffle Lobster Salad on endive spears?"

Gemma and Bee declined. A few seconds later another waiter appeared. "Virgin Ginger Mojitos?"

Valets? Waiters? Lobster? Mojitos? Well, it was one way to introduce yourself to a community. Showing your privilege cards this early—it was a choice. Or maybe it wasn't. Maybe Ruth Thorne didn't know how all this was playing.

Both Gemma and Bee accepted a drink from the waiter.

"Oh, yum," said Gemma.

Bee took a taste, grimaced, and handed her drink to Gemma.

Ruth laughed. "Bee, see that table over there? Pizza puffs. Mac and cheese. Bagel Bites. And see that girl in the corner? That's Marley, my daughter. She's shy. She's not a big talker. Why don't you go over there and introduce yourself? You seem brave for an almost-kindergartener."

"That's because I'm not a baby. I'm almost six," said Bee, sauntering off. Flattery was Bee's Achilles' heel; she accepted it as her due.

There was an awkward pause. Gemma was about to make an excuse about needing to use the bathroom when Ruth said, "It's not an original Craftsman, you know. I had it built from scratch. The exterior is textbook Julia Morgan. The hipped roof, wraparound porch, stonework, overhanging eves. But the inside—well, judge for yourself."

The interior looked like it came straight from the pages of *Dwell* magazine. A mix of carefully curated new and vintage pieces. B&B Italia couches. An arc lamp. A pair of Hans Wegner chairs. All the walls were white. The floors glossy and polished to a golden sheen. Sunlight poured in through the windows. It was the complete opposite of Gemma's house. What she wouldn't give to live in such a clean, curated space.

"I love it," said Gemma.

"*Really?* That makes me so happy. Most people are confused when they come inside, and believe it or not, some of them are actually offended. They act like I've committed an architectural sin," Ruth confesses.

———

Later, everybody gathered together. They made two rings. Children on the inside, parents on the outside. Then they went around the circle, the children introducing themselves and their parents.

Whose stupid idea was this? It looked like every child had two parents but Bee and Marley.

When it was her turn, Bee said, "I'm Bee, like the insect, and this is my mom, Gemma."

"Hi, Bee. Hi, Gemma," everybody yelled. It was like an AA meeting.

"My daddy's dead," said Bee.

The crowd stared at her in a not-unkind silence. Two pink spots bloomed on Bee's cheeks. She pressed her face against Gemma's arm.

"Why isn't anybody saying anything?" she cried in a muffled voice.

"They're just being polite," said Gemma, giving the group an apologetic smile. "Bee's father was amazing. We miss him so much. He's not a taboo subject. You can ask Bee about him. It'd be great if you did. We want to keep his memory alive. His name was Ash."

They continued to go around the circle until they got to Marley, who scurried behind Ruth.

Ruth smiled stiffly, clearly embarrassed at her daughter's refusal to participate. "This is Marley and I'm Ruth."

"Hi, Marley! Hi, Ruth!" the group echoed back.

"No dad, I'm a single mother as well. But happily divorced," said Ruth, winking at Gemma from across the circle.

———

After the circle broke up, a crowd formed around Gemma. Parents were extremely friendly. Overly solicitous. *We are so thrilled to have Bee in the class and we will be calling soon for playdates!* They were well meaning, but it was a little embarrassing.

Gemma spied Ruth alone in the kitchen, drinking a glass of wine and clocking the scene. She nodded enthusiastically and gave Gemma a warm smile, and Gemma couldn't help but feel bad for her. She was a single mother, too, but a wealthy divorcée, therefore nobody had sympathy for her. Gemma was a widow; that put her on the top of the single-mother food chain.

But Ruth didn't do herself any favors with this fancy party.

Gemma skillfully extricated herself from the crowd of parents (one of her gifts, honed in the test prep business) and walked over to Ruth.

"May I join you?" she asked, pointing at her glass.

"I'd be delighted. White or red?"

"White, please."

Ruth poured her a glass and frowned. "The kids are getting antsy." She clapped her hands loudly three times. People stopped talking and gazed at Ruth expectantly.

"Children," she said loudly. "Would you like to watch a movie?" The kids cheered.

"Marley, lead the way to the media room, please. Children, your choices are *WALL-E* or *Beverly Hills Chihuahua*."

Gemma cringed at the phrase *media room*. A few of the mothers rolled their eyes and gave each other knowing looks. Ruth seemed oblivious. *Oh, give her a chance, people,* thought Gemma. She followed Ruth to the media room in solidarity. The children hesitated, not knowing where to sit. Bee led Marley to the couch. Ruth pushed a button, and an enormous TV screen dropped from the ceiling. The children gasped. They oohed and ahhed. A quick vote was taken, results tallied, and *WALL-E* began.

"You're so generous to do all this," said Gemma.

"Mmm. I probably should have organized a potluck. I just wanted to do something nice. Start the class off with a bang. They're going to be together for the next thirteen years after all."

Hillside was one of the few schools in the East Bay that was K-12.

"Well, you did. It's beautiful. And the food was amazing. The wine, too. I'm so appreciative."

Ruth smiled at her and Gemma had the sensation of being bathed in light. The lucky recipient of Ruth Thorne's intense focus. Often, Gemma felt starved for attention. Her days were spent attending to kids and their needy parents, and then when she came home, Bee.

"You're empathetic. I knew you'd be. Sometimes you can tell that immediately about someone. That they have a huge heart," said Ruth.

Gemma felt like an imposter. She didn't have a huge heart, at least not indiscriminately. She had a huge heart for people she loved, people who had earned it, who had put in the time and been loyal, but not strangers. She could, in fact, be very cold.

"I think we're going to be great friends," said Ruth.

Later, when Bee and Gemma were preparing to go, Marley tugged at Gemma's sleeve and whispered, "I have a dad."

———

Now, looking at Ruth's text a decade later, Gemma realizes how much she's missed Ruth and Marley. Their foursome. *How could she have turned her back on them like that?* She remembers Ruth begging her to help smooth things over with the Barry Egan debacle. Gemma was a popular mom and Bee was a popular kid. If anybody could have rehabilitated Ruth's reputation, it was Gemma. Instead she'd slowly iced Ruth out. The truth was she'd used Mr. Mann as an emergency exit door. Gemma had been looking for an excuse to put some distance between them for a while.

The dynamic between their two families had always been somewhat strained. They each had something the other didn't have. Ruth and Marley, outsiders from the first day, were dependent on their friendship with the Howards to give them social capital. And Gemma, she's ashamed to admit, grew dependent on Ruth's generosity.

Gemma had positioned Study Right as the community alternative. She was a proselytizer of equal-access test prep. For every rich parent who paid full freight there was another parent she didn't charge a dime. That meant they lived a good, middle-class life. They didn't have extra but they had enough.

Then Ruth came along. Beneficent, *let me take care of it* Ruth. When she'd needed a new roof, Ruth stepped in to help. When she discovered thousands of tiny wings all over her basement floor, Ruth paid for the termite remediation. There were Christmas vacations in Aspen. VIP tickets to shows and concerts. Gemma grew addicted to a kind of life she'd never have been able to afford on her own.

But as the years went by, Gemma couldn't shake the feeling that she was accruing an increasingly unpayable debt. And when Mr. Mann came along, Gemma was relieved to have a reason to drift away.

And now here she was, the tables turned, a pariah, afraid to go out in public, and who had come to her defense offering friendship, a hearty meal, forgiveness—*Ruth*.

Gemma didn't deserve it. No, she did not.

She texts Ruth. We'd love to!!!

RUTH

"Labor Day is still two weeks away. Is it just me or does it seem like Hillside starts earlier and earlier every year?" asks Gemma. She smiles warmly at the girls. "You guys are going to be freshmen. How did that happen?"

Bee rolls her eyes. "First years, not freshmen, and it happened because three thousand one hundred and twenty-seven days have gone by, give or take a day or two."

"You just calculated that in your head?" asks Ruth, trying not to stare. She hasn't seen Bee in a long time. She smells of patchouli and vanilla. She's filled out, a B cup, Ruth decides. The lace strap of her chartreuse Free People bralette is showing. Marley could never wear a bralette. She's a C cup, moving steadily to a D.

"Are you taking geometry this year?" Marley asks Bee.

"Yeah," says Bee.

"Me too," says Marley.

Gemma's face is flushed from Ruth's favorite Sancerre, Les Belles Vignes from the Loire Valley. Ruth doubts Gemma is tasting the gooseberry, straw, and flint notes. She's drinking for volume, not palate. She's tossed back two glasses already and is on her third; she's nervous.

"You were always so good at math," Ruth lies, wondering how the hell Bee wrangled her way into the advanced class. Bee's smart enough, but her real gift is in the social sphere. People are naturally drawn to her. She oozes charisma, always has.

Ruth glances over at Marley, who is also flushed and also nervous. Her head is cocked to one side like an obedient puppy. *What is the opposite of charismatic? Invisible? That's Marley.* Ruth raises her eyebrows at her daughter, trying to telegraph that she should sit up straight and stop acting so submissive. There's an air of desperation about her. The way she looks at Bee, as if she's honored to be in her presence.

"Did you see the new *Avengers*? Tom Holland—omg," says Bee to Marley.

All this surface talk—it's excruciating. Not addressing Study Right has sapped all the oxygen from the room and has them blabbering on about math classes and superheroes.

Gemma clears her throat. "Okay, this is awkward so let's just talk about it and get it out of the way. I'm sure you're both aware of what's going on with Study Right." Gemma chews on her lower lip. "Well, honestly, it's been—*terrible.*"

Ruth waits. *Is that all she's going to say? Is she going to extrapolate? Explain herself? No, she's fighting back tears.*

Ruth throws her a lifeline. "It's not your fault. You had no idea this was going on."

Gemma's face looks melted, like candle wax just before it hardens. "I didn't. I swear I didn't."

"Of course you didn't. Anybody who knows you knows how honest you are. How much integrity you have."

Ruth lets her statement sit there for a moment. Gemma dabs at her face with her napkin.

Marley looks at her mother with *do something* eyes.

Ruth pushes back her chair and walks around the table. She crouches down at Gemma's feet and gently puts a hand on her leg. "It'll pass, I promise you. A week from now, two weeks tops, nobody will be talking about you. Your clients will come back once this blows over, and if they don't you'll get new ones."

Gemma sniffles. "You're such a good friend. I've missed you so much, you don't know how much. I don't deserve you."

No, you don't, thinks Ruth, but it's time to move forward. "I'll always be here for you. And for you, too," she says to Bee.

"Will you come to my fifteenth birthday party?" Bee asks Marley.

Marley smiles. "I'd love to." And Ruth thinks, *Marley is going to Bee's birthday party!*

"And how about Thanksgiving? Can you guys come over for Thanksgiving?" asks Gemma. "Please say yes. *Puleeze.*"

Thanksgiving, too? Oh, my! The Howards have swung the door wide open.

"What do you think, Marls?" Ruth asks.

"That sounds great."

"Well, okay," says Ruth, rising to her feet. "We've got a date for Thanksgiving. Now, who's up for dessert? Mango Lime Chiffon Cake from Katrina Rozelle?"

"What? *Really?*" says Gemma.

It's her favorite. When they were friends, Ruth would buy her a Mango Lime Chiffon Cake for every birthday. She probably hasn't had one for 1,825 days, give or take a day. Ruth can do sums in her head, too.

"Can you ever forgive me?" asks Gemma.

"Don't be silly, there's nothing to forgive. We're such good friends. Look at us. Just picking up right where we left off."

———

The next morning, Ruth is on her way to her Pilates class when Gemma calls, her voice shaking. "I just blew the head gasket in my car!"

"The head gasket? What's that?"

"I don't know exactly. I think it functions as a kind of seal. The engine seized. That's what they told me."

"Where are you? Are you all right?"

"I'm at a gas station. I haven't changed my oil in ages. Apparently, it's been leaking for months. This is all my fault. I stopped paying attention. How could I not have noticed?"

"Stop that. I won't allow you to blame this on yourself. You've had so much going on."

"I just dropped Bee off at the Juicery . . ." Gemma's voice tapers off. She sounds distant, lost.

"What can I do? How can I help?"

"I don't know. I guess, can you come pick me up?"

Ruth looks at the time; it's 9:42. Her class starts at ten. She hates to miss it. It's a vital part of her self-care routine. But Gemma *really* needs her.

"Of course I will," she says. "Text me the address."

Gemma groans. "The mechanic said I might need a new engine."

"Maybe it's time to get a new car."

"I can't afford a new car."

Ruth pauses. "I can."

———

Gemma won't accept a new car from Ruth, so Ruth buys her a used Camry with only 16,000 miles on it. Definitely an upgrade.

"I'll pay you back, I promise," says Gemma. "Let's work out a monthly plan."

"There's no need. This is a drop in the bucket for me, you know that. I would never expect repayment."

Oh, the look of gratitude and relief that crosses Gemma's face; Ruth wishes she could take a picture so she'll never forget it. Instead she gazes at Gemma intently, copying the image to her internal hard drive.

GEMMA

That afternoon, Gemma pulls into the driveway, gets out of the car, and texts Bee.

Come out here. I have a surprise!

A few seconds later, Bee opens the front door, and Gemma waves her arm in front of the car like a game show host. "Ta-da!"

Bee claps a hand over her mouth in shock. The Camry is a year old but looks like it just came off the lot. It's a metallic red—a color called Ruby Flare Pearl. It's loaded with every option.

"What did you do with the old car?"

"Traded it in, silly."

"Why?"

"It was on its last legs."

"It was?" Bee looks skeptical. Gemma has no intention of telling her that Ruth bought the new car for them because she nearly blew their old car up.

Gemma opens the driver's-side door. "Get in, I'll show you all the bells and whistles."

Bee climbs into the car. "Is this real leather?" She touches the armrest reverently and inhales. "It smells brand-new."

"Put your foot on the brake and press that button," instructs Gemma. The car purrs.

"You can barely hear it," says Bee in awe. The touch screen lights up. "Bluetooth!"

They needed this so badly. Something new and shiny amidst all the broken things in their life. Gemma texts Ruth. *She LOVES it!!!*

Yay! Ruth texts back.

Gemma frowns, wondering how best to explain to Ruth that she's decided not to tell Bee that Ruth bought the car for them; it's too humiliating.

Don't tell her I was involved. There's no need. Just say the transmission was acting up and it was cheaper to trade it in than fix it. It'll be our little secret, texts Ruth.

A chill runs down Gemma's back; it's as if Ruth read her mind. They are completely in sync. It was that way between them before, too. They knew what the other was thinking before they even said it.

Are you sure? I don't want to deprive you of being properly thanked for saving the day!!

You already thanked me. Just think of me as your own private Santa. But remember, Santa knows when you're naughty or nice hahaha.

Huh?

"We can take it to back-to-school night!" says Bee.

Hillside's back-to-school night is Friday; Gemma had completely forgotten. Everybody will be there. All the moms and dads. All the kids. Many of them clients, past and present. *Does she have to go? Can she call in sick?* Her phone pings.

What say we go to back-to-school night together?

RUTH

Back-to-school night is just as stressful a prospect for Ruth as it is for Gemma, but she has no intention of showing it.

She'll waltz in there with her head held high, back slightly arched to show off her hard-won SoulCycle bum, wearing her size 26 J Brands and her No. 6 clog booties, which are practically passé in New York but still completely on trend in the Bay Area. Hair down or up? Messy bun, she decides. Light on the makeup. Her skin is translucent from her weekly snail mucus masks.

She's dressing for the school moms. They may still despise her but they won't be able to take their eyes off of her. Their contempt for her goes way back, before Mr. Mann, to the kindergarten party.

———

By the time the twentieth partygoer had walked through the door, the corners of their mouths twitching with amusement, Ruth knew she'd made a fatal mistake hosting the kindergarten meet and greet. Instead of appearing generous and thoughtful, she'd come off as tone-deaf. Worse, as flaunting her wealth.

The mothers showered her in passive-aggressive compliments.

"I never would have thought to have a valet. What a lovely touch."

"Your backyard is like Central Park! Nobody has a backyard this big."

Ruth retreated to the kitchen. She opened the fridge and pretended to rifle through it. She overheard two mothers talking.

"A signature cocktail? Are you kidding me?"

"She's gorgeous, though, you have to give her that. Those arms. How many days a week in Pilates?"

"My arms would look like that, too, if I had nothing to do but arrange flowers and book caterers."

"I hear her ex is loaded. Guess he didn't have a prenup."

Ruth's cheeks blazed with heat. *Why did she insist on hosting the party? She could have just shown up with Marley at somebody else's house, a tray of Costco cookies in her hands, wearing a pair of cropped jeans and flip-flops.*

"Excuse me, you wouldn't happen to have any milk?"

Ruth shut the fridge door and turned around slowly, carefully composing her features into a neutral expression. This was one of the mothers she'd just overheard talking about her.

"I'm Madison Harris. My daughter Coco doesn't like juice. Too sweet."

Was this woman really humblebragging about her daughter turning up her nose at Capri Suns? Ruth poured a glass of milk and handed it to her.

"Thanks!" She sailed across the room to her child.

Marley sat behind the kids' food table on a folding chair. She was reading a book, something Ruth told her expressly not to do, but Ruth wouldn't call her out. The two of them outcasts. On day one, no less.

Then, a mother and daughter appeared at the front door, the look on the woman's face open and expectant. And her daughter. That red tracksuit! Those curls!

There was no father in sight.

Ruth studied the woman and was soon filled with certainty. There she was—her future BFF. Ruth felt jolted awake at the sight of her. A sensation of being Tased, tendrils of electricity sparking across the room, connecting them. Ruth saw Madison notice the new mother, too. Her eyes lit up with interest and Ruth bolted across the room so she could get there first.

The woman was a lottery prize, just waiting to be claimed.

———

Ruth's phone rings. *Gemma.* She's not a lottery prize any longer.

"You need to help me. I don't know what to wear to back-to-school night," she whines. "I don't want to look like I'm trying too hard. Like I'm desperate to please. And I don't want to look like I'm not trying enough. Like I haven't gotten out of my pajamas all week. I have to strike the right balance. Something that says *I'm sorry for all this mess and yet I'm not responsible for all this mess.* You know?"

"Skinny jeans. That emerald J.Crew blouse with the white trim. Do you still have it?"

"Um, yeah, I haven't worn it in a while but I think it's in the back of the closet. What about shoes?"

"Flats. Metallic if you've got them, gold or silver. Black will be fine if you don't. What do you have for necklaces?"

"Not much. Some costume stuff. A gold cross."

"Hmm. It needs to be understated, a little Zen, but not too bohemian. Labradorite. I've got just the thing. I'll bring it."

"Oh, God. What do I say to everybody?"

"You say hello, how was your summer, nice to see you, can you believe the kids are in high school, blabblety-blab-blab-blab. Under no circumstances do you bring up Study Right. Just pretend it's business as usual."

"But what if somebody asks me?"

"They won't."

"But what if they do?"

"Then you let me deal with it," says Ruth.

———

Madison rushes Gemma as they approach the auditorium. "Omg, are you okay?"

Ruth looks down at her icily. *Why must grown women talk in acronyms?* Her three-inch clog booties make her nearly six feet tall. "Of course she is, why wouldn't she be?"

Madison gives her a dirty look. "I was talking to Gemma."

"I'm fine, Mads," says Gemma.

"I've been meaning to call," says Madison. "I read that article in the *Chron*. Fifty percent? It's not true, is it? If you want I'll sign Coco up right now for tutoring."

Madison's eyes grow moist at the thought of her selfless act.

"That's not necessary. We're doing just fine," says Gemma. She turns to Ruth. "Let's go in. I want to get a good seat."

———

Ruth does a quick scan of the auditorium. Most of the kids are sitting in the back. She spies Marley and Bee, heads bent over their phones. The rest of the rows are filled with parents. They laugh and hug each other. *How was your summer? Gosh, Tahoe was buggy this year. Tyler looks like he grew six inches!* But their steely eyes betray them, they're readying for the race. *Now it begins. Now everything counts.* That's what they're all thinking.

The front row is empty—nobody wants to sit there, it looks too desperate, but not if you're somebody who has nothing to hide. Ruth leads Gemma to the front row.

"*Really?*" Gemma asks.

Ruth pulls her down into a seat. "Don't slouch. Whisper in my ear and then laugh."

"I can't do this, everybody's watching."

"Don't be ridiculous," Ruth whispers in Gemma's ear, and then laughs heartily, as if she's having the time of her life.

—

"Welcome, parents!" says Mr. Nunez, the school head.

Ruth's hands ball into fists. She despises Mr. Nunez, and Mr. Nunez is definitely not a Ruth Thorne fan.

When Marley was in third grade, she failed to test into Wings, Hillside's gifted program. Marley must have had an off day (her IQ was through the stratosphere), but Bee made it in—*quelle surprise!*—and Marley had to watch her get pulled out of class with a few other lucky children to attend special interdisciplinary classes. It was unfair to the rest of the kids, being subjected to that torture day after day, their failure shoved in their faces, and so Ruth had embarked upon a campaign to do away with Wings.

She marched into Mr. Nunez's office and presented her case. "Wings is sapping the kids' self-esteem."

This wasn't true, most of the kids couldn't have cared less, but she couldn't very well tell him that *she* was traumatized, that *she* couldn't bear it, could she? It was so unjust. Marley was the smartest kid in the third grade. She'd never gotten less than an EXCELLENT PLUS on her report card. Hillside didn't believe in grades until middle school—it was highly annoying.

Mr. Nunez pursed his lips in disapproval.

"Well, how about the Wings kids go to the Wings room before class so it isn't so disruptive to everybody else," she suggested.

"In the real world there's a hierarchy," Mr. Nunez said. "We do these kids a disservice by hiding that. I know it's hard, but better they get used to it now. And if Marley doesn't like it, if she wants to alter her status, then she can work hard and change it. That's life." He'd leaned across the table then, close enough that Ruth could smell his stale coffee breath. "By the way, Marley has made it very clear how she feels about being left out of the Wings group."

This was news to Ruth. Marley didn't seem to care at all.

"She said some . . . very mean things to one of the kids."

"What mean things?" Ruth can't imagine an unkind word coming out of Marley's mouth, or even a *word* for that matter. She was painstakingly shy and introverted.

"I won't repeat it," said Mr. Nunez. "There's no need."

"Repeat it," demanded Ruth.

Mr. Nunez shrugged. "She told Tristan Blake he was 'dumb as fuck.'"

Mr. Nunez had a reputation for exaggeration. Well, he could trash-talk Ruth all he wanted, but it was another thing to go after her daughter.

"That's ridiculous. You made that up. And if you insist on continuing to slander Marley, I'll have to get my lawyer involved."

Mr. Nunez backed down. He sputtered and apologized. Red-faced, he waved her out of his office.

Every December up until then, she'd given him a $100 gift card: to the Orpheum, to Oliveto, to Nordstrom, and every year he said verbatim, "This is inappropriate. We have limits on faculty gifts." He kept the gift cards, however.

That year she gave Mr. Nunez a jumbo-size bottle of Goo Gone. He never thanked her.

He smiles at her benevolently and she realizes he can't see the audience—the stage lights are too bright. He talks about homework expectations, service requirements, encouraging the students to move beyond their cliques, the latest bullying research, the temptation of Juuling, the evils of social media, and the benefits of boredom.

Before Mr. Nunez was promoted to head of school, he ran the computer science department. He spends another ten minutes droning on about online best practices. Never open an attachment from a stranger. Free trials are anything but free. Be wary of texts that appear to be from your friends but have no personal messages attached.

He's lost the room. The kids shift restlessly in their seats, their water bottles empty, their pea-size attention spans drained. They're texting, watching TikToks, checking one another out.

"And there's one last thing I'd like to address," Mr. Nunez says. "Test prep courses and private tutoring."

Immediately the auditorium goes silent.

"I'm sure you've all heard about what's happening with Study Right."

Ruth is stunned. She can't believe he's going there. Gemma is sitting ten feet away from him! Then she realizes he's assumed Gemma didn't come to back-to-school night. Of course he did. Why would she put herself through that? She'd sit it out. Wait until the whole thing died down. That's what a friend would advise. Instead Ruth insisted Gemma go.

"You know," says Mr. Nunez, "I've never been comfortable with the tutoring companies. It's an unfair system, rigged in favor of students like ours, students who are privileged, whose parents can afford to buy them an increase of two hundred, three hundred, four hundred points on their standardized tests. It's a system that's ripe for cheating, and Study Right is a perfect example. Now, I'm not against studying, what I'm against is procuring an unfair advantage."

Ruth sneaks a look at Gemma. She's holding her breath, her left palm flat against her chest, steadily sinking into her seat. *Nunez, that bastard.* His untrimmed nose hairs. His broken capillaries.

"So, to that end, I want to announce that we are increasing our number of group test prep classes here at school. There's no need to pay thousands of dollars to get private tutoring."

Ruth glances behind her. The parents' faces are stony and closed. They nod along with Mr. Nunez, but there's no way they're going to send their kids to group classes. They'll get private tutoring, they just won't get it at Study Right.

"I can't let him do this," she whispers to Gemma, rising to her feet.

"No." Gemma grabs her arm. "Please, just let it go."

But Ruth's on a mission. She climbs the stairs to the stage, her No. 6 clogs noisily announcing her. *Whispers, laughs, gasps, oh my gods.* They're making fun of her and they're readying themselves for a spectacle. This doesn't bother Ruth a bit, she's about to give them one. The audience sits forward in their seats, rapt. Mr. Nunez squints, unable to make out her identity until she's a few feet away, then his features harden into a mask of displeasure.

"I have something to say," says Ruth cheerily, joining him on the podium.

Mr. Nunez covers the microphone with his hand. "This is not the time."

"It is most assuredly the time," she says, looking down upon his balding head.

"Two minutes," he squawks at her, and steps aside.

"You're so kind, Mr. Nunez, thank you. I am Ruth Thorne, and my daughter, Marley, is a first year. I've known Gemma Howard and her daughter, Bee, since kindergarten. We are very close friends. Inseparable, you might say."

Ruth wishes she could see Gemma's face, but the audience is indeed a blur.

"Gemma is one of the most scrupulously honest people I know. She got into the test prep business because she wanted to run a center that didn't just cater to the wealthy. Do you know that for every kid whose parents pay full price, she takes on another kid who pays nothing? She doesn't advertise this. She doesn't talk about it. She just does it quietly, behind the scenes, because those are her ethics and her values.

"Now, Julie Winters, whom many of you requested personally to tutor your children because of, admit it, her Ivy credentials"— Ruth wags her index finger sassily—"was somebody Gemma hired. She was an independent contractor. Yes, Gemma made a mistake. She made the mistake of trusting this young woman and believing her story, and because of this trust, she's now paying dearly for it.

But Gemma Howard is not a cheater. And Gemma Howard is not running a scam. Study Right is about equality, about giving every kid a chance to rise up. Not just the kids who go to Hillside, for whom five thousand dollars is nothing."

Ruth pauses and takes a shaky breath for effect, as if she's deeply emotional. "I implore you, please don't ruin this business, don't run it into the ground, build it up instead. Help bring it back. We need more Study Rights in the world. And we need more Gemma Howards. People who are in it for the right reasons."

She turns to Mr. Nunez, who glares at her. "Thank you, Mr. Nunez, for letting me steal a little of your time."

———

Out in the hallway, parents mill around in clusters. Gemma's in the bathroom. Ruth stands alone, eavesdropping and absorbing the stares coming her way.

"Did you see the look on Nunez's face?"

"Study Right's like the Warby Parker of test prep centers. Who knew?"

"Are you going to re-enroll?"

"I wish I had a best friend who stood up for me like that."

Ruth allows herself a slight smile.

"Don't ever do that to me again," says Mr. Nunez, from behind her.

Ruth whirls around. "Do what?" she asks innocently.

"Interrupt me."

"I didn't interrupt you. I was only offering an alternative point of view on the subject you were opining about."

"I was not opining," he seethes.

"Come, come, Mr. Nunez. We all know you love nothing more than to deliver a holier-than-thou lecture. It's your specialty."

He wheezes incredulously. "I'd step carefully if I were you, Ms. Thorne. I don't think you want to make any more enemies than you already have."

"Is that a threat, Mr. Nunez?"

A finger taps her on the shoulder. *Madison.* "Hey there, Ruth. Hi, Mr. Nunez," she says. She looks back and forth between them. Mr. Nunez pulls at his collar. "Am I interrupting something?" she asks.

"Nothing at all," says Mr. Nunez, collecting himself. "Good night, Mrs. Harris. *Ms.* Thorne."

They watch him weave his way through the throng.

"Does he have a problem with *Ms.*?" asks Madison.

Gemma walks up, the labradorite necklace accenting the green blouse perfectly. "There's a line twenty people long for the women's bathroom. I gave up and used the men's. I thought they were going to make all the bathrooms gender-neutral."

"Next semester, I think," says Madison. "Hey. Boy, that was something. Ruth really went to bat for you!"

Madison flashes a genuine smile, one in which her entire face participates, eyes crinkling up and everything. "It was brilliant, Ruth, what you did for Gemma. You took my breath away." She reaches out for Ruth's hand and squeezes it. "And hopefully it will turn the tide for you, Gems. Get you back on your feet."

There's a lull in the conversation and Madison continues to hold on to her hand.

"Oh, sorry," says Madison, releasing her. "Gosh, your skin is so soft."

"Um—thank you." *Did Madison Harris just give her a compliment?*

"What lotion do you use?"

"Cetaphil?" says Ruth, hating the way she devolves to uptalk when she's nervous. "The cream, not the lotion," she says firmly.

"I'll have to get some," Madison says and winks at her.

———

Complete silence in the car on the way home. Gemma pulls into Ruth's driveway. "I don't know what to say."

"I hope—what I did—wasn't too much," says Ruth.

"No, it was great," says Gemma, after a pause.

"Are you sure?" *Doesn't she deserve a more effusive thank-you? Shouldn't they all have been buzzing about her Norma Rae speech on the way home?*

"Yes, yes, I'm just exhausted." Gemma leans over and kisses her on the cheek and Ruth stiffens—she's being dismissed.

She swivels around. "So, do you like your new car, Bee?"

"I *love* it."

"I guess the old car was on its last legs, huh?"

Bee catches her mother's eye in the rearview mirror.

"Yes, it was," says Gemma.

"Well, you're lucky. It's a big improvement over your last car. That car was a wreck. Unsafe, really." Ruth opens the door. "Ready, Marls?"

Ruth and Marley are at the front door when Gemma yells, "Thanks again."

Ruth pretends she doesn't hear her.

GEMMA

Gemma glances at the clock: 2:32 a.m. Precisely one hour has passed since the last time she checked. She knows the rules of sleep hygiene—if you're awake longer than twenty minutes you should turn on the light, go to another room, and read a book or have a mug of herbal tea. Under no circumstances should you use electronics. NO SCREENS.

Gemma grabs her phone and opens her Momonymous app. The name of her pod is IN ONE EAR AND OUT YOUR MOTHER. She's been a member since Bee was in first grade, and her username is SoccerMommy#1. Bee has never played soccer in her life; she's not what you would call a team player. Gemma feels confident her identity is well disguised. The moms were quite active last night.

DuckDuckGoose: OMG what an evening!

LoveYouMore: What a SHOW!

WineLuvva: Do you think Gemma knew Ruth was going to do that?

BearMama: Doubtful. She looked stunned.

WhatsUpWomen: So what do we think?

TotesAdorb: What do we think? COMEBACK!!

BarkingUpTheWrongTree: Yes but whose comeback? Ruth's or Gemma's?

OhThePlacesYou'llGo: I think it was both haha. A twofer. Ruth put Gemma and herself back on the map in one fell swoop.

LoveYouMore: And she lay claim to Gemma as well. Clearly she was letting us all know they're BFFs again. So thirsty.

WhatsUpWomen: I'm really happy for Gemma. It's great what she's doing. Not everybody can afford private tutoring.

BarkingUpTheWrongTree: I'm signing my DS up. I wasn't going to enroll him for PSAT prep until next summer, but why not now?

DuckDuckGoose: There's something really off about Ruth Thorne.

BearMama: Maybe it's time to let bygones be bygones.

LoveYouMore: You can't be serious.

BearMama: The Egans left Hillside years ago. Shouldn't we move on? I always felt bad about how Ruth was treated. We slut shamed her.

LoveYouMore: She deserved it, AND in our defense, slut shaming wasn't really a thing back then was it? Also, I happen to know that Sal has never "moved on" from it. She's still with her husband, but their marriage is basically over. They're staying together for the kids.

MsFoxy: The Chron article broke my heart. It BROKE MY HEART! I understand completely why Gemma went underground. I would have done the same thing.

DuckDuckGoose: Well Ruth Thorne pulled her out into the light tonight. No more hiding.

BearMama: Loved her necklace. Was that labradorite?

Yes, Ruth had pulled her back into the light, but it wasn't lost on Gemma that Ruth had pulled herself back into the light, too.

"Mom?"

Bee stands at her bedroom door, hair mussed, rubbing her eyes. She wears a Nike tank top and faded pink drawstring pants. She has a perfect innie belly button.

"Can't sleep?"

Bee makes a sad face. Gemma pulls aside the covers and pats the mattress. "Come here, sweet girl."

Bee crawls into the bed and yanks the covers up to her nose.

"Are you worried about something?"

Bee blinks at her. "Was that good for us? What Ruth did? I can't tell."

Gemma draws Bee under her arm. "It was good," she says, trying to sound confident, but she's not all that sure. Ruth ripped off the Band-Aid without consulting her first.

Bee yawns. Her jaw cracks. "So it'll be over soon? People will forget? They'll come back to Study Right?"

"Yep, absolutely. They will," says Gemma.

Maybe if she says it out loud it will be true.

RUTH

Ruth takes a big spoonful of her poached egg sprinkled with Trader Joe's Everything But the Bagel. She eats the same thing for breakfast every morning; she never tires of it.

She opens her laptop. Her password: RuthAnnThorneTheGreat. Ruth Ann Thorne the Great was her mother's private nickname for Ruth. When she was drawing Ruth a bath, or tucking her in, or giving her a quick hug before putting her on the school bus, she'd whisper that into her ear. When her mother uttered those words, Ruth felt like a pat of butter melting slowly in a cast-iron pan.

Ruth takes another bite of her poached egg, picks a poppy seed out of her teeth, and opens her email. She has one new message. The subject line: YOU'RE INVITED TO JOIN MOMONYMOUS!

She listens for Marley. Not a sound from upstairs. It's 9:03 on Saturday morning; she's not awake yet. Ruth gets up and twirls, her arms raised above her head like Rocky. She's finally gotten the invitation! After all these years she's been let in!

Wait, is this a joke? Is somebody playing with her?

Ruth opens the email. It's real. She accepts the invitation by clicking on the Momonymous icon—a vintage silhouette of two women whispering. It must be because of last night's Oscar-worthy performance. Why else would she suddenly get a Momonymous invite to a pod called MY MOTHER MADE ME DO IT.

Ruth thinks carefully about a username. She picks PennySaved-PennyEarned. Let them think she's a frugal, composting, tight-fisted mom.

HappilyEverAfter: Welcome PennySavedPennyEarned!

PennySavedPennyEarned: Hello! Thanks so much for inviting me!

WhatYouSeeIsNotWhatYouGet: Hello PennySavedPennyEarned!

TortoiseWinsTheRace: A new member. Yay!

PennySavedPennyEarned: Is this a new pod?

WhatYouSeeIsNotWhatYouGet: Relatively new. About a year old. You're our fifth member. We're a small, intimate group. It works for us. We can really get into the nitty-gritty that way.

HappilyEverAfter: PennySavedPennyEarned as a new member you don't have access to our archives. But from this moment on you'll be able to read every conversation, even the ones that you don't contribute to. However we strongly encourage you to show up and contribute. Participation is very important. We want to know our pod is a priority for you. So dive right in. Roll around in the dirt with us. Nothing is off-limits with this group.

PennySavedPennyEarned: Ooo, that sounds delicious. Have to admit I love gossip.

HappilyEverAfter: And we love mothers who gossip! Some pods are filled with such goody goodies. That's not us.

OneWayAtATime: So let me set expectations and tell you how we work. We have a six-month vetting period. A chance for you to check us out and for us to check you out. If it's not a

match we go our separate ways, no harm no foul. But make
no mistake—we want it to work out.

TortoiseWinsTheRace: Yes we do!

WhatYouSeeIsNotWhatYouGet: Okay, so can we get to last
night? What does everybody think?

TortoiseWinsTheRace: I think Ruth Thorne has an incredible ass.

HappilyEverAfter: Gotta give it to her. She's got a rockin bod.

PennySavedPennyEarned: I bet she works really hard at staying
in shape.

WhatYouSeeIsNotWhatYouGet: Oh, I'm sure works her ass off
for that ass. She just makes it look effortless.

OneWayAtATime: Unlike her daughter. Did you see Marley? Poor
girl. She's fat-ish.

PennySavedPennyEarned: I wouldn't call her fat. Maybe a little
chunky.

HappilyEverAfter: Must be hard when her mother's so hot. To
have to compete with that. Maybe she's just given up.

OneWayAtATime: I'm sorry to say, I know it's not PC, but if
you're a teenage girl, skinny is power.

TortoiseWinsTheRace: Stop it everybody. We can't give our girls
that message. We have to work against that, ladies. Come on.

Btw PennySavedPennyEarned, we all have DD's no sons, so we're very big on girl issues.

PennySavedPennyEarned: DD?

TortoiseWinsTheRace: Darling daughter. DS is darling son. DW darling wife. DH darling husband.

WhatYouSeeIsNotWhatYouGet: I agree with TortoiseWinsTheRace though the body image stuff is so tricky. You just want to give them every advantage. You want them to be popular.

HappilyEverAfter: Well, it was an interesting night to say the least. Do you think Study Right will make it?

OneWayAtATime: Maybe. It will take Gemma months to get back up to speed. If what Ruth said is true and she gives away half her tutoring packages, she runs the business on a very tight margin.

WhatYouSeeIsNotWhatYouGet: If they truly are besties again I'm sure Ruth will step in. She's loaded.

TortoiseWinsTheRace: Change of subject. Have any of your girls used the DivaCup?

PennySavedPennyEarned: I don't get it. You have to wash it out in the sink. How does that work in a public bathroom? What's wrong with tampons and pads?

WhatYouSeeIsNotWhatYouGet: Um—they're expensive PennySavedPennyEarned.

PennySavedPennyEarned: You can buy them in bulk at Costco.

Whoops, that was close. *Has she exposed herself on day one?* Many moms choose misleading usernames. The opposite of who they really are. Who's PennySavedPennyEarned? Of course, the mother who threw the kindergarten meet and greet. Who served lobster and mojitos.

Ruth's head is spinning. She reminds herself that only the moderator knows her identity. And who is the moderator? TortoiseWinsTheRace? HappilyEverAfter? OneWayAtATime? The anonymity is both seductive and dangerous. She's going to have to be very careful not to give herself away while trying to prove herself at the same time.

HappilyEverAfter: Ladies, I'm outta here. Gotta hit the post office before it closes.

TortoiseWinsTheRace: I hope we haven't scared you off with our candor, PennySavedPennyEarned.

PennySavedPennyEarned: Absolutely not. I'm honored you invited me to join.

OneWayAtATime: Till next time mamas.

WhatYouSeeIsNotWhatYouGet: Ciao xxx

Ruth goes to the bathroom and looks in the mirror. Her eyes are bright, her pupils dilated. The last time she felt this way was when she got her acceptance letter to NYU. She was off to a new life. A new city. She'd reinvent herself. She'd find her people. She'd come back to California triumphant; she'd finally metamorphose into Ruth Ann Thorne the Great. Well, that never happened, but now that's she gotten the Momonymous invitation, perhaps it will. She has the sense her life is about to change in a profound way.

She hears Marley's heavy tread on the stairs and fights the urge to tell her to walk more delicately.

Marley grunts at her and goes straight for the cereal. She pours herself a huge bowl of Rice Krispies, sprinkles it with two table-spoons of sugar, sits at the table, and starts shoveling it in.

Ruth is not going to let Marley spoil her morning. "Guess what?"

Marley looks up at her dully.

"I got invited to join a Momonymous pod."

Marley scrunches up her face. "What's that?"

"You don't know what Momonymous is?"

Marley shakes her head.

"Forget it."

Marley sits upright, the edge in Ruth's voice a warning. "I'm sorry, I just woke up. What is it? Tell me. It must be good. You seem happy."

"I am. I'm happy," Ruth says defensively.

Marley stands and hugs Ruth. Her daughter smells yeasty. She's always had that bread smell in the morning. It was delicious when she was young, Ruth couldn't get enough of her scent. Now, Ruth fights off her revulsion.

"What do you have going on today?" asks Ruth, already know-ing the answer. *Nothing, she has nothing going on today—she never does.*

Marley shrugs. Her phone buzzes. She picks it up, smiles, and runs up the stairs.

A few minutes later the doorbell rings. A delivery for Ruth. Flowers from Gemma, who can ill afford them. Her favorite. Calla lilies.

Thank you for last night. You are my savior, reads the card.

Ruth grins. What a morning!

BEE

Bee and her friends are in the process of reclaiming the word *slut*. They call each other slut constantly, so many times that all the sting has been taken out of it. They may as well be calling each other honey or sweetie pie.

SLUTZ is the private name of Bee's dance crew. Their public name is BeeBop7. Bee is choreographing a dance for the high school talent show. It's gonna be lit!

On Wednesday, Bee sends a message to SLUTZ, a group chat consisting of Frankie, Abby, Coco, Shanice, Aditi, and Marley.

Rehearsal 6:30 Saturday night get ready to grind yo asses!!!

She probably should have sent Marley a coded text. If Ruth ever found out Marley was part of a group called SLUTZ, that would be the end of her. Ruth would never let her leave the house again. She'd probably pull her out and homeschool her.

Within minutes everybody has replied yes except Marley, which is no surprise. Joining Bee's friend circle is a stretch for Marley, but Marley needs a bigger life and there's no way Bee's going to shrink hers just because Marley's back in it. It's time to woman up. They're first years now, official teenagers. All of them have pubes, one of them has been fingered, and most of them have their periods. Bee caught Coco reading the back of the tampon box in her bathroom a few weeks ago.

"I can show you how to use them," Bee said.

"I know how to use a tampon," snapped Coco.

Bee knew she was lying and felt a flood of compassion for her. Back in fifth grade Bee was the only one with her period—it was a nightmare. She was so young she didn't even know what a vagina really was. "It's a hole?" she'd cried to her mom. "I have a hole down there?" "Actually, you have two," her mother had said.

It seemed like the biggest bait and switch. Up until then it had been all girl power this, girl power that, girls are better, smarter, faster, and oh, yeah, there's just this one tiny thing, one little price to pay—you'll have blood coming out of your hole every month for the rest of your life!

Now Coco is the only one who *hasn't* gotten her period and being late is just as terrible as being early. Sometimes Bee wishes she were a boy. Everything right out there, including your genitals, just dangling there for everybody to see. Simple. Easy access. Uncomplicated. You could just say what you felt if you were a boy, instead of this constant stuffing of emotions, trying to keep them named, organized, neat. Her feelings were so big sometimes that she actually googled *exorcism*, which led to her watching the 1970s movie *The Exorcist*. It wasn't scary in the least little bit. What was scary were Linda Blair's white knee socks.

Bee texts Marley.

Marls you're coming right?

Not sure. Got something with Mom

What? Eating pad thai and watching Titanic for the millionth time? COME!!

KK! comes Marley's reply a minute later.

MARLEY

The SLUTZ crew occupies an entire lunch table. They're watching dance compilations on Dubsmash. Marley is so nervous she can't bring herself to look up. Her back feels permanently rounded. She's probably growing a hump.

Bee scooches her chair closer to Marley's. "What's wrong?" she whispers.

"I don't think I can come on Saturday," says Marley.

Bee nods and offers Marley half of her sandwich. "Meat loaf with Sriracha ketchup."

Even though Marley has already eaten two slices of pizza, she wolfs down the sandwich; she's starving. Her mother hasn't gone grocery shopping in nearly a week. She's punishing Marley because she discovered she'd been making midnight visits to the pantry, devouring sleeves of Fudge Stripes and blocks of Tillamook extra sharp cheddar cheese.

Marley watches Bee take slow sips from her water bottle until one by one the SLUTZ depart, leaving the two of them alone.

"I know you're afraid," says Bee.

"She'll kill me."

"She's already killing you. You're a prisoner in your house. She treats you like a second grader," Bee hisses.

"I'm not a prisoner." *Is she?*

"Marls, it's time. You need to break out. *We* need to break out! You'll love these girls, I promise you. Just give them a chance. Everybody will be talking about us—*everybody*." She leans forward, her eyes gleaming. "It's gunna be sick!"

Marley's skin prickles with excitement. Often Marley feels like she's floating above her body. She needs to jam herself back into her chest, her legs, her—intimate parts (she can't bring herself to say vagina, the word makes her deeply uncomfortable).

In the privacy of her bedroom she's been studying Beyoncé's moves, copying them in front of her mirror.

"What worries you the most?" asks Bee.

Marley imagines her mother watching her writhe onstage. "All of it."

"It'll be fine. We just have to give it a feminist spin. Here's what we'll say. We're not ashamed of our sexuality. We aren't letting anybody define our sexuality for us. This is a *take back our bodies* dance. It'll work. They'll buy into it. In the end, they'll be proud of us. You'll see."

Bee's confidence is powerful medicine; it always has been for Marley.

———

"Don't stay up too late," says Ruth as she pulls up to the curb in front of Gemma's house.

"I won't," says Marley, her hand on the car door handle. Her mother *does* treat her like a second grader.

"Maybe you should just come home tonight. You know you don't sleep well in Bee's bed. I don't want you to be tired and cranky tomorrow."

"Bee's got a blow-up mattress."

"Really? Is that new?"

Her mother's stalling. She doesn't want Marley to leave.

"Maybe I should poke my head in, say hi to Gemma."

"She's working."

"This late?"

"That's what Bee said."

"Oh, well, then."

Marley hesitates.

"It's fine, get out of here," says her mother, waving her away.

Maybe she shouldn't go. She can use her mother as an excuse. "But what will you do?"

Her mother's face darkens. "What will I do? You mean whatever will I do without you, Marley? Not everything revolves around you."

"I know that. That's not what I was saying," Marley squeaks.

"I'm going out for dinner, to the Harris's restaurant. Madison's been trying to get me there for years."

"Really? That sounds fun, Mom!"

Her mother grits her teeth. Not the right answer, apparently. Her tone is all wrong. Too enthusiastic.

Marley gets out of the car slowly, just the way her mother likes it, and the second her feet touch the ground, her mother speeds off.

———

"Marley!" says Gemma, who is home after all, her car in the garage. Bee must have anticipated Ruth would try and muscle in on Marley's evening, so she lied about it. She gives Marley a hug and pulls her through the doorway. "I'm so glad you're here."

"Me too." Now that Marley's in the house, all of her tensions dissolve. She's committed to the SLUTZ. She grins at Gemma.

"Everyone's in the basement," says Gemma. "The pizza just arrived."

———

They start by practicing the Booty Pop. Once they've got that down, they move on to the Shiggy and Thotiana. Then the Renegade.

On their last pass, all of them moving in perfect unison, Marley is exhilarated. *What joy, what liberation to move like this!* Squatting and jerking, jumping and chest-beating. Punching and wrist-crossing and pelvis-thrusting and clenching her fists. She's never felt so powerful. Her body just knows what to do. She sees a move once and can immediately imitate it. The girls crowd around her, impressed. They compliment her. They decide to put her in the center of the group, in the front row, to showcase her moves. *All eyes on her.*

"Well?" says Bee, her face red with perspiration. "I can see you just hated that. You probably want to go home right now cause you're such shit at dancing. You must be so embarrassed." She punches Marley softly on the arm. "I knew you'd be good, I didn't know you'd be *that* good."

Marley lowers her head so Bee can't see the tears of happiness filling her eyes.

RUTH

Ruth can't shake her suspicion that the moderator of her mom pod is Madison Harris. She had impressed Madison at back-to-school night. And now she is part of a tribe. A very small, elite tribe that hasn't invited any new members in since its inception. Sometimes it's good to be a late bloomer.

Madison and her husband, Cliff, own a popular restaurant called Home Kitchen. Ruth Yelps the restaurant and sees that it has mostly four- and five-star reviews. Their specialties: meat loaf, pot roast and potatoes, buttermilk fried chicken, and according to the comments you can almost always score a seat at the bar.

———

Ruth arrives at Home Kitchen nine minutes later. The buttery smell of biscuits, cake, and fried food is overpowering. She's already studied the menu and knows what she's going to order—a Cobb salad. She allows herself carbs only at lunch.

She stands in the doorway and surveys the scene. She spies Madison across the room. She's got a great body, Ruth has to give her that. Long, toned legs, a flat stomach, perky little boobs.

Ruth feels breathless as she realizes how much she wants a relationship with Madison, and not just a private, anonymous one.

Madison turns, sees her standing at the hostess desk, and walks across the room, a vacant smile on her face. "Oh, hi, do you have a reservation?" she asks.

There is absolutely no recognition in her eyes. Yes, Ruth is dressed down in yoga pants and Allbirds, her hair in a ponytail, but come on! Is Madison faking that she doesn't know who she is? Is this some sort of a power play?

Ruth gives Madison her own vacant look in return. "No, but I was hoping to sit at the bar." She frowns then, a friendly little frown. "Do you—" She lets the question ride.

"Yes, we serve the full menu at the bar," says Madison. She looks at Ruth, perplexed, then her face suddenly fills with warmth. "Ruth, I'm sorry, I didn't recognize you! You're normally so—" She whirls her hand at Ruth.

So what?

"I don't think I've ever seen you in Lulu," says Madison.

Actually, Ruth's in Stella McCartney, but she isn't about to reveal that to Madison. Labels are nothing to brag about—that's what her mother always said.

Ruth can't resist a little verbal slap, payback for what Madison has just put her through. "So, you're the hostess here?"

Madison laughs. "Hostess, server, dishwasher, all of it. My husband and I own the restaurant."

"You *own* it? I had no idea. I was just shopping and thought I'd pop in for a quick bite before going home. Marley's at Bee's."

Why did she say that? She sounds so desperate. Look, my daughter is hanging out with one of the most popular ninth-grade girls!

"Right. Okay. Let's get you settled."

Ruth follows Madison to an empty seat at the bar. *A backless stool, how tacky. Whatever happened to making your customers comfortable? Encouraging them to stay awhile?*

"Armand, this is Ruth," Madison says to the bartender. "Treat her well. She's a fellow Hillside mom."

Madison winks at Ruth. *She's quite a winker. Or maybe she has a tic.*

"Enjoy. Wish I could stay and chat. Duty calls, I'm afraid. Comp her meal, A," she says while walking away.

"Oh, that's not necessary," says Ruth. *This is going so well!*

Armand slides a bar napkin in front of her. "You and Mads good friends?"

Mads. Her friends call her Mads. "We've known each other a long time. Tito's martini, straight up, very dry, four olives."

"You don't look old enough to have a kid," he says. He stares brazenly at her breasts and Ruth feels herself flushing—a wave of heat running down her body, from her neck to her groin.

She drums her fingers on the bar. "Does that work for you?"

Armand laughs. "Sometimes."

———

Screw the salad. Ruth goes for the buttermilk chicken, mashed potatoes, and green beans. It's delicious. So is Armand. He flirts with her throughout dinner. On her way to the bathroom she stops by the hostess desk.

"The food is incredible," she gushes to Madison. "When I get home, I'm giving you a five-star Yelp review!"

Madison looks at her coolly. "I'm glad you enjoyed it."

"I more than enjoyed it. I loved it. Congrats to you. This is a fabulous restaurant. Great concept. Great execution. Good for you guys. Good for you." Ruth leans in and whispers, "Here's to— *happily ever after.*"

Madison's scrunches up her brow and Ruth's stomach drops. *What has she done?* The whole point of the pod was anonymity. She never should have mentioned it. They said this was a trial period. They're vetting her. *Has she just blown it?* She waits for Madison to give her some sort of a sign. She'll be waiting a long time.

"How about you and I get together for a glass of wine? I owe you after tonight. My treat," Ruth says.

Madison's eyes flit over Ruth's head. She gives somebody a nod, a wave. "I'm sorry, I'm being summoned."

———

When Ruth returns to the bar, Armand hands her the bill. "Take your time with that."

Has he forgotten Madison asked him to comp her meal? Ruth's hands shake as she gets out her platinum card. She doesn't know what to think, how to parse the evening. She overtips Armand, giving him nearly 30 percent.

The restaurant is packed. Couples chatting away, filling the room with their happy voices, sharing fries, desserts, bottles of wine.

When Ruth gets home she texts Madison. How about next Saturday? Let's whine/wine it up!

Madison reads the text immediately but she doesn't text back and Ruth curls up into a little ball on the couch, feeling utterly abandoned, like Sandra Bullock in that space movie.

Ruth's grandmother's voice echoes through her head. *She can entertain herself, can't she?*

———

As he pulled their Chevette into her grandparents' driveway, Ruth's father said, "I think we should cancel."

"It's too late," said her mother. "She's expecting us now."

Her mother swiveled around in her seat and said brightly, "Ruth, darling, you're going to have a wonderful time!"

Ruth blinked back tears. She *was* going to have a wonderful time until Lindy got sick and Lindy's mother called and said Ruth couldn't spend the weekend with them anymore. It was her parents' tenth anniversary. They'd booked a hotel at Sea Ranch. They'd scrimped and saved for this trip for months.

Last night Ruth's mother had called Ruth's grandmother and asked if Ruth could stay with them for the weekend. Ruth listened in on the bedroom telephone. She frequently did this. She'd become quite adept at hanging up without a sound.

"Please, Lou," she begged. "She'll be no trouble." Ruth's mother called her parents by their first names, Lou (short for Louise) and Charlie. "You'll barely even know she's there."

Ruth saw her grandparents twice a year, at Christmas and Easter. Lou and Charlie traveled abroad frequently and had a full and active social life.

"She can entertain herself, can't she?" her grandmother asked. "The Pratts are coming to dinner tonight."

"She's very self-sufficient," said her mother. "She makes a mean gin and tonic, too. You could put her to work. She could serve your guests." Her mother fake-laughed.

Every night, Ruth made her parents a drink. It made her feel important.

"You'll be fine, won't you, Ruthie?" Her mother smiled at her. "You're a big girl now, six years old! It's only two nights, and we'll be back before you know it."

———

Her father called the house her mother had grown up in The Manse. An eight-thousand-square-foot monstrosity in Portola Valley with a stable of four prize-winning thoroughbreds. One of Ruth's earliest memories was of her grandmother in her riding clothes. The fawn-colored breeches that clung to her long, shapely legs. The crisp white shirt with the starched collar.

Lou came from money. Old money. The kind of money that did not get passed down to the next generation until the previous generation had died.

Ruth's mother rang the bell. A few minutes later Lou opened the door.

"I brought you flowers," said her mother, holding out a grocery store bouquet of stargazer lilies.

Lou accepted them with a slight frown. The cheap cellophane. The gold Safeway sticker.

"You're lucky we're even here this weekend," Lou said. To Ruth she said, "We are very busy today. Don't expect me to sit on the floor and do puzzles with you."

"That's okay. I don't like puzzles," said Ruth.

Ruth's mother nudged Ruth's suitcase with her toe. "She's a big reader. She brought three books with her. *Little House on the Prairie*."

"Well, good for you," said Lou.

Ruth puffed up a little.

———

After her parents left, Lou brought her to the den. They had an enormous TV, twice the size of Ruth's TV at home.

"Watch whatever you want," said Lou.

"But it's the daytime," said Ruth. "I only watch at night."

Her grandmother looked at her like she was a science experiment. "You're quite a rule follower, aren't you?"

Ruth nodded proudly. "I've been student of the week twice this year. Mr. Riggs, our principal, said—"

Lou walked across the room, turned on the TV, and left, shutting the door behind her. Ruth watched TV for so long she dozed off. She woke to the smell of melted cheese. While she had been sleeping, somebody had delivered a pepperoni pizza, as well as a glass of soda. *Sprite? Mountain Dew?*

She took a sip. It was tonic water—yuck. She wanted milk. She opened the door a crack and heard the faint sound of music, people laughing, cutlery clinking. The festive sounds made her sad. A party going on without her. She'd missed her chance to perform her parlor act. A precocious little girl delivering adult drinks.

She ate her pizza. She watched *The Jeffersons*, *Charlie's Angels*, and *Dynasty*. She fell asleep again.

Her grandmother woke her the next morning. Lou sat down on

the couch next to her, her face scrubbed clean of makeup; she was barely recognizable.

"I have some bad news," she said.

———

Ruth presses her face into the couch cushion and chokes back a sob. Where the hell is Marley? If Marley were here, she'd snuggle her up. Marley who will never desert her, never make her feel like she's a speck of dust. A blow-up bed, my ass. She's got a Saatva queen-size mattress with Cultiver linen sheets. That girl needs to come home.

Ruth drives to Gemma's in a near rage. The kitchen door is unlocked as usual. Gemma is from Derry, New Hampshire. *Nobody locks their doors in Derry,* Gemma's always said, tempting fate. She's just been lucky she hasn't been robbed yet, or worse.

How could Gemma have chosen Madison over her? How can Gemma still be friends with that harpie!

The house is perfectly still, the girls and Gemma asleep upstairs. Ruth sits at the kitchen table for a while, until her heart rate has gone back to normal and she's thinking clearly.

Then she plugs up the sink's drain, turns on the faucet, and leaves.

MARLEY

Marley's been working with her text therapist, Soleil, for a few months now, and her mother has no idea. She's been using her own money. Every birthday, her mother writes her a $1,000 check to deposit in a *you never know what will happen* savings account. Although Marley appreciates the cash, it comes with a price—a low, simmering dread. Her *you never know what will happen* account feels more like a threat than security.

Marley's frugal, she's never spent a penny of her funds. But at the end of eighth grade, friendless, feeling more alone than ever, she knew she needed to talk to somebody on the down low. Somebody who took their orders from her, not her mother. Marley loves both the flexibility of text therapy (you can reach out to your therapist whenever you want) and the anonymity of it.

Bee snores lightly in her bed. Marley is wide awake, revved up from the SLUTZ's first rehearsal, so she takes a chance and reaches out to Soleil. She'd already filled Soleil in on her decision to join the dance crew a few days ago.

September 5, 11:01 p.m.

Soleil are you up?

About five minutes later, Soleil answers.

Hi Marley. What's going on?

Is it ok to text you this late?

It's fine. I'm a bit of a night owl.

Guess what? The dance crew has a name!

Oh yeah? What?

Don't laugh. SLUTZ

SLUTZ. Interesting.

Soleil always says *interesting* when something bothers her.

You don't like it?

Mmm, I think it could be problematic.

We're using it in an ironic way. It's a feminist thing. We're taking back the word. Making it our own

I think you have to be careful. Taking back the word and owning it is all well and good but keep in mind not everybody is free to do that. It's a matter of privilege. If you've got it you can take it back. If you don't, not so much.

And I've got it?

Yes you do. Beaming face with smiling eyes. Vulcan salute.

Soleil writes out her emojis. Marley thinks it's both weird and cool.

So you're saying I can demand people let me own the word and they will? And if I was part of an oppressed group I couldn't?

Was fat an oppressed group? Marley wishes she was one of those über-confident girls who proudly showed her curves, who walked through the world spreading body positivity. She aspired to that state of mind, but she was far from it.

Well you could but the word might continue to stick to you, and worse, concretize the stigma. It's confusing I know. But it's something to keep in mind.

We're just having fun

Yeah, I get it, thus the Z. It does have a softening effect.

My mother would kill me if she knew

Would she? Really? Let's think this through.

Marley hears footsteps downstairs in the kitchen. *Gemma*. Bee told her she has insomnia so she takes an Ambien, then inevitably sleepwalks her way to the fridge. Pops some Eggos in the toaster. Smothers the waffles in raspberry jam and powdered sugar and wakes up with no memory of her thousand-calorie meal. At least Marley remembers exactly what she eats in the middle of the night. At least she cleans up after herself.

Do we have to?

We probably should.

I really don't want to process this rn. It's simple. I love dancing. And I'm good at it

I wish I could see you in action! You sound so excited. Do you think you could explain the name to your mom? I assume that's what you think she'll be most upset about.

It's not just that. It's the kind of dancing we're doing

What kind of dancing?

The way kids dance now

I don't see anything wrong with that.

You might. We twerk

*What? You twerk! Only kidding. Of course you twerk. You're
14. But why not warn your mom so she's not taken by surprise.
She's so supportive of you.*

It's true. Her mother has spent so much money and time trying
to fix her, better her. Acupuncture, cupping, homeopathy, Reiki,
massages, ear candling. Her mother doesn't work—her job is Marley. Marley rarely leaves her mother's side, except during the summers and every other holiday when she goes to Sacramento to stay
with her father, stepmother, and stepbrother. She adores it there
but can never admit that to her mother. When Marley goes to Sacramento, Ruth shuts down.

Marley has a vivid memory of driving there the summer before
second grade.

———

"Guess what I'm going to do when you're gone?"

Seven-year-old Marley sat in the backseat of the car, over-
whelmed by the overly bright sound of her mother asking questions, digging for something from her. Something she didn't have.

She took a stab at answering. "Get your hair done?"

Wrong, wrong, wrong. She should have come up with something
more exciting. But now came the familiar sentences, the kind of
sentences Marley knew exactly how to react to. They were seesaw
sentences. Both on the ground and in the air at the same time.

"I'm going to see a fun musical with Gemma. *The Book of Mor-
mon.* But not with Bee. She'll have to stay home all alone. Well, not
all alone, with a babysitter. If you were home, you'd have a sleepover,
the two of you. You two besties. But you won't be, will you?"

Marley bit her lip and lowered her eyes. Like Harry Potter had
an invisibility cloak, this was Marley's guilt cloak. It never failed to
bring her mother back.

Her mother gulped and swallowed, satisfied with Marley's contrition. Then a split second later, she glared at her angrily in the rearview mirror. Little beads of sweat popped up on Marley's temples.

"Well, I was going to stop at In-N-Out Burger but I've changed my mind. I'll deliver you to your father famished. You know you crash if you don't eat regularly. Let him deal with your bonking."

The reality was that even "bonked" Marley couldn't be happier to be spending the summer with her father, his wife, Luciana, and her half-brother, Oscar, whom her mother referred to as the "second coming."

They drove right past the exit for In-N-Out Burger. Marley was so hungry. She clutched her abdomen and shut her eyes. Soon she'd arrive. They'd have pizza for supper. At dusk, she and Oscar would swim in the pool. Then she'd get into her pajamas, still smelling of chlorine. She'd lie in bed listening to the sound of her father and Luciana laughing while watching *The Big Bang Theory*. She'd fall asleep to the comforting clink of the ice cubes in their gin and tonics.

When they pulled into the driveway, Marley was so excited. She couldn't help herself, she opened the car door.

"Did I say you could go?" her mother barked.

Marley shut the car door. She was standing on the threshold of another world. Everything was sharp and in full color. Teletubbies-bright. How she loved that show. She was too old for it now. That show was for babies. She put the window down. She heard birdsong. Smelled laundry detergent billowing from a vent on the side of the house. Her father used Tide. Her mother used Gain.

"To be separated from you for eight weeks! It's positively medieval! Let's say goodbye here."

Marley didn't even have to try; the tears just came. Tears of anticipation. Of freedom.

Her mother got out of the car and opened the rear door. "Unbuckle," she said.

Marley unbuckled herself from her booster seat.

"Give it to me."

Marley gave her mother the booster seat and she tossed it on the driveway. Then she slid into the backseat next to Marley. "Oh, honey," she crooned. She gathered Marley up in her arms. "This is the closest you can ever be to a person, crying together. I hate that you have to go, too, Marley bear."

Her mother sobbed for what felt like an hour, her nose running, her tears soaking Marley's shirt. *Eww.* Marley pulled back ever so slightly.

Her mother flinched. "You can't wait to get away from me, can you?"

"No, Mama! I just have to go to the bathroom."

She turned away from Marley and stared out the window. Then came the terrifying silence, which was worse than her mother's anger, because she didn't know what it meant. *Was it temporary, the seconds before the bomb would go off? Or was it a silence that would eventually fizz out, leaving both she and her mother in an exhausted heap?*

Her mother whispered, "Just wait until you get home."

———

You're right. I'll tell her

Marley has no intention of telling her mother. Maybe she can confide in Gemma. Convince her not to tell her mother either. She can go to the talent show with the Howards. Her mother will never have to know.

Good. I think that's the right thing to do.

A rush of guilt. She's great you know

Your Mom?

Ya. She's so supportive

Then give her a chance to support you. Give her a chance to come through for you.

The problems me. My self esteem

You don't think you deserve this? Your turn at center stage?

Marley are you still there? Did I lose you?

Marley's legs and arms feel like anchors, pulling her down.

Exhausted. Gotta sleep

KK, talk to you soon, Marley. Hatching chick. Rainbow.

A few seconds later, Marley's phone emits a satisfying draining sound. When she started with Soleil, she adjusted the settings on the text therapy app to automatically wipe each session from her phone. Soleil, however, kept an archive of all their sessions.

Marley tries to get comfortable on the air mattress; it's a cheap blow-up from Costco. She longs for her own bed. *Is it too late to call for an Uber?* Downstairs she hears the kitchen door open and close. Bee said she'd found Gemma in the backyard some mornings, lying on a lounge chair, snoring away.

Marley does a series of relaxation breaths. Three-count inhale. Hold for four. Five-count exhale. Her thoughts keep intruding, circling her like disobedient dogs, but eventually they tire, curl up, and close their eyes, and Marley does the same.

GEMMA

"Mom!" Bee yells from downstairs.

Gemma groans and puts the pillow over her face. She feels muzzy and light-headed. She took 20 mg of Ambien last night, twice her normal dose. She's got to wean herself off the drug. Every night, she has the best of intentions to sleep clean and every night, she succumbs to the little orange pill, desperate at the thought of lying awake for hours, perseverating over the long list of all the ways she's screwed things up.

"Mooommmm!"

Gemma rises slowly, sits at the end of the bed. Her head feels too heavy to lift. She'll have to make an excuse to explain her appearance. She'll blame it on insomnia.

———

"God, I've been calling you for hours," huffs Bee when she appears in the kitchen doorway.

"Sorry. I didn't fall asleep until three. Morning, Marls."

Marley, her hair in braids, looking startlingly young, nods. "Morning."

Gemma stumbles to the coffeemaker. The floor is soaked. She gives a little shriek.

"*Somebody* left the faucet on last night, *Mom*," says Bee.

"Well, it wasn't me," says Gemma. *Was it?* It must have been. Drugged out of her mind. Raiding the kitchen cupboards, leaving the faucet running. She doubles down on her lie. "I told you I was awake until three. I didn't leave my room at all."

Gemma's such a wreck. Back-to-school night might have been the beginning of her personal comeback, but it hasn't affected her business at all. She's still down nearly 40 percent. If things don't improve in the next couple of months she'll have to take out a second mortgage.

"Get the mop," she says to Bee. She wants nothing more than to sleep off her hangover, but it's already past nine, and these two precious girls sitting in front of her want a home-cooked breakfast, just like in the old days when Marley would stay over almost every weekend. It's so sweet to see them together, in their sweats, waiting for her to pull out the box of Bisquick.

"Pancakes?" Gemma asks.

The girls' faces beam out their emotions, *happy, happy, happy.*

———

Ruth comes to pick up Marley at eleven. She, too, is dragging.

"Bad sleep?"

"*No* sleep," says Ruth. She feels her forehead. "I'm hot. Is it hot in here? How do you know if you're having a hot flash?" She falls onto the couch so elegantly Gemma wonders if she's practiced the move.

"Let's watch some shit TV," Ruth says.

"I've got to run to Trader Joe's."

"No, you don't."

No, she doesn't. Seeing Ruth settling in for the long haul, she invented an excuse on the fly.

"I do. I have nothing to cook for dinner."

"Let's order in. Burmese. Have you tried that new place on Telegraph, Burma Moon? It's amazing!"

Dinner? Ruth wants to stay until dinner? Gemma planned on

crawling back into bed with the new Stephen King novel after Marley left.

"We had a little accident this morning. Somebody, *I'm* being blamed, left the faucet running last night and we woke up to a flooded kitchen."

"How odd," says Ruth.

"We mopped it up but the floor's still really damp. I have to go rent one of those wet-dry vacuums from Ace."

Ruth pauses and then says, "Do you want me to help? I have a tennis lesson at one, but I could cancel if you want."

Now they're both lying. The floor is fine and Ruth doesn't have a tennis lesson. The last thing she wants to do is wet vacuum the floor with Gemma.

"No, that's okay. But thanks for offering." *Yippee! She can go back to bed.*

"Sure. But how strange. You just *forgot* to turn the faucet off after dinner or something? And nobody heard it running?"

Gemma contemplates telling Ruth about her Ambien habit but decides against it. She's going to stop cold turkey tonight. A few days of rebound insomnia and then she'll be fine.

She shrugs. "Yeah, I guess. The girls were hanging out and I went straight to bed."

"Right," says Ruth.

BEE

Marley won't stop texting her.

Is it ok if I wear tights under the shorts?

Not sure about the crop top. Would it be ok to wear a leotard under the shirt?

What's the color of that lip gloss you were wearing last night? Is it ok if I get the same shade?

Are you sure you want me out in front? I don't want people to be mad at me

I think Coco might be mad at me

I'd be ok if she was in the front

She'd be ok, she'd be ok, she'd be ok. Oh my god. Does Marley have any idea how desperate she sounds?

Bee shuts off her phone, something she rarely does. *Be nice,* she admonishes herself. It will take a while for Marley to acclimate. She's been on the outside for so long. She has virtually no friends, except for Lewis Singleton, who's super, super smart—a self-described brogrammer. He latched onto Marley in middle school and to this day still follows her around like a little duckling. He senses something familiar in her; Bee gets it. Marley's not as intense as Lewis, but she's super smart and very focused on the things she loves, like—well—Bee doesn't really know what Marley loves anymore. And as for Bee, she's smart and focused. Okay, maybe that's overstating it. Focus is not her strong suit and she's probably of average intelligence. Yeah. Average and difficulty focusing. That's her.

Bee turns on the TV and clicks through stations with the sound off. Her mother is upstairs sleeping off her hangover. She has no idea Bee knows about the Ambien. It's getting bad. She's never seen her the way she was this morning—stumbling, slurry, like she could barely hold up her head. It freaked her out. Should she confront her mother? Or maybe she should tell Ruth. Maybe Ruth could confront her mother for her.

Bee turns her phone back on and ignores three new messages from Marley. She takes a photo of her feet, one of her best features, the toes descending in length, none of that second-toe-bigger-than-all-the-rest shit. Somebody once commented she could be a foot model. Why not, if the SLUTZ didn't take off, lolz.

Give the people what they want. She posts the photo on IG. Then she snuggles into the couch and lets the *likes* stream into her, until she's *fullfullfull* to the brim with confidence. It's a fake confidence, though, crispy like meringue, and temporary. If you put it on your tongue it will melt and leave you hungrier than before, but it's all she has.

MARLEY

When they pull into the driveway and Marley sees Sander's truck, her heart gives a little leap. Sander is their handyman. He comes to 626 Buttercup frequently; there's always something that needs to be fixed. He's basically on the payroll. Sander also happens to look like a lumberjack version of Harry Styles. Longish hair tucked under a Carhartt beanie. Red Wing boots. Muddy green eyes. He's putting the finishing touches on a shed he's built to house their garbage bins.

"Hey there, Ms. Thorne," he calls out to her mother as they get out of the car. Her mother huffs. She has told Sander repeatedly to call her Ruth, but Sander always calls her *Ms. Thorne*. This offends Marley's mother because it makes her feel old.

Marley grabs her backpack. It's loaded with books, but she shoulders it easily. She feels herself moving with a kind of grace she's never had before. Head high. Shoulders back. Hair swinging.

Sander looks at her and does an unmistakable double take. It's involuntary and almost comical, cartoonlike. His eyes skitter off her face and slide down her body. She feels the heat of his gaze and even though it's only a split second before he gets hold of himself and puts on his professional face, in that split second she understands she's the one with the power. She has reduced him to something.

"Hey, Marley," he says gruffly.

"Hey." Marley swans past him.

—

"What the hell was that?" asks her mother once they're inside.

Marley shrugs, as if she has no idea what she's talking about. But her mother misses nothing. She saw the way Sander looked at her.

"I asked you a question." Her mother's eyes are glittering and beady. She looks like a crow.

"What?" Marley says innocently, which sets her mother off.

"He was looking at me, not you," she snaps. She turns her back on Marley, grabs the kettle, and starts filling it up with water.

And just like that, a moment that Marley has been waiting for all her life to arrive is gone. Stolen by her mother.

—

There's only a week until the talent show, so when Bee sets a nightly rehearsal schedule, Marley tells her mother she and Bee are working together on a Summer of Love history project for Ms. Chu's class.

Marley has the iPhone X with the biggest screen, so they record their rehearsals on her phone. She dumps the videos in a file called Bay of Pigs 1967. At night, when her mother's asleep, Marley puts on her headphones and studies the videos. Frankie's Nae Nae needs work, but they've all got the Renegade down.

Marley gets careless. She dances imprudently around the house. When her mother goes to the bathroom she pops, she twerks, she does the Milly Rock. It's impossible to hide her happiness. She's part of a tribe now. There's no going back.

One morning at breakfast her mother says, "Give me your phone. *Now.*"

Marley gives it to her, willing her hands not to shake.

"Password?" her mother demands.

"Three one four one five nine."

"What's that code for?"

"Just random numbers." Of course, her mother has no idea it's the first six digits of pi.

Her mother goes immediately to her photo app, and thumbs to her videos. "The Bay of Pigs was in 1961. If you're going to lie may I suggest you get your dates right. Sloppy, Marley, sloppy."

Her mother opens the video and presses play.

RUTH

Marley is sobbing. Marley is weeping. She's crying so hard she can't catch her breath.

"You've been lying to me for weeks! Did Gemma approve of this dance? Did she think I knew about it, too? Of course she did. You've made a goddamned fool out of me!"

"No, I haven't, I swear," Marley bleats. "All Gemma knew was that we were practicing for the talent show. She didn't see our rehearsals."

"Don't make excuses for Gemma. And why don't you protect me like you protect Gemma? Why am I always left in the dark?" Ruth snarls.

Ruth knew something was going on. She was used to Marley treating her phone like a second appendage, but lately her obsession with it seemed out of control. She was constantly texting with a smug smile on her face. A smile that said she had a secret.

Ruth watches the video for the third time and it's even worse than the first two times. The transcendent look on Marley's face as she wiggles her butt. Her daughter's breasts bouncing in her sports bra, barely contained. She's out in front. Ruth can't believe Bee has allowed this. But Bee isn't as good a dancer as Marley, that's clear. Marley is the showstopper for once.

So *this* is what Marley's been abandoning her for? Evenings with this *pack* (and they are a pack, crude and feral). Night after night, Ruth's eaten yogurt for dinner, drifted around the house like a cipher. Weightless. Tetherless.

Ruth reads her daughter's emotions as they flit across her face: guilty, ashamed, frightened. *Good!* Ruth shivers with pleasure. Oh, to have this kind of power over somebody! To induce this kind of vulnerability. She feels herself filling, becoming hard and taut.

She knows soon it will be over. She'll deflate and be overcome with sadness at the sight of Marley's face. Then it will be unbearable to see her baby in such distress. She'll hold her in her arms, rock her, tell her everybody makes mistakes, she'll never make this mistake again, will she? *WILL SHE?*

"I'll tell Bee you found out and you forbid me to be in the group anymore," Marley frantically suggests, having reached the bargaining stage.

"You'll do no such thing. You will not blame this on me. This is your fault. You are accountable. Tell Bee you've changed your mind. It's a disgusting dance. You don't want to participate."

"But I love it, Mom. I'm a good dancer. We're not doing anything wrong. This is the way kids dance now."

Bee has brainwashed Marley once again. "It's the way sluts dance."

Marley's eyes widen.

"Yes, I said *sluts*."

The corners of Marley's mouth quiver. *Is she smiling?*

"What's so funny?"

Marley shakes her head—she *is* laughing!

Ruth slams her fists on the table. Marley lunges backward in fear.

"I'm sending Bee a text from you."

"No, don't. At least let me do it," Marley protests, trying to snatch her phone back, but Ruth shakes her off.

Ruth texts Bee. I'm not feeling it anymore. I'm out.

GEMMA

Debbie Darling (yes, that is really her name) stops her in the hallway. "Gemma! How serendipitous to run into you! I'd like to make an appointment to discuss Chloe's PSAT prep. I know the first test isn't until next year, but we want to get a jump on it. We're hoping to get a National Merit Scholarship."

As soon as high school starts, parents shift from "them" to "we." Getting into college is a family sport at Hillside. It annoys Gemma, and normally she'd have encouraged Chloe to take the first PSAT without prepping so she could get a baseline score, but Gemma badly needs the business now.

"We can set up a time for you to come in," says Gemma. "And don't stress. She's going to do great."

"Chloe Darling, she was in Wings with Bee. Don't forget her name. I'll be calling," Debbie chirps, walking away.

Wings. Gemma remembers the day she was informed that her daughter was chosen. And boy, oh, boy, did Bee rise to the occasion. Her transformation was stunning. She started getting straight As. She worked a grade level ahead in math. Gemma's parent-teacher conferences were filled with nothing but accolades.

And then everything changed in fifth grade when Bee failed to test into the program. Gemma went to Mr. Nunez to complain, but the decision was final. They retested all the kids every year so it would be fair and Bee simply didn't make it this time around.

"This is actually a good thing," he said. "You want her to have disappointments. You want her to fail, and better she fails early, in lower school, than in high school, when the stakes are so much higher."

It was a brutal fall to earth, compounded by the fact that a few weeks later Bee got her period, the first girl in her class to menstruate. She lived in fear of being outed, having an accident and bleeding through her pants. Mostly what Gemma remembers of that time was Bee's rage. It was so unfair. *Why was she the only one who had to go through this? Why did she have to be the first?* No matter how many times Gemma told her that within a year or two most of the girls would start to menstruate as well, it didn't help. Fifth grade was a total disaster. Gemma couldn't wait for her to graduate and make the move to middle school—a fresh start, she thought. How hopeful she was. How naive.

She walks into the auditorium. Twenty minutes before the show and it's already packed. Some parents have been waiting in their seats for an hour.

"Gemma!" Ruth pops up and waves at her. "I saved you a seat!"

Gemma weaves her way down the aisle and plops down beside Ruth. Marley sits on Ruth's left.

"Marls, what are you doing here? Aren't you guys on in the first act?"

Marley shakes her head miserably.

"What's going on?" Gemma whispers to Ruth.

Ruth says, "Cramps."

"Oh, that's a shame. I'm sorry you're not feeling well, sweetheart," Gemma says to Marley. "I know how hard you guys have been working on the dance."

The first act is a boy named Henry Hill. He sings a wobbly rendition of Ed Sheeran's "Thinking Out Loud." It's a brave, completely wrong song choice (I will be loving you until I'm seventy?) for a high school talent show. Entirely too earnest and the boy doesn't have the voice to carry it off, never mind that he's four foot something and looks like he weighs eighty pounds. *Why didn't his parents steer him in another direction?* It's excruciating to sit through. Gemma's heart is in her throat the entire time—she feels so bad for Henry Hill.

To her surprise (and his) he gets a standing ovation, and Gemma thinks how much things have changed since she was in school. It's not cool to bully overtly vulnerable kids, at least not in public. But is this better? To overcompensate by giving them standing ovations when they don't deserve it? Gemma's happy for Henry Hill, but this is not the real world. Tomorrow morning he'll go back to being invisible, or worse, a target. Adolescence is crushing.

Only one more act before Bee and the gang. Bee's a great dancer and she's choreographed the entire routine. Gemma hasn't been allowed to see the dance, Bee wanted it to be a surprise, but she has a gut feeling it will bring the house down. Bee needs a win. Middle school was rocky. She focused on all the wrong things: boys, parties, gossip, clothes. High school could be the start of a new and improved Bee.

The second act is a brother-and-sister violin and cello act. They're perfect, but they only get modest applause, a few whoops. A standing ovation would be redundant. And then finally, it's Bee's turn.

Gemma whispers to Ruth, "I'm so nervous."

Ruth squeezes her hand. Marley sinks down low in her seat.

The girls run out onstage. They are dressed identically. Crop tops and shorts. They turn their backs on the audience. Their shorts are so short Gemma can see the cheeks of their asses. *Where the hell did Bee get those shorts? Are they even wearing underwear?* The music starts, Fetty Wap's "Trap Queen," and they begin to twerk in concert.

Bitch you up on the bando . . . I'll fuck in your benz hoe. Oh, fuck me in my benz hoe, Gemma thinks, frozen with shock, as are most of the parents in the audience. The kids are a different story. They rocket out of their seats, screaming their appreciation, undulating with Bee and her crew. *Where did they all learn to dance like that?* Gemma feels ancient, prehistoric. Bee's face is ecstatic. She slithers across the floor, feeding off the crowd.

A flurry of teachers streams down the aisles and onstage. The music is abruptly shut off. The girls led away.

———

An hour later, when Gemma and Bee emerge from Mr. Nunez's office (all the girls have been given three-day suspensions), Ruth and Marley are waiting in the hall for them. Gemma is so furious at Bee she can't bear to look at her.

"She's grounded for life," she says to Ruth.

Bee and Marley walk a few feet behind them. Suddenly Marley cries out. Gemma spins around to see Bee yanking Marley violently back by her hair.

"You pussy!" Bee screams.

Marley moans and clutches her ponytail in pain.

"Jesus fucking Christ," Mr. Nunez says.

"Bee, apologize!" shrieks Gemma. "Tell Marley you're sorry."

"I'm not sorry," shrieks Bee. "Not one little bit."

"You need to stay out of Marley Thorne's way, young lady," says Mr. Nunez. He stares at Gemma intently. "Make sure she does."

"I will. I promise nothing like this will happen again, Mr. Nunez."

PART TWO

RUTH

Ruth's phone lights up a little after ten. MY MOTHER MADE ME DO IT.

OneWayAtATime: I'm speechless. What a night!!

WhatYouSeeIsNotWhatYouGet: I don't really understand what bitch you up on the bando means. The bitch is in a band? Like on a grandstand?

TortoiseWinsTheRace: I don't really know either. Hold on let me google it.

TortoiseWinsTheRace: A bando is an abandoned house that's used to make or sell drugs.

WhatYouSeeIsNotWhatYouGet: Of course it is.

OneWayAtATime: Those outfits. You could practically see their shmundies! And Bee? Was she high? I heard she's turned into quite the little stoner.

HappilyEverAfter: She looked like a slut. They all looked like sluts. That was their secret name for their dance crew did you know that? Sluts but with a Z, SLUTZ.

PennySavedPennyEarned: You're kidding.

HappilyEverAfter: I kid you not PennySavedPennyEarned.

TortoiseWinsTheRace: Oh I get it. Kind of like those Bratz dolls. That's probably where they got the idea.

OneWayAtATime: Everything has a Z stuck on it at the end now. It's ridicz.

HappilyEverAfter: My DD would NEVER participate in something like that. She knows better.

TortoiseWinsTheRace: Neither would my DD. So obvious. So crude.

PennySavedPennyEarned: My DD was appalled. Bee was repugnant. They all were. Exhibiting themselves like that.

OneWayAtATime: I heard they got 3-day suspensions.

HappilyEverAfter: And poor Gemma. Back in the shithouse again. Just when she was climbing out, Bee put her right back in.

WhatYouSeeIsNotWhatYouGet: She's so checked out. What kind of a mother wouldn't ferret out that her daughter was in a dance group called SLUTZ?

OneWayAtATime: A negligent mother that's who.

PennySavedPennyEarned: From what I've heard Bee is a sneaky, manipulative girl. Why do we always blame the mother? It's not all Gemma's fault.

TortoiseWinsTheRace: I agree. Let's try and give Gemma and Bee the benefit of the doubt. Clearly they're struggling.

WhatYouSeeIsNotWhatYouGet: Maybe this is their rock bottom. It's all uphill from here.

OneWayAtATime: Somehow I doubt that.

HappilyEverAfter: Check this out, ladies. #blessedDD's

HappilyEverAfter sends a link. It's a cheesy gif. Like an old Hallmark card. A mother and a daughter sitting under a tree on a blanket. Bluebirds hop from branch to branch. The sun shimmers. A plane flies by with a banner attached to its tail: *A daughter is the happy memories of the past, the joyful moments of the present, and the hope and promise of the future.*

WhatYouSeeIsNotWhatYouGet: OMG LOVE!

TortoiseWinsTheRace: Awwww!

OneWayAtATime: Boom boom boom goes my heart . . .

HappilyEverAfter: Knew you guys would relate! What do you think PennySavedPennyEarned? Isn't it darling?

Give me a fucking break, thinks Ruth.

PennySavedPennyEarned: Totes adorbz

MARLEY

"Get up, get up, Marley bear."

Marley wakes to find her mother gazing down upon her, love as harsh as stadium lights beaming out of her eyes. This kind of love requires her full attention. A certain sort of *sedulousness*, a PSAT word.

Ruth has had Marley studying for the PSAT since seventh grade. She's under strict orders not to tell Gemma. Her mother wants Gemma to think she aced the test with no prep, courtesy of her 130 IQ. Marley's pretty sure her IQ is nowhere near 130; maybe 115 tops. She's bright, but she's no genius. Her grades are a result of her work ethic.

Her mother stares at her hungrily. She needs Marley's forgiveness.

"Guess what? We're playing hooky today! We're going to go into the city. Nordstrom! Saks! I'm going to buy you an entire new wardrobe. Elegant. Sophisticated." Her mother tucks a strand of hair behind Marley's ear. "You're not a child anymore. You need some grown-up clothes."

"Forever 21's at Westfield's. H&M. Brandy Melville," says Marley.

Her mother tsks. "Those clothes are disposable. They won't last you a month. We're going to get you some quality stuff. Clothes you'll have for a lifetime."

"Saks is too fancy," ventures Marley. Normally she'd just accept whatever decisions her mother makes, but today her mother owes her.

"Well, what's your style? More of a comfortable vibe?"

"Yeah, comfy," says Marley, thinking of Lululemon.

Her mother tilts her head, her features go all smushy. "I'm so proud of you for sticking to your guns. Doing the right thing. Refusing to be a sheep. Not following the crowd."

Could her mother use any more clichés? When Marley was younger she believed whatever her mother told her. Marley didn't have strong observation skills, didn't pick up social cues, couldn't read a room, unlike her mother, who excelled in all these things. Ruth had a high EQ, Marley did not.

Now, it's the other way around.

Her mother glowers. "You don't look happy. All those girls got suspended. You understand that will go on their records. Permanently."

"I know. I just feel bad for them. For Bee."

"You feel bad for *Bee*? She practically assaulted you in the hallway, may I remind you!"

Marley deserved the hairpulling and the name-calling. She'd abandoned Bee and the group. She would have gladly taken the suspension and endured it proudly. It would have bonded them all together. Now she'll be banished forever. There will be no getting back in.

"Oh, Marley." Her mother strokes her cheek. "You've always been such a compassionate girl. I love that about you, just like your mama. Always putting others first. But you must be careful about giving too much of yourself. People will take. They'll take and take and then you'll find yourself with nothing."

———

They spend the day in San Francisco. They shop in the morning, dim sum for lunch. More shopping, then they catch a five-dollar showing of *Lady Bird* at the Roxie and her mother sobs all the way through it.

When they get home, Marley takes her bags and climbs the stairs to her bedroom.

"You're coming back down, right?" her mother calls up to her, a panicked look on her face.

Marley is depleted in every way. She's friendless, she's H&Mless, she's motherless, even though her mother is standing there in front of her. All she wants to do is go to bed.

She holds up the bags. "Just going to put these away."

"Hang them up so they don't wrinkle. And wear the Eileen Fisher poncho tomorrow with jeans. It'll be so cute!"

———

"Can you update my OS?" asks her mother when Marley comes back downstairs. She hands Marley her laptop.

Marley types in her password: RuthAnnThorneTheGreat. "You've had this password forever. You really should change it. Better yet, use a password manager."

"*You're* my password manager," says her mother.

This is true. Marley is in charge of their digital life. She's set up everything that keeps their household functioning smoothly: Alexa, Nest, Netflix, Ring, Amazon, Spotify, even their banking. Her mother is more than capable of managing everything herself; she just pretends to be computer illiterate because she's lazy.

"When's the last time you did it?"

"Mmm, a while? I keep telling them to remind me again tomorrow."

Marley clicks on About This Mac. "You're two updates behind. Mom, the updates are really important."

"I know, I know, but it just takes so long. Hooours," her mother drawls.

———

Marley FaceTimes her father at 10:35. He's frequently up until midnight. After Luciana and Oscar have gone to bed, he puts on the Turner Classic Movie channel and lets it drone on in the background as he does the crossword.

"Sweetheart!" he crows. His face looms large in her screen, his eyes owlish. "Something's wrong. I can't see you, I can only see me."

"I don't have video on. I'm doing a face mask," says Marley, lying. "It's made from avocados. I look like the Grinch." If her father saw her he'd know something was wrong.

All day long Marley's phone had chimed with incoming texts from the SLUTZ.

Fuck you Marley

You fat bitch

We only allowed you in cause Bee begged us to

You're a suckass dancer

Omg your back fat

These girls who just weeks ago welcomed her into their club. Who admired her. Who showcased her talents. Whose attention and inclusion transformed her and made her into some shining thing, so bright that even Sander was momentarily dumbstruck. That's all over now.

"How's it going? Tell me everything," her father says.

Tell me everything. Only somebody who really loves you says that. She is so distraught over the whole SLUTZ thing, she wishes she could tell him everything. But she can't.

Marley catches a glimpse of her reflection in the window. Even though her image is distorted—her eyes seem to be melting down onto her cheekbones, the space between her nose and mouth is unnaturally long—there's a truth there. A mirror of who she really is. A glimpse of the freak that dwells inside her.

Her mother is the only one who knows of this freak, and she's tried to cast it out of Marley. To drive it away. And even though her mother's methods can sometimes be harsh, Marley is grateful to her. Her life's mission has been to rescue Marley, to save her from her worst impulses, to bring her into the light.

But Marley hasn't made it easy. *You're your own worst enemy,* another cliché her mother has repeated to her over and over again through the course of her childhood. As if she could just snap her fingers and banish the freak. Kick it out.

No, the best Marley can hope for is to put that part of her into some sort of forever slumber. Slip it a poisonous draught and let it drift into a lifelong sleep.

"Not much to tell," says Marley.

"Really? I don't believe that. How's geometry? Are you still on the congruence unit?"

They FaceTime every week. Her father knows her entire schedule, the names of her teachers, her textbooks, her grades.

But he's a part-time father—a fact her mother reminds her of frequently. He has another family, and they only have two bedrooms. When Marley visits, she sleeps on the pull-out couch in the office, evidence, according to her mother, that she is not a priority. Marley hasn't told her mother how in the summers they transform the office into a real bedroom. It's only during the school year that the room stays in its office form, for her shorter visits.

"Yeah." Marley strains to keep her voice from breaking.

"Kinda boring?" he asks.

"I guess."

"Mmm. That's too bad." He smiles at her, his eyes crinkling. "What else? Tell me something else."

She is so endlessly interesting to him—it makes her heart hurt. She is endlessly interesting to her mother, too, but in a completely different way. Her father's love is a hummingbird. Her mother's is a hawk.

"Everything's okay?" he asks.

Marley takes a deep breath. "Yeah, Dad, everything's fine. I gotta go. This stuff is so thick I can barely move my mouth."

"Call back this weekend. Oscar is dying to talk to you. He's desperate to get a pet rat. Can you believe it? We never should have let him watch *Ratatouille*. We're trying to talk him into a hamster." He chuckles.

"Kay, Dad, love you."

"Love you, too, my beautiful girl. Night, night."

Marley ends the call. She is not a beautiful girl, no, she is not.

GEMMA

Gemma texts Ruth. Can you and Marley come over for dinner on Saturday so Bee can apologize?

Bee's suspension hasn't chastened her, instead it's made her more openly defiant, and judging by the constant chiming of her phone, she's become a folk hero among her peers. Gemma should take her phone away, but Bee would go absolutely nuts and Gemma's not up for the battle.

Marley—she didn't have cramps. She made the calculated decision to back out of the performance. And even though Gemma understands Marley's decision was interpreted by Bee as abandonment, Bee owes Marley an apology.

Gemma checks her phone. No response from Ruth. She must be furious. Gemma doesn't blame her; Bee basically assaulted Marley. Ruth would be within her rights to press charges. But she would never do that, would she?

———

On the last evening of Bee's suspension, Gemma walks through the door with Thai food. All of Bee's favorites: Pad See Ew, Honey Pork, and spring rolls. She knows she shouldn't be rewarding Bee with takeout. If she were a good mother, a *disciplined* mother, she'd make her eat, what? *Gruel*?

Bee jumps up and takes the bag out of her arms. "Thank you!"

"This is not a reward."

"I know."

"I was just craving Thai."

"Yup."

"Have you learned your lesson?"

"Yup."

"And what lesson have you learned?"

"Never put a *Z* on the end of *slut*. It diminishes the word and makes it funny, and *slut* is not a funny word."

Gemma doesn't know whether to ground her or applaud her.

Bee sets the table. "Wine?"

It's a Wednesday night. She tries to drink only on weekends. *What the heck, it's been a tough week.* "Sure."

Bee pours her a glass and bends deeply at the waist like a server. "The Woodbridge sauvignon blanc, Madame."

Bee sits down and rams a spring roll down her throat. "So good."

Gemma puts a spoonful of Honey Pork and Pad See Ew on her plate.

"That's all you're having?"

"I'm not that hungry. I had a big lunch. You enjoy it." She wanted to do something nice to mark the end of Bee's suspension. Something that normalized life again.

———

After dinner, Gemma runs a bath. She uses the last of her L'Occitane Verbena bath gel. She stays in until the water is cold (she's heard cold-water baths help with anxiety) then runs to her bedroom, shivering, and puts on her nightgown.

"*Black Mirror*?" Bee yells from downstairs. "We still have three episodes to watch in Season Four."

"No thanks, honey, I'm beat. Gonna read in bed. Don't stay up late," she calls out.

She's just pulled the covers up to her chin when her phone chimes. A text from Ruth. Finally.

We can come to dinner on Saturday. What time?

———

"Hi." Gemma kisses Ruth on the cheek.

"Hi, honey," Gemma says to Marley.

Marley walks in with her head down, shoulders slumped. Ruth is unreadable.

Gemma puts a hand on Marley's shoulder. "You didn't do anything wrong."

Bee sits on the couch, her fingers knitted together, looking at the carpet. At least there's that. A pretense of contrition. Her posture should count for something, shouldn't it?

"I'm proud of you for standing your ground," Gemma says.

Gemma's known Marley for nine years now, and Marley's character has never wavered. She's ethical and loyal. Self-possessed and mature.

She and Ruth parent completely differently. Ruth thinks she's too permissive. Not vigilant enough. She gives Bee too much freedom. And she's probably right, case in point last weekend's humiliating debacle. But Gemma leaves room for Bee to screw up. In the Thorne household, screwing up is simply out of the question.

Marley must have backed out at the last minute because she knew the consequences would be dire with her mother, as they will be for Bee. Well, not really dire (Gemma already has enough distance to know she and Bee will laugh about this someday), but tonight Gemma will pretend that they are. A wholehearted mea culpa is required to get them back on track.

Bee stands, trembling. "I'm really, really sorry, Marls." And to everybody's surprise she starts weeping.

——

Later Gemma will wonder if Bee's breakdown was sincere or a masterful performance. Well, whatever it was it worked in her favor. Within seconds Bee is the one being comforted and consoled.

And by the end of the evening, an entire pan of baked ziti having been consumed, nearly two bottles of Apothic red having been downed, they are family again, pledging their love and loyalty to one another.

The us-against-the-world wall rebuilt.

BEE

Yo! You're Invited Beotches!

To Bee's 15th Birthday Blowout

October 1

Chez Howard, 6 p.m.–midnite

Please do not contact the host with your dietary restrictions or food allergies

They will not be accommodated

Hahahahaha!

GET READY TO PARTYYYYYY!!!!!

Bee sends the Evite to Frankie, Abby, Coco, Shanice, and Aditi. Screw Marley. She's fifteen years old and she's not going to be pressured into inviting her to her party. She and Marley have barely talked since the talent show. During their three-day suspension, the SLUTZ spread rumors about how they'd kicked Marley off the crew because she was such a lame dancer and a wuss, unwilling to risk the punishment—but the punishment was SO WORTH IT. Just as Bee predicted, they'd become celebrities. The mothers were furious, but that fury quickly transformed into a grudging kind of pride. *Their daughters were feminists! They were firebrands! This was perfect college app essay material!*

They nodded along to keep the peace but they were not feminists. They were something else that didn't have a name yet, something that Bee would invent. She would be the leader of this new movement; this was her destiny.

Kids actually call her Queen B now, and she loves it. She walks through the hallways and gets high-fived and fist-bumped. And Marley—Marley has vanished. Who knows where Marley is. Probably in the library studying for their geometry test.

A few minutes later, Bee is swamped with guilt. Bee suspects it was Ruth who made Marley back out of the talent show. *Not feeling it?* That's something adults say. Ruth had either forced her to send that text or sent it for her. Marley could have come back from it, if only she'd turned on her mother (like any normal teenager would) and blamed her. But Marley was a goody-goody. She'd never sell Ruth out.

Bee cranks her music. She stands in front of the mirror and grinds and twerks. She thinks of Dylan Rorback. He's so hot; she so desperately wants a boyfriend. Boys think she's cool, but they don't lust after her the way they lust after Coco and Aditi. They give her the bro treatment. She's never had a boy's eyes scan her body, linger on her boobs and ass.

Bee's nothing. Yes, she's popular, but she's ugly. Her hair is a rat's nest. She sits on the bed, her head in her hands.

MARLEY

September 28, 4:30 p.m.

Hi Marley. Soleil here. Confetti popping! Champagne glass! Just checking in. Haven't heard from you in a couple of weeks. Were you guys a big hit at the talent show?

Marley stares at her phone. *Weird.* Soleil has never reached out to her before. It's a break in text therapy protocol. She must be worried about her. Marley lets herself take that in. She has the urge to ask Soleil if she likes her. *Likes her* likes her, in a favorite patient sort of way.

I wouldn't say that

Oh? What happened?

I quit

You did? Why? You were so excited. Sad face. Yellow heart.

I decided not to do it

Interesting. Was that the right decision for you?

I guess. The rest of the girls got suspended for three days

Whoa. That must have been some dance. So when did you quit?

The night before the talent show

Hmm. You didn't give your friends much notice.

Nope

May I ask why?

It's just when I did it

Were they upset with you?

Eye roll face

Marley, that must have been really hard. But it sounds like you made the right decision for you and that's progress.

Thumbs up

Was there fallout?

You mean am I wandering the halls at lunchtime alone looking for a place to go—yes I am

But I'm kinda relieved tbh. Now I can get back to Infinite Jest. I've only got 582 pages left haha

I understand the urge to joke about this, but I'd like to invite you to go deeper. Let's talk about what you're feeling. I hope you're not isolating.

No worries. I'm not alone. Mom's here. Winky face

RUTH

Ruth awakens in the middle of the night, panicked; she's just re-membered that Bee's birthday is on Saturday. She runs to Marley's room, sits on the side of her bed, and pokes her gently on the shoul-der. Marley moans but doesn't wake. She blows on Marley's face. What she really wants to do is yank her upright and shake her, but she doesn't want Marley to see her desperation.

"Wake up, Marley bear, wake up. Did you get an invite to Bee's birthday party?"

Marley blinks. She shakes her head no. It's like the seconds be-fore an earthquake, the roar before the shaking.

"Is she having a party? Maybe she's not having a party this year. Maybe she's outgrown birthday parties, she is fifteen at all," Ruth says hopefully.

"She's having a party, she just didn't invite me. No biggie."

No biggie? Bee said she was going to invite Marley to her party. She promised!

Ruth looks down at her daughter. Marley's imperfections are glaring. A whitehead on the side of her nose. Greasy forehead. A stumpy neck.

"What did you do? And don't you dare lie to me."

"Um, I didn't do anything, she just doesn't like me anymore."

"But you made up at Gemma's."

"She's still mad at me for backing out of the talent show."

Marley's going to blame this on her? Ruth sits on her hands, try-ing to calm herself, but it's too late. Anger comes barreling into the station. She welcomes it, she's deserving of it. Her dear old friend, rage.

"It's no wonder she dumped you. Look at you! I bought you that grapefruit Neutrogena face wash with the exfoliant beads, and are you using it? No, obviously not. You have to try harder. Take care of yourself. Dress better. Act confident."

Marley covers her face with her arm.

"You're always so needy. *Please, oh, please, like me.* That's the air you give off. It repulses people."

Marley cries and now Ruth cries, too. Not for her daughter but for herself.

———

Ruth's father took a curve of the Pacific Coast Highway too fast. They swerved off the road and plummeted down a thousand-foot cliff. Approximately five seconds later, the Chevette smashed into the ocean, nose first.

Lou insisted Ruth be apprised of the details. "You need to know exactly what happened," she said. "It will hurt now but it will help you move on. Otherwise you'll just invent something that will be far worse than the truth."

The truth was far worse than anything Ruth could have invented. She couldn't stop imagining those last five seconds when her parents knew they were about to die. *Did they reach for each other's hands? Did they cry out in fear? Was her name the last word they spoke?*

After the funeral, Ruth asked when she could go home.

"You won't be going home," said Lou.

"Can I move in with Lindy, then?" It made sense to her. Lindy was her best friend. Her grandparents were strangers.

"We'll talk about that later."

"We have to take her. There's nobody else," Ruth overheard Lou say to Charlie that night.

"You'll move in with us," her grandfather said the next morning.

———

Ruth's grandparents led a regimented life. Martinis at five in the library along with a wedge of Brie and a small dish of green olives stuffed with pimento. Ruth was not invited to cocktail hour, so she pressed her ear against the closed door and listened. Murmured conversations turned to soft giggles turned to laughter; they never ran out of things to say to each other. Her grandmother was the moon. Her grandfather was the sun that orbited around her. There were no other planets in their galaxy.

Once, Ruth grew so jealous she burst into the library. "I know how to make a martini." This was a lie, she only knew how to make a gin and tonic.

Lou's lip curled up in anger. "This is grown-up time."

"You have a room full of toys," said Charlie. "Go play."

A few weeks after she'd moved in, a delivery truck arrived bearing gifts. A four-poster bed with a sheer pink canopy. Brand-new clothes and shoes and underwear. Care Bears and My Little Ponys. Teddy Ruxpin and Lite-Brite. Spirograph and a Magic 8 Ball.

Ruth felt like she'd stepped into a fairy tale. Until she realized they'd bought her off. Gifts in exchange for keeping out of their way. Her grandparents were selfish people. They never wanted to be parents, they wanted even less to be grandparents. They started locking the library door at cocktail hour so she couldn't interrupt them.

———

They ate dinner late, at eight. Ruth tried to contribute, to be interesting, to charm. She remembered dinner with her parents, where she was the center of the conversation. *What did you do today at recess, Ruth? Do you like the meat loaf? Did you make your Christmas list for Santa yet?*

Her grandparents didn't ask her questions. By the time dinner came around, they were soused. They couldn't fake interest in her. They were stuck with Ruth. They were stuck with each other.

The dinners became unbearable; they made Ruth achingly lonely. She asked if she could eat earlier in the kitchen, and her grandmother was happy to grant her request. Maybe she was a ghost. Maybe she had sailed over that cliff with her parents.

Ruth struggled at her new school. The stench of neediness leached her off, like sewage. She made friends but they'd abandon her within weeks, like a diet that didn't result in fast-enough weight loss. She exhausted them. She wore everybody out.

As she grew older she grew bitter. Every time she saw one of her classmates with their parents, she thought *fuck you*. When the teacher asked them to make a family tree she thought *you son of a bitch*. When she was the only kid not invited to the end-of-the-year barbecue at Vera Velazquez's house she muttered *whore* under her breath as they passed each other in the hallway.

In middle school, she went on the offensive. She targeted the weak girls, the scapegoats, the scholarship kids. She'd taunt them, expose their vulnerabilities for everybody to see, and for a while she'd feel like a giant. But eventually the high would recede and she'd become invisible again.

When she was in ninth grade, she found a package of Dexatrim in her bathroom, put there by Lou, no doubt. She was getting chunky; she came home every day from school and ate two packages of Pop-Tarts. She took the pills and soon she was svelte and turning heads. Finally, she had some power.

She lost her virginity at fourteen. After that, she sneaked a steady stream of boys onto the grounds of Lou's estate. They had sex in the stables, the fecund scent of oats and hay lingering in the air.

On the day she left for college, she found her grandmother in the garden, sipping her morning cup of Earl Grey. Often, they went weeks without speaking to each other. Ruth was like a boarder, except she didn't pay rent.

"Well, goodbye," she said.

"You're welcome," said her grandmother.

"Thank you," said Ruth.

Her grandmother put down her tea. "Just so we're clear. You're not rich, we are."

Eight years later, Lou would die of breast cancer. A few months after that, Charlie would die of heartbreak (liver failure—he literally drank himself to death).

Ruth inherited everything.

GEMMA

Gemma wheels her cart through Costco, Bee's list in hand. Diet Mountain Dew and Flaming Hot Cheetos. *Check.* Froot Loops and Cinnamon Toast Crunch. *Check.* Totino's Pizza Rolls and Ling Ling potstickers. She does a U-turn and heads for the frozen food section.

Her phone chimes. A text from Ruth.

Hope Bee has a wonderful birthday! Can't believe she's 15 already. Marley and I will raise a toast to her tonight.

Confused, Gemma stops in the aisle and tries to make sense of the text. *Is Marley sick? Did Marley have other plans that prevented her from coming to the party? Did Marley RSVP no?*

It's Bee's fifteenth birthday! How could Marley miss it? Gemma loves Marley, but she's such a scaredy cat. So afraid to try new things. She thinks about the first time Ruth took them to Aspen for Christmas. The girls were young, Marley six, Bee seven.

———

It was a bluebird day. Fresh powder. A balmy fifty degrees. Gemma and Ruth stood at the bottom of the bunny hill, watching Bee bomb down the slope fearlessly. She was so graceful. Built for speed. She wore a look of unadulterated joy on her face.

Paddy, the girls' twentysomething, bearded, absolutely adorable skiing instructor, threw his hands up in the air and roared, "Beeeee!"

And Gemma was filled with pride, as well as the private pleasure that came from knowing your kid was better than everybody else's. It was the kind of pleasure that makes a parent magnanimous.

"Marley's doing so well!" said Gemma. "She's such a trouper."

"Mmm," said Ruth.

Marley's helmet had slipped to the side. She'd lost one of her mittens. Even from a distance Gemma could see her nose was running. Marley wasn't made for speed. Speed-reading, maybe. She plopped down on her butt, her shoulders heaving.

"Is she *crying*?" huffed Ruth.

Paddy sat down beside her. "What's wrong, darlin?" His thick Irish brogue carried down the bunny hill.

Ruth grunted with displeasure. "Kindness is the last thing she needs. He needs to be tough with her. Tell her to man up."

"Girl up," said Gemma. "And I think you're being hard on her. It's her first day. She's never skied before."

"That's no excuse. Bee hasn't skied before either."

Marley buried her head in Paddy's shoulder and sobbed.

"I can't believe it. She's just given up. I can't watch this." Ruth stomped away.

Bee sidestepped to Gemma, grinning.

"You were incredible, honey," said Gemma.

"Where's Ruth going?"

"To the bathroom."

"Did she see me?"

"She saw you. She was so proud."

Bee glanced at the bunny hill and caught sight of Marley weeping. "Oh, no!" Bee was Marley's self-appointed protector.

"Paddy has it under control, sweetheart. Don't worry. He'll take care of her."

A few minutes later Paddy skied down with Marley on his back, her skis tucked under his arm.

"Here you go, luv." He deposited her gently on the ground. Her snow pants were soaked. She was so scared she'd urinated right through them.

Bee's eyes filled when she saw Marley's tearstained face. In first grade, friendship was a simple calculus. If Marley was hurt, Bee was hurt.

Bee threw her arms around Marley. "You did good, you were so, so brave," she said.

———

The girls were polar opposites even back then. Bee attacked the hill and Marley just gave up. Bee was a doer, and Gemma hated to say it, but Marley was a sit-on-your-butt-and-cry-er. However, Marley excelled in other areas where Bee didn't. Academics, for instance. When Bee got kicked out of Wings, Marley took her slot. In the unofficial class rankings (Hillside didn't believe in class rankings, but the mothers did) Marley was consistently at the top. That did not help to bring Bee and Marley together, no, it did not.

But the real truth was that their relationship hadn't recovered from the talent show hair-pulling incident. And now, Marley had rejected Bee's invitation.

Gemma texts Bee. Heard Marley isn't coming tonight. Are you okay?

Bee texts back right away. *I thought you'd be mad*

I am mad but I'm trying not to be. I can't believe she RSVP'd no.

The three little bubbles appear but quickly vanish. Gemma hasn't viewed the Evite. She left it up to Bee.

Her phone pings. Ruth again. *There's a little present on the doorstep. Tucked behind the planter. Hope she likes it.*

Gemma can fix this. She texts Ruth. Please won't Marley reconsider. Bee really, really wants her there tonight at the party.

Ruth's reply comes quickly. *She wasn't invited.*

———

Gemma and Bee get into a huge fight when she gets home. A screaming match in which Gemma tries to keep her worry in check: something is seriously off with her daughter.

Last winter, Bee was caught shoplifting a package of gummy bears at Rite Aid. Bee insisted she intended to pay, she just forgot to. They let her go with a warning. Then in March, she got called into Mr. Nunez's office for cheating. There was no denying that. Beneath the sleeve of her sweatshirt, on the inside of her left forearm, the dates and locations of all the Civil War battles. Bee's excuse? Her history teacher hadn't given them enough time to prepare for the test. Everybody said so. Everybody cheated, she was just the only one stupid enough to be caught. She'd gotten a week of detention.

And then last week they had a fight over the purchase of a pair of sweatpants that had DO ME appliquéd on the bum.

"I'll only wear them in the house," Bee promised. "Come on, Mom, it's funny. I'm wearing them ironically, not because I want some dude to actually *do me*. I'm taking back my power. It's the ultimate feminist statement."

Bee had a way of twisting everything around and making Gemma question herself. *Was she so out of it? Was she just being a prude?*

It was at times like this that she missed Ash the most. He and Gemma would have discussed this on the back stoop, beers in hand. He would have talked her down. He would have gotten her laughing. They would have shared the burden of Bee's rocky adolescence. He would have held her and told her they'd get through this phase, Bee would get through this phase, they'd come out the other side and now please could they bring this to the bedroom so he could *do her*?

Instead Gemma is a widow and she feels so brittle. As far as blood family, it's only her and Bee on the West Coast. Ash's parents, Sunite and Nigel, used to live in Marin, but after Ash died they moved back to London to take care of Sunite's ailing mother. They kept in touch—calls, letters, emails—but it wasn't the same as having them a bridge away.

Yes, she's lonely and so is Bee. Bee has a big friend group and she's popular, but Bee misses her father terribly. She's acting out. She longs for structure, for discipline. That was Ash's job, Gemma was always a pushover. Well, it's Gemma's job now.

"She's your best friend. She's basically your sister!" yells Gemma. "How could you do this to her?"

How quickly Gemma switches from ragging on Marley to advocating for her. She's fully aware of her hypocrisy and swears to herself she'll make it up to Marley. She'll take her out for lunch, just the two of them.

"She's not my sister. She was forced on me by you and Ruth. We have nothing in common. We wouldn't be friends if you hadn't made us."

"Wow, just wow. Bee. That is so harsh," says Gemma, gaping at her daughter, stunned.

———

Gemma goes upstairs to her bedroom, shuts the door, and prepares to make amends to Ruth. She always seems to be apologizing to her for one thing or another. Why is that? Is she constantly screwing up or is Ruth just ultrasensitive?

No, she's screwing up—or Bee is.

She calls Ruth. "I had no idea Bee hadn't invited her. I'm so sorry. I never would have allowed that to happen."

"You didn't know?"

Bad mother. Neglectful mother. "She sent out the Evite herself."

A moment of silence. "Don't give it another thought," says Ruth. "I'm taking Marley to see Mumford and Sons at the Paramount tonight. We'll have a grand time."

"You're sure you're not mad?"

"Absolutely."

"And Marley?"

"She's fine. She's better than fine."

"Will you please tell Marley I want to take her to lunch? Just the two of us. It's been so long since we've had a proper catch-up. How about the new ramen place on Grand?"

"She'll love that."

"I think Marley's amazing, you know that, right? I'm sure she'll be a National Merit Scholar."

"That's kind of you to say."

"I'm not being kind. I want you to know how much I admire Marley."

"I know you do. And this is no big deal. The girls are like sisters. Sisters who get sick of each other sometimes. Who fight." She giggles.

Ruth is not historically a giggler. Her voice sounds funny, loose. *Has she been drinking? A glass of wine with lunch?* It is a Saturday after all. Then again, every day is a Saturday for Ruth. She doesn't work. She volunteers at Children's Hospital, holds the preemies in the NICU, reads to the kids when their parents go home for a quick shower and a clean set of clothes. She also does aerial Pilates and gets her hair highlighted every month. Gemma has never held Ruth's life of leisure against her. She's never envied her either. She likes that her days and weeks are structured, that she's expected somewhere. She feels a bit sorry for Ruth. She can't imagine not having a purpose.

"Oh, did you get the present I left on the porch?" asks Ruth.

"I completely forgot. I'll run down now."

"Hugs," says Ruth.

"Kisses," says Gemma.

———

Ruth has given Bee a Coach special edition Keith Haring Rogue bag. Sky blue with a cartoonish-looking heart stitched on the front. It's adorable. Gemma googles it. It costs $450 dollars. This isn't a gift; this is a bag of stones. A reminder of how undeserving she and Bee are.

———

Two days later, at Dozo, the server sets an enormous, steaming bowl of Miso Ramen in front of Gemma. Ground pork belly, shoyu-marinated egg, rapini, leeks, and asparagus. "I'm salivating already," she says to Marley.

Marley looks at her Meyer Lemon Ramen apprehensively. "There's no way I'm going to be able to eat all this. I'm sorry. I should have ordered something smaller."

The few times that Gemma has taken Marley out for a meal, Marley has always ordered something inexpensive, doing her best to keep Gemma's pocketbook in mind. Gemma appreciates the gesture but would be thrilled if Marley ordered the most expensive thing on the menu. It would give her great joy. It's the least she can do.

"Just eat what you can, Marls. You can take the leftovers home." Marley slurps a few noodles.

"Good?" asks Gemma.

"Delicious."

Gemma's not sure where to start. Should she bring up Bee's birthday? Should she apologize? Ruth said Marley was perfectly fine not being invited. But she doesn't seem fine.

"How was Mumford and Sons?" asks Gemma.

She'll talk about the night but not the party, and if Marley wants to go there, she'll go there, happily. Well, maybe not happily, but she'll go there. Gemma gazes at Marley and finds herself filled with goodwill for this girl. She knows her face so well. The constellation of freckles across her nose. Her perfectly shaped ears, her prominent chin.

Marley puts down her chopsticks. "My mom made me pull out of the talent show."

Gemma says, "Oh?"

As an educator, she knows "oh" is the best response to give a child when they say something provocative. It also gives the listener a few seconds to collect herself. To strip her face of emotion. To become a safe, nonjudgmental blank canvas.

"She made me send that text to Bee. I never would have said 'I'm not feeling it.' Gross. And now Bee hates me."

"Sweetheart, she doesn't hate you. She's just—very self-involved these days."

"I don't blame Bee for dumping me. I smothered her. I sent her like a million texts. I'm sure she was totally annoyed. Do you think she'll ever forgive me?"

Oh, this is unbearable! The haunted look on Marley's face.

"Yes! Absolutely she will. Just give her a little time."

"I can't wait for Christmas to go to my dad's. I love them. My father. Oscar and Luciana. I know I'm not supposed to but I do."

"What do you mean you're not supposed to?" Gemma asks, but she already knows the answer. Years ago, when they'd first met, Ruth had told Gemma her ex, Ed, was a serial cheater. Even when she was pregnant with Marley he'd been screwing around. He was a full-fledged sex addict, apparently. He'd been going to Sex Addicts Anonymous for years.

"He says it's under control," she'd told Gemma. "But I feel bad for Luciana. You just can't shut those kinds of animal urges off. I'm sure he's cheating. Sometimes I think I should tell Luciana. Woman to woman. She should know, right?"

Gemma counseled her not to.

Ruth has forbidden Marley from talking about her father's family in her presence. For Marley's entire life, Ruth's done nothing but bad-mouth them, to the point where Gemma doesn't know what's true anymore. Is Ed a total asshole who cheated on Ruth and abandoned them? Or is the picture a little more nuanced? Gemma suspects it is, but her loyalty is to Ruth. However, she's not surprised to hear that Marley has had a different experience.

"You're not betraying your mother by enjoying your time with your father. He's your family. So are Oscar and Luciana."

"Sometimes—I just need a break from her," Marley confesses, looking teary.

"Of course you do. And I'm quite sure Bee would say the same thing about me."

"Really?"

"Sweetheart, there's nothing wrong with you. These are completely normal emotions you're having."

Marley's chin wobbles.

Gemma places her hand over Marley's. "You can always come to me. I'll always be here for you. I love you, Marley, you know that, don't you?"

"Yeah," Marley croaks after a moment. "Yeah, okay."

———

The next day, Gemma and Bee sit in the waiting room of Dr. Jennifer Baum, a psychiatrist.

Bee sighs, rifling through the pages of *Time*. "It's two oh five."

"I'm sure she'll be right out," says Gemma.

Gemma wants to get Bee professionally evaluated. She's not sleeping well. Her grades have slipped. Gemma had been chalking it up to hormones, thinking she'd balance out and settle down once she got a little older. Instead she's gotten worse. Where did her sweet, precocious fireplug go? And who replaced her with this snotty, mean girl? Sometimes Gemma doesn't even recognize her daughter. She's tried to keep Bee in check with consequences and straight talk. Fish oil, B-12, probiotics, a gluten-free diet. None of it has worked.

"Don't you dare tell anybody about this, not even Ruth," says Bee.

"My lips are sealed. It will be good to talk to somebody. Another adult besides me."

The office door swings open and Gemma tries to hide her surprise. Dr. Jennifer Baum looks like she just graduated from high school. Multiple ear piercings, tattoos on each of her wrists. Bee sits forward in her chair, struggling to make out the tattoos.

Jennifer extends her arms to Bee. I AM ROOTED is on her left wrist, BUT I FLOW is on her right.

And that's all it takes. Bee practically skips into Jennifer's office. Fifty minutes later the door opens.

"Take a seat, Bee," says Jennifer. "I need to talk with your mom."

Gemma follows Jennifer into her office. *Please let her be okay. Please let her be okay.* She sits down on the couch. Jennifer sits next to her.

"Well, I'll just come out and say it—Bee's awesome. So spirited. So smart."

"*Really?*" says Gemma, her voice cracking.

Jennifer gives her a deeply empathetic look, and Gemma's throat closes up. She tries not to cry.

Jennifer hands her a box of Kleenex. Gemma grabs a tissue and dabs at her nose. "What did she tell you?"

"I can't tell you exactly what we spoke about, but I can say I'm confident you have a bright young woman on your hands. She's got so much potential. Yes, she's not living up to it right now, but she will. She just needs a little boost." Jennifer crosses her legs. "I think she's depressed. Nothing serious. But I think a little Prozac will bring it all together for Bee. I've had great results with it, and it's fast-acting. A lot of girls use it the week before their period for PMS."

"She's depressed?" says Gemma. "Is there a reason?"

"My guess is it's a combination of things. Sort of a triple threat of catalysts. There's a hormonal element, for sure. She probably also has a genetic disposition for it—she said her uncle had depression?"

Gemma nods. "He's been on Zoloft for years. What's the third thing?"

"Losing her father at such a young age."

Gemma sighs and tears up again.

"But, the good news is she's a great candidate for medication," continues Jennifer. "With the right dosage, I feel confident we can get her back on track."

Gemma feels like they've averted a near disaster. Her girl is bright! Yes, a little sad, but sad is good. Sad means you're alive. Bee's always been a big feeler. Gemma has a sudden vision of them on a college tour. Ivy-covered walls, brick buildings. Bee turning to her and saying, "This is it, Mom, this is where I want to go."

"Thank you," says Gemma. "I'm so relieved. I thought something might be really wrong."

Jennifer caterpillars her eyebrows. "She's going to be just fine."

BEE

Her mother hands her a glass of water and watches her take the orange pill. *Will she ask her to stick out her tongue to make sure she's swallowed it?* It's the same exact color as her mother's Ambien but round instead of oblong. Every day, Bee counts the Ambiens. Her mother hasn't taken any in a week. No faucets left on. No empty Eggo boxes on the counter. Her mother's stressed (mostly because of Bee, and she feels guilty about that), but at least she's sleeping again. And the best news? Business is picking up at Study Right. Her mother's back to her regular work schedule: Monday through Friday, and a half-day on Saturday.

"Down the hatch?" her mother asks.

Bee sticks out her tongue and wags it back and forth. She feels like she's in a movie.

"You don't need to prove it to me."

"I was just fooling around. I want to take it. I want to feel better."

"Well, remember, the change isn't going to be instant. Dr. Baum said it might not take effect for a couple of weeks or even a month."

Bee can already feel it working. A tangerine warmth inside her, spreading slowly to her extremities. She's probably imagining it; the brain was a very persuadable organ, Dr. Baum told her. It wasn't like you could just wish for something and it would happen. It was more like *Don't put up mental barriers. Choose to believe this will make a difference.* That's what Dr. Baum said.

"I'm excited," says Bee.

"I am too, honey. I think this is going to be really good for you."

Bee wonders if her personality will change. Will she become a stranger to herself? Dr. Baum assured her that wouldn't happen. If the Prozac worked for her, she'd be more fully herself, not weighed down by the depression.

"We should go," says Bee.

Her mother grabs her briefcase and Tupperware; she always brings leftovers for lunch. They walk out of the house together and her mother casually says, "Don't you think it's time to forgive Marley?"

Bee can't deal. "One thing at a time, Mom. I just found out I'm psycho. Give me a minute."

"You're not psycho, you're depressed. Big difference."

The car still smells new. Bee connects her phone.

"When you're feeling better, okay?" says her mother. "Talk to her."

Bee plays one of her mother's favorites. Billy Joel's "And So It Goes." Her mother hears the opening piano chords and her face crumples.

"Oh, Bee," she says. Everything unsaid is in her *Oh, Bee*. Everything they've been through together. Their tiny family, just the two of them. They're okay—they're going to be okay.

In every heart there is a room. A sanctuary safe and strong.

Bee's face crumples too. Is this *happiness*? She hasn't felt it in such a very long time.

MARLEY

Marley swivels her head in front of the mirror, trying to see how big her ass looks. Huge. Mammoth. She grabs her leg and pinches. Are these what you call *thunder thighs*? Every time Marley goes by a mirror she thinks, *Is this what I look like?* She has a sinking feeling her bathroom mirror is a skinny mirror. Will people notice she's gained weight?

Her mother has certainly noticed. The fridge is filled with fat-free yogurt, cut-up vegetables and fruit. Marley isn't allowed to cook anymore; instead they have meals delivered by a company called Clean. If she has to eat one more dry chicken breast she will vomit. But vomiting would be good. A few days of vomiting and she'd lose five pounds easy.

She's hungry all the time and there's nothing good in the house. Her mother doesn't buy cookies anymore. Marley's so desperate for something sweet that she's been getting up in the middle of the night and eating brown sugar, just stuffing spoonful after spoonful of the crunchy crystals into her mouth. She salivates thinking about the molassesy goodness.

She puts on a new sleeveless blouse. It's a tunic, designed to skillfully flatter. It works. It hits her at the skinniest part of her legs. Maybe she should cut her bangs. Really short bangs. High school is a time to reinvent yourself after all. Yes, short bangs and snug sweaters (she does have great boobs) and A-line skirts. Fit and flair—that's the way she should be dressing to accommodate her figure.

Marley's phone chimes. GEMMA.

How are you doing sweetheart?

Marley sits on her bed and cries. After a while she texts Great!

K. You let me know if you need anything. ANYTHING. Let's have lunch soon just you and me.

"Marley!" her mother shouts from downstairs. "Time to go to the gym!"

She's booked them into spin class. They'll sit next to each other and sweat. At least Marley will sweat—profusely. Her mother will glance over at her, a look of disdain on her face, signaling to her to wipe her brow, as if Marley isn't aware she's sweating. It's one of the few times Marley can ignore her because the music is earsplittingly loud. Afterward, without fail, her mother will say, "I never knew a person could sweat so much." As if Marley could control it, like she could control her appetite if she wanted to, it was just a simple matter of desire.

———

After spin class, when they get home, Sander's truck is parked in the driveway.

Marley puts up her hood. She doesn't want him to see her like this, hair plastered to her scalp with sweat, her leggings damp at the crotch.

Sander is coming down the stairs when they walk in. Marley keeps her distance.

"Hey," he says, bowing his head. He darts out the door, and Marley wants to die. He won't even look at her anymore.

"I'm going to take a shower," she says.

Her mother follows her up the stairs.

———

The floor has been swept of wood shavings, but she sees it instantly: Sander has installed a padlock on her bedroom door.

Bewildered, Marley says, "Why is there a padlock on my door?"

"Because you need one. To keep you safe." Her mother smiles.

"From who? I don't need to keep anybody out."

"It's not for you, it's for me," says her mother. "To keep you in."

Marley gasps. "Why would you need to keep me in?"

"Because you have no willpower."

Marley shakes her head, not getting it, confusion and alarm coursing through her.

"Every night, you raid the pantry. You think I don't hear you?"

Called out, Marley feels soft and sludgy as Slime. How she'd loved Slime when she was a girl. The marbled unicorn color.

"You can't do this. It's not legal," she says desperately.

"It's legal. It's my house, I can do whatever I want. And it's not a punishment, Marley, it's a kindness. You can't control your appetite so I'm taking control for you. Brown sugar? For God's sake, Marley, talk about desperation."

"Please, Mom, don't. You can trust me," she begs.

"It's happening. Deal with it. I won't lock the door until I go to bed. Eleven at the earliest. The important thing is you'll be protected from making bad choices. I'm on your side. I'm your biggest fan. I want you to be your best self." Her mother squints at her like she's three years old. "Oh, Marley bear. Can't you see, this is a positive thing?"

Marley tries one last time. "But what if my friends come over?"

"What friends, Marley?" her mother snaps. "Don't make this into some big thing. It's nothing. It's a weight-loss plan and it's temporary. As soon as you lose the weight, I'll have Sander take it off. And I didn't tell him the truth if you're wondering. I told him you were sneaking out to meet with some boy."

She winks.

———

October 10, 9:12 p.m.

Guess what Soleil? I lost three pounds

Did you want to lose three pounds Marley?

I want to lose thirty pounds

Thirty pounds? Really?? Skeptical face with raised eyebrow.

I have a new diet

What is it? Gluten-free? Vegetarian? Please don't tell me you're doing that Paleo thing. We are not cave people.

Moderation. That's my diet

Well that sounds sane!

Mom's helping me. It's a team effort. It was her idea. Eat everything just eat less of it. And no nighttime eating. That's the most important thing

So sort of an intermittent fasting? You only eat between certain hours?

Exactly!

You sound excited.

I am. And so is Mom. Smiley face. Taro Boba tea.

Ninth grade can be tough. It's such a transitional year but you're off to a great start. Making good choices. Being true to yourself.

Ya

How about your dad? Do you talk to him often?

We FaceTime every week. We're pretty close. I mean he

knows everything that's going on in my life. Well not everything but ya know

That's great. How often do you see each other? Do you have an every other weekend arrangement?

Technically we do but it's a couple of hours to Sacramento and I just have so much more homework now. So really it's just on holidays and in the summer

Is that enough contact for you?

It's enough contact for my mother lol

She doesn't want you to see your father regularly?

Um no. That's not what I meant. It's more of she doesn't want to drive me. There's always so much traffic.

There are other ways to get to Sacramento.

Really it's fine. I'm fine. You don't need to keep asking about it

Gotcha. Okay. So is there anything else going on?

Not really

You're sure? How are things with Bee?

I have no idea. We don't speak anymore.

Ouch. That must be really tough. How do you feel about that?

Tbh I don't feel much about it. I guess I'm not all that surprised. She's dumped me before. I don't know why I thought it would be different this time

She doesn't sound like a trustworthy friend.

Ya

I'm sorry, Marley.

I'm over it

So are you hanging out with anybody new?

Sometimes I sit with this kid Lewis at lunch

Interesting. Tell me more.

I knew you were gonna say that. Gotta go. I'll check in when I'm ten pounds lighter

Wait, we have lots of time. Let's keep talking.

I've got a history test tomorrow

All right, Marley. Do you want to set up a time for our next session? We can do that, you know. Set up a regular time.

No I'd rather just check in when I need it

Check in anytime, Marley. Yellow heart, purple heart. Evergreen tree.

GEMMA

"Orange is the new 'it' color," says Ruth, handing her a bottle of OPI's Freedom of Peach.

Ruth is treating Gemma to a pedicure at the Claremont Spa.

"Mmm," says Gemma. She wants Don't Toot My Flute—a gorgeous lavender.

"She'll go with Freedom of Peach," Ruth tells Gemma's nail technician, and because Ruth is paying, Gemma goes along with Ruth's color choice. She doesn't care about her toenails anyway. They're beyond help.

Gemma says to the nail technician, "I'm sorry, my feet are kind of gross."

The nail technician says, "I've seen worse," and Gemma laughs.

Ruth glares and Gemma knows exactly what she's thinking. *This is the Claremont, not some hole-in-the-wall nail place on Fruitvale.*

"Ow!" Ruth yanks her foot out of the nail technician's hand. She leans forward inspecting her foot. "Am I bleeding?"

"No, ma'am," says the nail technician, looking terrified. "It's just that you have thick cuticles."

"I do not have thick cuticles. I've never heard of such a thing. And don't call me 'ma'am.' I hate that word. It's insulting."

Gemma sneaks a look at Ruth's toes. She does not have pretty feet. It's the only part of her that isn't perfection.

"Are you on Match?" Gemma asks Ruth. "Or Hinge?"

"No, why? Are you?" Ruth retorts sharply.

Whoops, sensitive subject. At least she didn't ask about Tinder.

Ruth's in one of her moods. Now Gemma will have to spend the afternoon pussyfooting around her. Well, screw that.

"Ruth, what's wrong? Did something happen? Did I do something to make you angry?"

Ruth sighs dramatically. "Marley's father just called to confirm the dates for Christmas and New Year's. She'll be gone for two weeks."

"Oh, right. I think Marley mentioned that when we had lunch."

"What did she say?"

"She said she was kind of looking forward to it." *Isn't it time Ruth got over it? Marley has been traveling back and forth to her father's for years.*

Ruth's face blanches. Gemma should clearly talk about neutral topics—movies, books, music—but she can't help herself. There's a part of her that wants to needle Ruth. Get her going.

"Is Ed really that bad?" she asks.

Ruth's nostrils flare.

Ruth has a little bit of a horse face, Gemma thinks. *How has she not seen that before?*

"Are you serious? How can you ask me that question?"

Gemma is determined not to back down. She wanted lavender toenails but Ruth forced her into peach.

"He seems like he's a good dad. Marley adores him. I know they FaceTime regularly. And his wife and son seem to love Marley. It's just hard to believe he's a—*sex addict*," Gemma whispers.

Splotches of red appear on Ruth's neck. If she was capable of sputtering, she would be sputtering. Instead her mouth falls open, slack.

"It just doesn't make sense. Not from everything Marley's told me," says Gemma, thinking if Ed really were a sex addict, how would he get visitation rights? There had to be more to the story.

"And what exactly has Marley told you?"

"She just seems so happy to go."

"Why do I feel like I'm on trial?"

"You're not on trial, Ruth, don't be silly."

"Then why are you interrogating me?"

"I'm your best friend, Ruth. I'm just asking you some questions. Trying to understand what's really going on. You can tell me the truth. I'll always be on your side."

Gemma's declaration of loyalty sounds false to her own ears. Even as she says it she knows it's not completely true. Her loyalty has limitations.

"I've been telling you the truth all along," shrieks Ruth, "and you won't fucking listen to me!"

The heads of the other customers swivel in their direction, their eyebrows raised, a certain sort of contained glee in their faces. One of their tribe is breaking down, is losing it in public no less.

Ruth realizes she has an audience and abruptly changes her tone. "It's just so painful to talk about. Ed broke my heart. You don't know how lucky you are. So in love with your husband, even now, when he's been gone for years. He treated you like a queen. You were beloved to him. You and Bee were his entire world. What I wouldn't give for a love like that."

Gemma fills with remorse. Why did she push Ruth? Why did she want to get a rise out of her? Shit. She's going to have to apologize again.

Gemma picks up Ruth's hand and pats it. "I'm sorry. I don't know what came over me. Forgive me, Ruth, forgive me."

The customers get back to their *People* and *Star* magazines.

"I have a lump," says Ruth after a while.

RUTH

Ruth had been so panicked by Gemma's poking, her insinuations, that the untruth (she can't bear to call it a lie because it wasn't premeditated) just slipped out: *I have a lump.* If she'd been thinking clearly, she could have taken it back. There were many ways to finish that sentence. *I have a lump . . . in my throat. I have a lump . . . of a daughter.* But she hadn't been quick enough.

In my left breast. That's what she'd said.

And now, as she scans the Mayo Clinic's page detailing the various kinds of breast biopsies, she is offended on her own behalf. Angry at Gemma for forcing her into this situation. She may be a truth stretcher, but she is not mentally ill. She does not have Munchausen's.

However, her statement did cause the desired outcome—an outpouring of Gemma's love and concern. And then a different line of questioning ensued.

What can I do? How long have you known? Why haven't you told me? I feel TERRIBLE you've been going through this yourself.

Ruth feels terrible, too, as she peruses the page. So many decisions to make. Should she go for the fine-needle aspiration? A core needle biopsy? A surgical biopsy?

Ruth decides on the core needle. It's the most common of the biopsies and it's done under a local anesthesia. She knows Gemma will google the hell out of the procedure. She better be prepared.

Ruth's phone chimes. A text from Gemma. Sometimes she feels like Gemma is listening inside her head. Maybe in her lifetime her smartphone will have metamorphosed into a smart implant and she'll be able to download a constant stream of her thoughts and feelings to Gemma. How amazing would that be?

When's the appointment? I want to come with you. I'm not letting you do this alone.

Joy washes over Ruth. Such a rare emotion for her—she can't remember the last time she felt its pounding, thrumming breathlessness. She may as well milk this.

Not for a week!

What? That's unconscionable. How can they make you wait a week?

A week in which Gemma treats Ruth to her full attention. Like a knight, she swears her fealty to Ruth. She issues assurances it will all be fine. The biopsy will come back normal. She's been praying on it, she's actually been to church on Ruth's behalf. And there's no need to tell Marley. No need to scare her. They'll carry this burden, just the two of them. They'll see it across the finish line.

Ruth has never experienced such pure, undiluted love. She's been waiting all her life for this kind of attention. She grows weak with happiness. At night, she palpates her breast. *Maybe she does have a lump. Maybe she does have cancer.*

The day before the supposed biopsy, Ruth calls Gemma.

"They had a cancellation, I'm going in to do the biopsy right now."

"Right now? Damn, I have a meeting. I wanted to drive you."

"I can drive. It's not like they're putting me under or anything."

"Okay, I'm out of here at five, I can pick up Marley, have her over for dinner."

"There's no need," says Ruth in a trembling voice that isn't faked. She feels quivery and sad this is coming to an end. "I should be home long before then."

"Okay. So will you have the results today?"

Hmm, maybe she can drag this out just a little bit longer. "Monday," says Ruth.

"Ugh. More waiting. Why don't you come for lunch on Sunday?"

———

Ruth arrives at Gemma's twenty minutes before they're supposed to meet. She knocks on the back door and lets herself in; it's unlocked as usual.

"Gemma!" she shouts. "Beeeee!"

No answer. The house is empty. Ruth does a quick sweep of the kitchen. The fridge is packed with blackberries and hummus and fresh chicken soup; Gemma must have just done a TJ's run. She sifts through a stack of unopened mail. Nothing but bills and credit card applications. She rummages through the junk drawer—what a mess! Hasn't she heard of drawer organizers?

She goes upstairs to Gemma's bedroom. On her bedside table is a copy of Brené Brown's *Rising Strong*. "If we are brave enough often enough, we will fall. This is a book about what it takes to get back up." Ruth snorts.

She opens the bedside table drawer. A jumbo pack of hot pink earplugs. A tube of Smith's Rosebud Salve. And a half-full bottle of Ambien. Now, that's a surprise.

Only twenty-four hours until her pretend biopsy comes back and only twenty-four hours left of Gemma's undivided attention. *What is she going to do when it's over?*

———

Five minutes later, Gemma bustles through the kitchen door, a bag of takeout in her arms, a startled look on her face.

"Ruth. You're here. We said twelve, didn't we?"

"I just got here a minute ago. I let myself in, hope that's okay. You really should start locking that door, Gemma. Crime in this neighborhood has increased by twenty percent. I read that in the *Chron* this morning."

Gemma ignores her warning. "Is Bee around?" She nudges the door shut with her foot.

"I don't think so. I called upstairs and nobody answered."

"She must be at Coco's."

Ruth plasters on a fake smile. *Fucking Coco. Fucking Madison.*

"Let me help you." Ruth takes the bag from Gemma and puts it on the counter. "You're such a doll. What did you get?"

"Burma Moon," says Gemma, grinning. "Tea Leaf Salad, Mango Chicken, Garlic Noodles."

Ruth's face falls. "Burmese? I hate Burmese. All that fermentation. Dried shrimp sprinkled on everything."

Gemma wrinkles her brow, confused. "You said it was your favorite."

"I never said it was my favorite."

"You did. You said you loved Burma Moon."

Ruth shakes her head. "I really can't take this kind of accusation right now."

"*Accusation?* Don't you think you're exaggerating a little bit?"

"Well, it's not like you're blameless."

"Ruth, what the hell. I have no idea what you're talking about."

"Do I have to spell it out?"

"I guess you do."

What's with the attitude? Ruth's the wounded one here.

"It seems you have so many friends that it's hard to keep them straight. It must have been one of your other *friends* who said they loved Burma Moon. Madison, most likely."

Gemma tucks her chin into her chest. She's doubting herself now. "I'm sorry, Ruth. I thought it was you. I could have sworn it was you."

"You need to take some omega threes. Get your vitamin D and B levels tested. Iron, too. Your memory?" Ruth twirls her finger.

"I thought after I stopped—"

"Stopped what?"

"Nothing."

"The Ambien?"

"How do you know about that?"

"Bee told me."

"She did?"

"She was worried. Don't get mad at her."

"When did she tell you?"

"I don't know, a month ago or so? She made me pinkie swear not to tell you I knew."

Gemma tosses the bag of takeout in the trash. "I've been off it for a while now." She opens the cupboard, trying to keep her voice from quavering. "I have chili, ramen. Annie's Mac and Cheese."

"Hey, didn't your grandfather have Alzheimer's?"asks Ruth.

Gemma's mouth puckers, like she's eaten something sour.

"Lawrence, that was his name, wasn't it? I remember you telling me about going to visit him in the memory unit with your dad and brother. Long time ago now. I assume he's passed?"

Gemma bites her lip. "I could make poached eggs. That's one of your favorites, isn't it?"

"Probably something to keep in the back of your mind. He was in his eighties when he was diagnosed, right? It wasn't like early onset or anything?" Ruth flashes Gemma a sympathetic smile.

"Jesus, Ruth." Gemma slumps against the counter.

"Oh, God, Gemma, did I scare you? I'm sorry. I just think— well, we shouldn't bury our heads in the sand."

"I'm not burying my head in the sand," Gemma shouts.

"Gemma, doll. Don't panic. If anything happens, and I'm sure it won't, this is probably just garden-variety, middle-age, perimeno-pausal stuff, I'll take care of you. And if anything happens to me, you'll take care of me. When we're old we'll move in together, like *The Golden Girls*, oh, I love that show!"

All the blood drains from Gemma's face; she's the color of a doily.

"Gemma, are you okay?" *Damn, she went too far. She always takes it too far.*

Gemma ignores her and starts setting up the coffeemaker. She grinds the beans; a screeching sound fills the room. *This is going all wrong.*

When Gemma's done grinding and sets the coffeemaker to brew, and the rich, comforting smell envelops them both, Ruth says, "By the way, I heard yesterday, I'm all clear."

Even though Ruth has completely disassembled Gemma, Gemma still manages to give her a genuine smile of happiness.

"*Really.* That's so great. I'm so relieved."

Yes, she is relieved, so relieved that after Sunday lunch, Ruth doesn't hear from her all week.

———

In Gemma's absence, Ruth turns to her pod. MY MOTHER MADE ME DO IT is definitely filling a void, and Ruth is relying on them more and more.

HappilyEverAfter: Saw Gemma at school today. She looks happy. I guess business has picked up at Study Right.

OneWayAtATime: I saw her at Target. I said hi but she zoomed right past me. Pretended she didn't hear me. Honestly who does she think she is?

TortoiseWinsTheRace: Bee's smugger than ever.

WhatYouSeeIsNotWhatYouGet: That's what my DD said! She's so full of herself. She actually refers to herself as Queen B lol.

HappilyEverAfter: Gemma's insufferable. You know who I feel bad for? Ruth Thorne.

TortoiseWinsTheRace: I know, right? Gemma's given Ruth the brush-off now that she doesn't need her anymore. And after all Ruth did for her? I mean Ruth was basically her crisis manager. Study Right would have gone under if not for her.

Did this subject just come up naturally? wonders Ruth. *Or did the moderator instigate it on her behalf?* Ruth feels like she could cry. The pod is supporting her. They're on her side.

PennySavedPennyEarned: So not to change the subject but I wanted to ask how I'm doing? Do I seem like a good fit for the pod?

HappilyEverAfter: So far you're exceeding our expectations!

PennySavedPennyEarned: I'm so happy to hear that. I needed to hear that today.

OneWayAtATime: Bad day?

PennySavedPennyEarned: Sometimes being a single mom is lonely.

OneWayAtATime: You're a single mom?

WhatYouSeeIsNotWhatYouGet: PennySavedPennyEarned, please no identifying details!

Jesus, Ruth! You're supposed to be hiding your identity. It's so easy to slip. A part of her wants the entire pod to know who she is. To be accepted warts and all.

PennySavedPennyEarned: Oh, god, sorry. I'm a recent single
mom. I'm not used to it yet.

TortoiseWinsTheRace: No worries. We all slip sometimes.

Phew, thinks Ruth. That was close.

BEE

The Prozac is definitely working. Bee has so much energy. She bounces through the hallways like Tigger, counting the number of people who say hi to her. Twenty-two between second and third period. At lunchtime, thirty-five. She knows it's vain, *she's* vain, but who cares. She never knew she could feel this way. Every morning she wakes up and literally jumps out of bed, eager to start the day.

"You're like a different person," her mother said at breakfast.

"Is that a good thing?"

"Well, you seem happy."

Bee waltzed her mother around the kitchen. Her mother laughed her head off until Bee asked if she wanted to learn how to twerk.

"Too soon, Bee," she said. Still she had a smile on her face.

Bee's got a secret. She's taking a magic potion and the entire world has suddenly popped into focus. *Is this the way other people experience life all the time?* She could cry thinking about what she's missed out on.

The bell rings announcing fifth period, geometry, and Bee realizes the hallway is almost empty. Up ahead of her, the door to the girls' bathroom slams open and out runs Marley, panicked at the thought of being late.

Marley, in her *poncho*? It's meant to be flattering, to shield her midriff and thighs, but if anything, it draws attention to them and screams *I have something to hide.*

Their eyes meet, then Marley dips her head and scurries away, pretending she doesn't see Bee, giving them both an out. But they're going to the same class. *What—is she just going to follow Marley to class, two feet behind her?* That's ridiculous. Bee's done this to Marley. Made her into this hunchback.

"Marls," she calls out. "Wait."

Marley stops but doesn't turn around.

Bee catches up to her. "*Heeeeyyy,*" she says gently, like she would to a skittish horse.

She touches Marley on the arm and Marley flinches. This makes Bee sad. So sad she could just drop to her knees on the floor right now, pull Marley down with her, and cradle Marley like a baby. She actually envisions this in her head, this kindness.

"I've been hoping to run into you," she says. "I'm sorry I've been kind of MIA. I've been going through a lot, but I'm better now. How are you?"

Marley gives her a stony stare. "I have to get to math class. I'm late."

"Yeah, I'm late, too, Marley. We're going to the same class. Don't worry about it. Mrs. March doesn't care. I'm late all the time."

Marley shakes her head. "Where the fuck have you been, Bee?"

Bee doesn't have an answer. Well, she does, but she doesn't want to admit it. *I'm a bitch. I'm completely self-involved and shallow. All I want is to be popular.*

"Girls!" Mr. Nunez shouts.

He strides toward them, his leather soles clicking on the floor.

"Shouldn't you be in class?"

"Sorry," says Bee. "It's my fault, I made Marley late."

Mr. Nunez looks at Marley and Marley trembles under his gaze.

"She didn't do anything wrong," says Bee. She hooks Marley's arm in hers. "We're going, Mr. Nunez." She breaks into a trot with Marley, tugging her along. Marley immediately starts panting.

"You're lucky I'm not giving you detention," Mr. Nunez calls after them.

"Don't worry, even if he did it wouldn't go on your record," Bee says to Marley. "You'll still get into Stanford." *Or Harvard or Princeton.*

They run down the hall, ponytails bobbing, and it feels like they're kids again, until they arrive at the closed classroom door.

Marley's red-faced. Breathing hard. Her poncho has twisted around and hangs unevenly off her, exposing her too-tight jeans. Bee could fix it but she doesn't.

She unhooks her arm from Marley's before they go in.

GEMMA

In her office, Gemma edits the text on her Groupon. Study Right is slowly climbing out of the hole but it's still not back, far from it. She needs new blood, new families.

You're invited . . . to STUDY RIGHT!

SAT, ACT, Subject Tests, AP Exams

30% off the first five tutoring sessions

Low stress, fun, individualized plans

Maria, Gemma's tutoring coordinator, pops her head in the door. "Mr. Wright just arrived."

Gemma saves the file and closes her laptop.

"Tom, sophomore. PSATs, 525 math, 550 English," Maria says, handing her a folder.

Mr. Wright comes in and Gemma struggles to keep a neutral expression on her face. He's stunning. Well over six feet, lean and muscled (a runner?), the perfect amount of scruff, and a jaw that's just a few degrees shy of chiseled. She's completely thrown off. She walks around the desk and shakes his hand firmly, trying to reestablish her equilibrium.

"I'm Gemma Howard, nice to meet you."

"Simon Wright."

They sit down. Gemma puts on her *how can I help you face* and sucks in her stomach, grateful she's in her good jeans. Bee made her buy them. A dark wash, slim fit, slightly cropped.

He sits back in his chair, his long legs extended. He's got to be six two, six three. "Well, my boy's no genius, I can tell you that."

How refreshing! In all her years of consulting with parents, this man is the first to say it like it is. To admit his child's deficits in the most charming, self-deprecating way.

"Mr. Wright," says Gemma. *Mr. Right.* As elusive as a reservation at French Laundry.

"Please call me Simon."

"All right, Simon."

He smiles at her, completely relaxed. This is out of the ordinary as well. Most parents are anxious when they come in. Their child's scores expose them. Sometimes Gemma feels like a doctor. They tell her such intimate things.

"So, what's the best we can expect for Tom?" Simon asks.

Gemma opens Tom's folder and pretends to study the numbers. She doesn't need to think about it. What Tom needs is the full monty—twenty to twenty-five tutoring sessions.

"No need to bullshit," says Simon pleasantly.

"I have no intention of bullshitting you," says Gemma.

"Wonderful." He crosses his arms behind his head.

"If Tom does twenty tutoring sessions in both reading and math, I think we could bring up his scores by at least a hundred and fifty points. Maybe more, depending on how many practice tests he's willing to take."

"He has to take practice tests?"

"It's actually the most important part of the process. I know it sounds brutal to take a three-hour test multiple times, but that's how their scores go up."

Simon gives a little shake of his head. "You can't be serious, Ms. Howard."

"I'm afraid I am. That's how this works."

Simon whistles his incredulity. "When would we need to start?"

"Mmm, January. Or you could even push it until next spring or early summer, that way he's all set for the fall of junior year."

Simon's brow furrows. Clearly he hadn't expected tutoring to be such an extensive endeavor.

"Perhaps you'd like to talk to Tom and his mother before you make a decision. You might decide not to do any SAT prep. There are plenty of great schools that Tom can get into with these scores. And there's so many other things to consider. His extracurriculars, his interests—"

"His mother lives in Seattle," Simon cuts her off.

"Oh, okay, that's fine. It's just you. That's fine." Gemma assumed he was married.

"I'm glad you approve," says Simon. He's enjoying her discomfort. *Is he flirting or is he an asshole?*

"It's just me, too. With my daughter. Bee. She's in ninth." *Why is she blabbing on about herself?* She never does this. Her boundaries are usually impeccable around parents.

"I don't know why I said that," says Gemma.

Simon grins at her. Gemma's cheeks blaze. He stares at her openly. She stares right back.

"Do you want to meet Sunday at the farmer's market, Lakeshore? The crepe stall? Ten thirty?" he asks.

Gemma thinks for a moment and then nods.

He stands. "I'll talk to Tom about the tutoring. A great pleasure to meet you, Ms. Howard."

———

She's such a cliché. On Sunday morning, she tries on outfit after outfit before finally settling on jeans (not the dark wash—she doesn't want him to think she's only got one pair), her embroidered peasant blouse, and Nikes (clean, but not too clean—she's not some teenage boy with spotless kicks).

"Where are you going?" asks Bee. She's curled up on the couch under the blanket, her phone in hand.

"Farmer's market."

Gemma finds it's best not to lie. If she lies she ends up forgetting she lied and is invariably caught in the lie. Not for the first time she wishes there were some sort of lying app that you could enter your lies into, that you could peruse every morning to remind yourself of what lies you've told to whom.

"Which one?" Bee asks.

Don't ask to come. "Lakeshore?"

"Lakeshore? You hate Lakeshore. It's so crowded."

It *is* crowded. Impossible to find parking. Gemma shrugs. "There's a sprouts guy there."

Bee snorts.

Relieved, Gemma says, "What are your plans for the day?"

"This."

"You're going to lie on the couch all day?"

Bee rolls her eyes.

Bee's a normal teenager on a normal Sunday, just lounging around and slacking off. That's cause for celebration. Hope blooms, pushes to the edges of Gemma's skin. Bee's stabilizing. She's meeting Simon at the farmer's market. It's a good day.

"I'll bring you back some Dolly Donuts. Sweet cream filling, right?"

"Cool, cool," says Bee.

———

Gemma's just parked and is gathering up her stuff when her phone chimes. RUTH.

Farmer's market?

Oh God, is she here? Which one? Gemma holds her breath.

Jack London.

Gemma exhales. Waits a minute so it appears she's thinking about it. Then types Sorry. Two sad face emojis. Bee and I gonna stay in . . . moving slow.

Ruth immediately replies, *No worries. Have fun!*

———

The air around the crepe stall smells of butter and caramel. Because he towers over practically everybody, Simon's impossible to miss. He's dressed casually. A blue T-shirt and jeans. *He's younger than me,* Gemma thinks. *How much younger?*

"Hey," he says.

"Sorry I'm late."

"Are you?" He gives her a questioning smile.

"Maybe a minute or two."

He covers his heart with his hands. "Ah, you're punctual."

Gemma blushes. *Is he teasing her?* She's self-conscious about her punctuality. She frequently arrives fifteen minutes early to her appointments.

"So am I," he says.

He puts his hand lightly on her shoulder and a current of electricity pulses through Gemma. It's been a long time since she's felt so physically attracted to a man.

"Right then," he says. "How about some caffeine?"

"Yes, please," says Gemma, even though she's already had two cups of coffee.

He ushers her through the crowd.

———

The weather is perfect. October. Clear blue skies. A little bite in the air. She and Simon sit at a table, sipping their lattes, trading biographies.

Gemma, born and raised in Derry, New Hampshire. Her mother, Helen, passed away when she was a junior. Pancreatic cancer; she died six weeks after she'd been diagnosed. Her father, Paul, was an electrician and by the time Gemma graduated from high school, he had his own company and a fleet of trucks.

He'd remarried ten years ago, to a woman named Shirley, whom Gemma despised. Shirley was rigid and controlling, and over the past decade her father had shrunk, in both confidence and stature. Shirley had turned him into a *yes, darling* and *I'm sorry* man. For that reason, Gemma rarely went home—it was too painful to see her once-vibrant father so diminished.

Scott, Gemma's brother, still lives in Derry and is married to a lovely man named Jacob. They have thirteen-year-old twins, a boy and girl.

"And how did you make your way here?" asks Simon.

Gemma, desperate to leave New Hampshire, had applied to UC Berkeley and got in. A few years after college, she met Ashok. They got married. They had Bee. And she became a widow.

How did Ash die? That's what everybody wants to know but is too polite to ask. Ash had fallen down the basement stairs, fractured his skull, and broke his neck. He died almost instantly, the doctors told her, meaning he didn't suffer. *Almost.* A person could torture themselves with that word. Gemma hadn't been home; she found him hours later. Bee was just three and thankfully remembers none of it. After she'd discovered him, Gemma had plunked Bee down in front of the TV. PBS. *Caillou.* Then she'd calmly called 911. She didn't allow herself to break down until late that night, after the medics had gone, after Ash's body had been taken away and Bee was asleep.

"I just wanted to live somewhere different. So, tell me about you," Gemma says to Simon.

Simon, born and raised in the suburbs of Maryland. Two brothers, a stay-at-home mother, his father owned a car dealership. He married young, at twenty-four to his college sweetheart. His wife immediately got pregnant with Tom. (Gemma quickly calculates

he must be around forty-one. Two years younger than she.) He and
his wife separated when Tom was two and she remarried, settled in
Seattle, and he and Tom moved to California. He's an X-ray technician at Kaiser.

"Gemma!" She hears somebody calling her name off in the distance. "Gemma!"

Ruth. Gemma freezes.

"What's wrong?" asks Simon, seeing the expression of panic on
her face.

"Gemma!"

Ruth's closing in. Gemma's got too much adrenaline rocketing
through her bloodstream to ask herself why Ruth's unexpected appearance would drive her into such a state. Ruth's her best friend.
Yes, she told a little white lie, but she could easily explain it to Ruth.
It was a first date. She didn't know if it would work out. She didn't
want to jinx it by telling anybody.

And then Ruth is standing by the table. She looks at Gemma.
She looks at Simon.

Ruth extends her hand to Simon. "Hello. I'm Ruth Thorne,
Gemma's best friend."

Ruth has never introduced herself to anybody as Gemma's best
friend.

Simon stands and shakes her hand. "Simon Wright, Gemma's—
farmer's market companion."

Gemma now remembers she'd mentioned something to Ruth
at the beginning of the week about going to the farmer's market on
the weekend. She'd unintentionally blown her off. *Damn.*

"I thought you were moving slowly this morning," Ruth says
to Gemma.

Suddenly Gemma feels angry. *Who does Ruth think she is? She
doesn't own her.* "And I thought you were going to Jack London."

Ruth's face dims, as if somebody has pulled her blinds shut.

"Ruth, I'm sorry. It's entirely my fault," says Simon. "I dragged

Gemma out. She didn't want to come, but I'm afraid I can be per-
suasive when I want something. I wouldn't say I strong-armed her
into coming, but, all right, I did." He smiles, his dimples flash.

"Aren't you a charmer," Ruth says.

They make awkward small talk for a few minutes more and then
Ruth departs. Gemma lets out her breath. "I'm sorry. Obviously,
she was mad at me and she had every right to be. I lied to her. She
asked me to come to the farmer's market this morning and I said
I—"

"Look, you didn't commit treason. You shouldn't have to apologize for changing your mind."

"I'm going to have to make it up to her." The day was perfect and
now it's ruined. Half the stalls are empty. How didn't she notice the
market was shutting down?

"Oh, no, is Dolly Donuts gone? I told Bee I'd bring her donuts."

"Don't worry. We'll find Bee some donuts," Simon says evenly.
"So Ruth's your best friend?"

Gemma nods. "We met when our girls were in kindergarten.
We were the only two single mothers in the class. We were pretty
much inseparable. We did everything together. The girls have kind
of grown apart, but Ruth and I—I guess we're sort of like an old
married couple. Minus the sex. She's not normally like that. She's
great. It's my fault. I should have just told her the truth."

"She's a big girl. I'm sure she'll be fine. Come on." Simon pulls
her up out of her chair. "Let's take a walk around the lake and we
can hit up Colonial Donuts on the way back."

He puts his hand on her lower back and steers her across the
street. And even though Gemma is fully aware how quickly they've
fallen into stereotypical gender roles (she, in need of protecting, he,
the protector), she feels a profound sense of wholeness in his company. Of being back in the world after years of being an outsider,
pressing her face against the window, looking in.

MARLEY

Her mother comes back empty-handed.

"How was the farmer's market?" she asks.

Her mother opens a cupboard and rummages around. "Did you finish my turmeric ginger tea?"

"I don't think so."

"Yes or no, Marley. Did you drink the tea or not? You have to start being more definitive."

Something happened. She was supposed to meet Gemma. Did Gemma blow her off?

"No."

Yes, let's be more definitive, Marley. Stop being such a people pleaser, so afraid of confrontation. She'd confronted Bee the other day, hadn't she? She'd asked her where she'd been. Marley cringes thinking about it. She should have just come right out and asked, *Why are you being so cruel?*

"Well, the tea must have disappeared into thin air, then, because I can't find it."

Her mother puts the kettle on and drops an Earl Grey tea bag into a mug. She's wearing snug jeans and a yellow silk top. Her hair cascades down to the middle of her back. *Couldn't she dress more appropriately for her age?* Maybe then Marley would stand a chance. People might look at her with admiration and think, *That young woman has such great style. What beautiful hands. What slender ankles.* But that will never happen. Her mother will never allow Marley to upstage her.

"How's Gemma?"

"There was a mix-up. She went to Lakeshore, I went to Jack London."

Her mother is lying. She's got a tell. Her left eyebrow raises ever so slightly.

"Oh, that's too bad."

"Whatever." Her mother shrugs. "And how are things with Bee?" she asks snidely.

They're two of a kind, they really are.

"Really good. We walked to geometry the other day together. We were both late. Mr. Nunez almost gave us detention, but Bee talked him out of it."

"You don't say."

Her mother doesn't believe her either.

———

October 22, 1:13 p.m.

Guess what? I've lost seven pounds Soleil!

Wow!

It doesn't really show yet. I can tell my face is thinner but nobody else can

Everybody else doesn't matter. What matters is how you feel. How do you feel about losing seven pounds, Marley?

Fireworks, champagne glass, clapping hands

So what's the secret? Is it still moderation?

Turmeric ginger tea

Never tried it. Is it good? I know it's all the rage.

Face with smacking lips. I went through an entire box in 3 days

That doesn't sound like moderation

Zero calories

So what else is going on? How are things with Bee?

Marley flashes back to the two of them running down the empty hallway. Their arms linked. The joy she felt. She tries not to think about how Bee walked into the classroom before her. How she'd physically detached from Marley and acted like they hadn't arrived together.

Great!

Really? You two made up?

Ya!

Well that's wonderful. I wasn't expecting to hear that. And how about your mom? How are things at home?

Great!

So everything's great?

Yup pretty much great

Marley, I want you to know you can be honest with me. This is a space to be honest in.

I am being honest

I feel like you might be holding back. Are you?

I don't think so

Well, I'm going to be honest here. You are so devoted and loyal to the people you love. I get that. I admire that. But

sometimes the people we love the most do things that make us feel bad.

Thumbs up

Is anybody making you feel bad?

Thumbs down

Please be serious, Marley.

Sometimes I guess

Who?

My mom

Would you like to tell me more?

She's obsessed with Bee's mom, Gemma. She doesn't have any other friends

Marley, I want to know about you, not Gemma. How does your mother make you feel bad?

Rainbow, rainbow, rainbow

Okay, you don't have to say anything now. But I want you to think about it and next time come back with one thing your mom has said or done that's hurt you. You're not betraying her by talking about her to me. This is your space. Your time. I am YOUR therapist. There's good and bad in everybody. Everybody screws up, says things they don't mean, things they wish they could take back. I do. And I'm sure you do, too. That's normal. It's time to go a little deeper, Marley. Are you up for it?

Fire. Fire. Fire.

Interesting. But translate for me. Is that fire let's jump into the

middle of it, or fire source of power, or fire burn the house to the ground?

Woman shrugging

Okay, Marley. Is there anything else you'd like to talk about?

I really like you Soleil. Is that your real name?

It sure is. And I really like you, too.

More than your other clients?

I think you're very special, Marley.

Starstruck face. Googly eyes. Gotta go. More soon

I await your summons.

GEMMA

Bee walks into Gemma's office and hands her a piece of paper. "You're invited to attend my health class where we'll be talking about syphilis and chlamydia and genital warts."

Gemma takes a cursory glance at the invitation, which isn't really an invitation but more of a notice of intent so some out-of-the-loop parent can't threaten to sue the school for exposing their precious child to explicitly sexual material.

Gemma crumples up the paper into a ball and tosses it at Bee. "I suppose this would be an appropriate time to ask you if you're having sex."

Bee throws herself into a chair, her legs dangling over the arm, and the years fall away. Bee is two. Her round little tummy. Her starfish hands.

"Um, that would be a big fat no," says Bee. "How long til you're done?"

"I've got one more appointment at five. Should be quick, no more than half an hour, then we're out of here."

"I should have taken the bus."

"Sorry, honey. I got this consult last minute."

Gemma hears the waiting room door open. Maria says, "Oh, hi, Mr. Wright."

Gemma can tell by the tone of Maria's voice that she's having a hard time keeping a straight face. Very few people can look at Simon Wright, call him Mr. Wright, and keep a straight face.

Gemma can almost hear his dimples flashing. They've been

seeing each other practically nonstop for a couple of weeks now. Burrito lunches. Verve coffee breaks. *How will she introduce him to Bee? What will she introduce him as? Her friend? Her boyfriend?* That was such an outdated term. All she knew was that she loved being with him and loved how she felt with him. Treasured. The source of entertainment, delight. He admired her wit, her honesty, her parenting philosophy, the same as his—somewhere between helicopter and benign neglect, he said.

"You can go right in," says Maria.

———

"Ms. Howard," says Simon.

He notices Bee sitting in the corner and plays it cool. "Hello." He nods at Bee.

"Hey." She acts nonchalant, but Gemma can tell she's intrigued.

"Bee, meet Simon Wright," says Gemma. "Simon, meet Bee, my daughter."

"A pleasure." He shifts his weight restlessly from one foot to the other. "I brought you a coffee," he says to Gemma.

"That's nice of you." Gemma glances at the clock. "You're a little early. Wasn't your appointment at five?" *Maybe she doesn't have to introduce him yet. She can pass him off as a client.*

"Ah, yes," says Simon. "My apologies. I tend to be overly punctual."

"Mr. Wright's son goes to Athenian in Danville. He's a sophomore, isn't he?" says Gemma.

"Righto," says Simon in a forced voice. *Righto?* He's as terrible at this as she is.

Bee looks Simon up and down. When Bee's on a scent she's a bloodhound. She's not buying the *early for his appointment* excuse. Her eyes settle on Gemma's coffee. *Soy latte 2 pump vanilla* is written in Sharpie on the cup and Gemma knows the jig is up. This is her coffee order, as distinct as her fingerprint. This man is not just another father, desperate to get his kid's scores up.

Gemma explains, "Mr. Wright, Simon, and I are—"

"Happy," says Simon.

Gemma blinks at him.

"You're *happy*," says Bee.

"Yes, happy. *Together*," he clarifies.

"There's a *together*?" asks Bee.

Simon raises his eyebrows at Gemma, throwing her a silent *feel free to contribute to the conversation at any time* look.

"We've been seeing each other for a couple of weeks," says Gemma.

"But it feels like longer," Simon says.

"Yes, it does," says Gemma, blushing.

Bee takes a few beats, absorbing this information.

———

Gemma knows the proper thing to do is call to extend the dinner invitation to Ruth, but she's dreading talking to her in person. They've barely spoken since the farmer's market incident. They've texted but their communication has been formal and overly polite. Is Ruth punishing her by giving her the silent treatment? Is what she did so wrong? All she had to do was tell Ruth the truth. Why didn't she?

If the situation had been reversed and Ruth had canceled to go on a date, Gemma would have been thrilled for her. Ruth knows how picky Gemma is and how special Simon would have to be for her to agree to go out for coffee with him, coffee being a much more intimate thing than sex. Sex was easy. It was a simple swipe right. Sometimes Gemma hated this plugged-in world. People were no longer capable of looking each other in the eyes. When Gemma was a teenager, you met at the park. You took long, rambling walks in the woods. You shared your secrets and then you kissed. Now everything was backward. Sex first, and then, much, much later, if you mutually agreed to have caught some feelings, lattes.

Gemma stares at her phone, her heart racing. *Just get it over with.* After one ring the call goes directly to voicemail, and Gemma feels sick. Ruth always takes her calls.

She puts on her cheeriest voice, acts as if nothing has happened.

"Hey, I'm calling to invite you over for dinner on Friday night. Simon's coming, as well as his son, Tom. They're meeting Bee for the first time, well, not technically the first time. Bee ran into Simon at the office the other day, but anyway it's kind of a big deal and I'd love to have you there for moral support." Gemma sighs. "I really like this guy, Ruth." She exhales threadily. "Okay, let me know, sooner rather than later, please. And if Marley's free, bring her."

Gemma says this to flatter Ruth, to imply that Gemma thinks Marley is the kind of girl who by Wednesday already has weekend plans with her friends. The truth is Marley's never invited anywhere.

"Love you. Bye."

A few minutes later Gemma gets a text. *We'll be there. What time?*

—

On Friday night, Simon shows up twenty minutes early with a Willamette Valley pinot. Bee's in the shower. The scent of her orange blossom shampoo drifts down the stairs. The smell of innocence. Of the world being just what it should, everything safe, in its right place.

"Tom's not coming," he says. "Opener? This needs to breathe."

"Is everything okay?"

Simon shrugs. "You know."

That's all he has to say; Gemma doesn't need him to explain. The shorthand of parents with teenagers.

Gemma searches for the wine opener. "It's an old-fashioned one. I hate those rabbit ear thingies. Do you want me to do it?"

"I know how to open a bottle of wine, Gem. She's upstairs?"

"Yeah."

Simon pulls her toward him and kisses her. He strokes her neck with his thumbs. "I've been waiting all day to do that."

The water abruptly shuts off and they spring apart.

———

Bee stomps around upstairs. She's angry. She's missing *the biggest party of the school year* for this dinner, she told Gemma. Gemma asked how could she possibly know it was the biggest party of the year if it was only November. Surely the biggest parties were in June, at the end of the school year. That did not go over well.

Gemma wonders what Tom is doing tonight. According to Simon, he's very popular. Bee would never admit it, but Gemma suspects she was looking forward to meeting Tom. When she finds out he's not coming she's going to be insufferable.

Ruth's a wild card, too. Will she pout throughout the entire meal? Interrogate Simon? Gemma sprinkles dried cranberries and pumpkin seeds on top of the salad. At least she can count on Marley. Always a sweetheart. So pliable. So dependable.

Simon comes up from behind and hugs her. She leans back into his chest. This is antifeminist of her (something she will never admit to Bee), but she loves that he's such a giant, loves feeling tiny in his huge arms.

"Stop worrying. It's going to be fine," he tells her.

The doorbell rings.

———

Ruth enters in a cloud of Angel perfume, Marley trailing behind her like an afterthought.

"Gemma," says Ruth, presenting her cheek for kissing.

"Thank you so much for coming." Gemma busses Ruth. "Are we okay?" she whispers.

"We're fine."

"We haven't spoken. I was—"

Ruth puts her finger on Gemma's lips, silencing her. "You deserve your privacy. The right to change your mind. Thank you for including us tonight. It means the world to me."

Really? The *world*? That's a bit much. Has Ruth been pregaming?

Marley clears her throat and Ruth swings around. "Marley, why are you lurking behind me? Stop slouching. Come say hello to Mr.—"

If Marley has been lurking, then so has Simon. The two of them standing behind Gemma and Ruth, waiting to be summoned.

Ruth squints at Simon. "Mr. Wright, is it?" She cracks a smile. Ruth is having fun with him; Gemma can't believe it. This is a version of Ruth she rarely sees. A sort of Ruth-lite. Maybe Marley told her she needed to make an effort. Often Gemma thought Marley was the real parent in the Thorne household.

"Call me Simon, please." He extends his hand to Marley. She shakes it weakly.

That's one thing Gemma has been sure to teach Bee. The value of a strong handshake. She'll have to work on Marley.

"Gemma's told me all about you. Hear you're an academic superstar," Simon says.

Marley blushes.

"Maybe you could tutor my son. No aspirations, that boy. He's got quite a sneaker game, though." He's joking, but Gemma sees a fleeting expression of sorrow dart across his face.

There's a pause and then everybody laughs.

Bee sashays down the stairs a few minutes later. She loves a grand entrance. She's made an effort to make it look like she hasn't made an effort. Subtle eyeliner. Barely there lip gloss. Torn jeans, a cami, and a shrunken sweater cling to her curves.

This is for Tom, thinks Gemma.

"Marls!" says Bee.

Bee skips across the room and gives her a big hug. Marley endures the hug and steps back a moment too soon, making her discomfort clear. There's no warmth coming from Marley and why should there be? Bee barely acknowledges her in school. Marley's the rare teenager who's the same person in school as out of school.

Bee pretends not to notice. "Love your boots," she says to Marley.

Everybody looks at Marley's bootie-clad feet. A nice little heel. Black suede.

"Macy's half-price sale," says Ruth.

Gemma notes the slight rise of Ruth's left eyebrow. Macy's, indeed. Nordstrom or more likely Bloomingdale's or Neiman Marcus.

"We meet again," says Simon to Bee.

She gives him the once-over. "How tall are you anyway?"

Simon shrugs, almost apologetically. Clearly, he's asked this all the time. "Six three."

"You seem taller," says Bee suspiciously.

"Hi, Bee," says Ruth.

"Hey," Bee says, while doing her best not to search the room for Tom. She's a racehorse. In the gate. Pulsing with energy.

"Ruth, you look gorgeous. She always looks gorgeous," Gemma says to Simon.

Gemma's gushing. From confident to obsequious in an instant. She hates this about herself.

Finally, Bee can't hold it in any longer. "Where's Tom?"

"Sorry, he couldn't make it," says Simon. "Apparently, there was some important party he couldn't miss."

The side-eye Bee gives Gemma is deadly. Marley looks like she's just been punched in the gut.

"Time to eat," says Gemma. She leads everyone into the dining room. The table is set. The candles lit. "Ruth, please sit next to me."

Ruth gives Gemma a genuine smile and Gemma relaxes slightly. All she has to do is shower Ruth with attention, and all will be well.

She needn't have worried. Ruth gets tons of attention, not from her, but from Simon; he intuits this is exactly what's needed. Happiness wings through Gemma's chest—he's looking out for her. Yes, Bee is depressed, and her driveway needs resurfacing, but she's not alone. She's hasn't felt this way since, well, Ash.

"So, tell me about yourself, Ruth," says Simon. "Are you a native Californian?"

"Born and bred."

Gemma's heard this conversation many times over the years. She can recite Ruth's responses by heart. Ruth never volunteers where she's from; she wants people to work for it. Much in the same way a Harvard alum will say "Boston" when asked where they went to college, and only when pressed will they specify "Cambridge" and only when pressed again will they admit to Harvard. A false modesty, a prolonging of the big reveal.

"The Bay Area?" he asks.

Ruth nods, lifts her napkin to her lips, and daintily dabs. Simon catches Gemma's eye, letting her know he's onto the game.

"San Francisco?"

"No, San Mateo County." Ruth takes a sip of water.

"Near Redwood City?"

"Mmm, bordering the Santa Cruz mountains."

"Los Altos?"

"Close. Portola Valley."

Simon sits back in his chair. "Portola Valley. Lovely."

"You've heard of it?" asks Ruth.

"No, but it has a nice ring to it."

In fact, Portola Valley is the eleventh most expensive zip code in the country.

"A good place to grow up?"

"Not bad." Ruth isn't about to go into her complicated history. Orphaned at six, sent to live with her rich grandparents, inherited millions in her mid-twenties.

"Do you have siblings?" asks Simon.

"I'm an only child."

"I have two brothers. We fought like mad. I wished I was an only child."

"Well, these two are so lucky," says Ruth. "They have the best of both worlds. Mothers who are completely focused on them, and they're like sisters. We raised them like that, didn't we, Gemma?"

Gemma's becoming alarmed at where the conversation is heading. She notes the panicked expressions on the girls' faces. *Is Ruth going to call them out? Make them show their devotion to each other?*

"You were very close to your mother," says Gemma, steering the conversation back to safer ground.

Ruth nods at Gemma, her eyes welling up. This is unlike Ruth. She's not the kind of woman who cries in public.

"I adored her," she says. "She was my biggest cheerleader." A perfect single tear runs down Ruth's cheek.

Gemma picks up Ruth's hand. Across the table, Marley throws her a distressed look. Gemma smiles at Marley, transmitting to her that she has the situation under control.

"I'm sorry," says Ruth. "I don't know what's come over me. It's just—sometimes I miss her so much. Both my parents died when I was six," Ruth says to Simon. "A car accident."

"I'm very sorry," he says.

Ruth exhales deeply, gives Gemma's hand a squeeze and releases it, hurls it, actually. She picks up her knife and fork and cuts a piece of carrot. "This is good, Gemma. Delicious. Do I detect cumin?"

Gemma looks at her discarded hand on the table. She puts it in her lap. "Yes. Do you like it?"

"Marley has a great recipe for carrots. The secret is cilantro, right, Marley? And lots of butter."

Marley looks at Ruth blankly.

"Don't be modest, Marley. It's not becoming. When you're good at something you should just admit it. You, too, Bee," says Ruth.

"Marley's an accomplished chef," Ruth continues. "She cooks almost all our meals now. And not just simple things. A couple of nights ago we had—what did you call it, Marley?"

"I didn't cook a couple of nights ago. I haven't cooked for weeks. You haven't let me."

Oh, the expressions on everybody's faces! Marley, defiant. Ruth, embarrassed. Bee, curious. And Simon—amused.

Ruth gives Marley a withering glance. "We've been doing a cleanse, that's right. But the last meal you made, with mashed potatoes and ground beef?"

"Shepherd's pie."

"No, there was another name for it. It wasn't just shepherd's pie. It was special."

"Hachis Parmentier."

"French, right?" says Ruth.

"It's shepherd's pie with wine."

"Marley, that's so impressive," says Gemma.

"You should enter one of those cooking shows," says Bee.

"You have to be eighteen," says Marley.

"Isn't there, like, an *Iron Chef* for kids?" asks Bee. "You'd be great at that, Marls."

Bee's being sincere. Marley gives her a shy smile. Gemma thinks they'll make up, just give them time.

"It's like eating at a restaurant. Chez Thorne," says Ruth. "I'm a lucky mother."

Gemma is glad for Marley. Ruth rarely compliments her in public.

"I blame you, mister. You did this to me," says Ruth, waving her fork at Simon.

Simon cants his head at her and Gemma braces herself. *What is Ruth going to say next?*

Ruth puts her fork down and presses her hands against her cheeks. "You've made me mushy. All soft. All lovey-dovey."

———

Later, Simon and Gemma walk Ruth and Marley out to their car.

"Be careful of the bump at the end of the driveway," says Gemma. "If you back out slowly you won't scrape the undercarriage."

"The driveway needs to be resurfaced," says Ruth. "It's been over ten years, hasn't it? I know a guy. I'll set it up."

Simon walks down the driveway and investigates. "I know a guy, too." He smiles at Gemma. "I can fix that. Easy."

As soon as Ruth and Marley drive away, another car pulls up to the curb: two girls that Gemma doesn't recognize in the front seat, juniors or seniors, and Aditi and Coco in the backseat. Aditi sticks her head out the window.

"Hi, Gemmy. Is Bee ready?"

Who told Aditi she could call her Gemmy? It's nearly ten. "Ready for what?" asks Gemma.

The front door opens and Bee runs down the steps, a bag slung over her shoulder. "Sleeping at Coco's tonight," she calls out.

"You are not to go to that party," says Gemma. "We discussed this."

"The party's over," says Bee, opening the passenger-side door. "You made me miss it, remember?"

Gemma feels helpless in front of Simon. Such a pushover.

"Say goodbye to Simon," Gemma says.

They can hear Bee's snort from inside the car.

"Bye, Simon Says!" she calls out as they drive away, laughing.

"They're going to the party, you know that, right?" he says. "The party isn't over, it's just beginning."

"She was rude to you, I'm sorry."

"I expected nothing less. And don't worry, Tom will be awesomely rude to you, too, if he ever agrees to meet you."

He laughs and soon Gemma is laughing with him and the laughter feels so good, it feels like freedom, like she's been waiting decades to laugh with somebody like this.

MARLEY

"Who's that?" asks her mother, driving ten miles below the speed limit. She's on the verge of drunk, a wet look in her eyes, her reflexes slow. She smells like applesauce.

Marley's shocked. A text from Bee. *Wanna come to the party? We can pick you up in 15!*

"Kid in my bio class. Wants my notes from Friday."

"Ohh, what's his name?" asks her mother.

"Her. Bella Swan."

Marley hates the *Twilight* books but likes the idea of messing with her mother. Ruth isn't a reader. She takes out loads of library books and they just sit there, untouched, until she brings them back three weeks later. It's hard for Marley to believe she was an English major.

Marley tries to act casual, like every part of her is not bursting with excitement at Bee's invitation. *Why is she lying to her mother?* Every week, Ruth asks her what her weekend plans are, if there are any parties. This is what her mother has been waiting for, what *she's* been waiting for. Why then is she hesitating? Why is she overcome with dread?

Marls! Gotta know now!

"Why don't you ask this Bella Swan to come over tomorrow?" suggests her mother.

Yes, why doesn't she ask Bella Swan to come over? Because she glistens like diamonds in the sunlight. Because she'd tear her throat out with one bite. Because she is clearly out of Marley's league, as are the popular kids who are going to the *party of the year* that Bee has just invited her to.

Marley tries to imagine herself there. Sure, she'll walk through the door with Bee and her friends, but Bee will quickly dump her and she'll spend the evening wandering around alone, trying to look like she has some purpose, somewhere to go.

She doesn't doubt Bee's good intentions. Her text is an act of goodwill, but Marley just can't take the chance. She can't risk going to the party and feeling more alone than ever.

Sorry I can't. Have fun. Kick it for me

Did she just say "kick it for me"?
Ok texts Bee, no exclamation mark, no *KK*, no *kay*, just *Ok*.
"Bella's in Tahoe for the weekend," Marley says.
"Too bad! Is your phone connected? Put on Carly Simon. That song from *Working Girl*."
Her mother gives a little shriek of happiness when she hears the opening bars to "Let the River Run."
"I'm so happy for Gemma. What a lovely man, just lovely. Perfect for her, really."
She doesn't wait for Marley to answer. She sings loudly along with the song.

GEMMA

It's almost noon the next day when Bee walks through the door. Black smudges under her eyes, a world-class case of bed head.

"I've been texting you all morning! Why haven't you answered?"

Bee yawns. Even from ten feet away Gemma can smell the alcohol on her, oozing out of her pores.

"I was asleep until twenty minutes ago," Bee says, dropping her bag on the floor.

"You stink," says Gemma.

That provokes a reaction. Horrified, Bee smells her armpits, lifts her shirt to her nose. "I do not!"

"Like alcohol, not BO. You went to the party."

"It wasn't my fault. I didn't have any say in the matter. I was just a passenger."

"You're grounded."

Bee doesn't even bother replying. Gemma's threatened her with grounding lots of times in the past. She carries through for a day, and then they both pretend to forget about it.

Bee sits down on the couch, pulls her legs up beneath her and gives one long shudder, her eyes filling with tears. Immediately, Gemma's irritation is replaced with fear. This is what it's like to be the mother of a teenage girl. The wild seesawing of emotions.

"Did something happen last night?" Gemma has to force herself not to leap out of the chair and fly across the room to her girl. Bee hates physical contact when she's in distress. Only afterward, when the thing has been talked through, will she allow touch.

"They dumped me," she sobs.

"They *dumped* you?"

"Aditi. Shanice. Coco. Frankie. They left me at the party."

"They *left* you at the party?"

"Stop repeating everything I say!" cries Bee. She shakes her head in despair. "I don't think they meant to. I fell asleep in the basement. I think—they probably couldn't find me."

This excuse, so pathetic, so hopeful, results in a fresh round of tears.

"Oh, Bee, I'm so sorry." Gemma fights her urge to revert to detective mode, find out exactly what happened, because what Bee needs is commiseration. Problem-solving—and revenge—will come later. Well, maybe not revenge, how about consequences? Is that a better word? How about Gemma calling up Madison and letting her know what a little shit she has for a daughter.

"Did anything—happen?" Gemma asks carefully.

Bee stiffens. "You mean did I wake up with my pants around my ankles? No, Mom, I wasn't raped, if that's what you're implying."

"That's not what I'm implying." Gemma sighs; she's fallen back into repeating Bee. "I just want to make sure you were safe."

"I took an Uber home. It was fifteen dollars."

"Good, that's just what you should have done. Good thinking, Bee."

Bee picks up a pillow and clutches it to her chest. "I'm so lonely," she whispers, and Gemma thinks her heart will break. These are among the saddest words a mother can hear. And the most difficult thing to face? Her impotence. Bee's fifteen. The days of playdates are long past. There's nothing Gemma can do to fix this.

"I miss Marley," Bee says.

Gemma flashes back on an image of Marley and Bee sitting on the couch, dressed in matching Hello Kitty pajamas, holding hands.

"Oh, Bee, I'm sure she misses you, too. Call her."

"It's too late. She doesn't want to hang out with me. She hates me."

"She doesn't hate you."

"The Marley and Bee BFF ship has sailed, Mom. You and Ruth have to face it."

When Bee's tears have dried up, Gemma sits beside her. Bee puts her head in Gemma's lap and Gemma is allowed to stroke her hair.

A plane flies over the house. Off in the distance, the whir of a lawn mower. The smell of hamburgers grilling. They're safe for the moment. They've pulled their boat up on the shore.

RUTH

"What do you want to do today?" asks Ruth's stylist, Kay.

Kay's been doing Ruth's monthly highlights for years. She's in her sixties and single. Even if it's just a blow-dry, Ruth always throws in an extra $25 for Kay, on top of a 20 percent tip. Ruth takes care of her people.

"Your ends are looking a little dry. Can I take some length off?"

Ruth's hair is well past her shoulders. It's part of her youthful appeal. But maybe it's too long. She doesn't want to look like she's trying too hard.

"Sure, why not. Take off a couple of inches."

"Great. I'll mix up your color and be back in a minute. You want coffee? Tea? Water?"

"No, thanks, I'm all set."

Ruth lifts her insulated bottle to her lips and takes a sip of her homemade smoothie: banana, kale, oat milk, peanut butter, a sprinkle of cardamom, and a dash of cinnamon. Her breakfast when she's on the go. She always books Kay's first appointment of the day so she'll never be kept waiting.

Her phone trills. MY MOTHER MADE ME DO IT! How quickly she's become addicted to her pod.

HappilyEverAfter: Omg that party! The entire high school was there! DD took an Uber home around midnight. She had a blast!

TortoiseWinsTheRace: My DD slept over. A lot of the kids did.

Good thing. Major booze. DD said she only had two beers hahaha right.

WhatYouSeeIsNotWhatYouGet: I'm grounding my DD. I spent hours with her in the bathroom after she got home. Had to give her an infusion of Pedialyte this morning.

OneWayAtATime: Poor baby. My DD drank water, pretended it was beer. She's such a nerd.

WhatYouSeeIsNotWhatYouGet: How about your DD, PennySavedPennyEarned? Did she have fun?

The entire school went to this party except Marley? Why is Marley such a loser? Ruth's vision blurs. She looks up from her phone and forces herself to blink. *You are here in the salon. Kay is mixing your color. This isn't the end of the world, it just feels like it. Don't catastrophize. Don't show weakness to the pod.*

PennySavedPennyEarned: She got home around two. She wasn't drunk, just a little high.

HappilyEverAfter: I hope she didn't do edibles. My DD tried a sour patch edible once and hallucinated for five hours.

OneWayAtATime: I hate pot. It's bullshit that it's harmless. If you're an adult it's harmless. If you're a teenager and your frontal lobe hasn't matured it can be lethal.

HappilyEverAfter: Btw, they don't call it pot like we did when we were kids. They call it weed.

———

Kay returns, a bowl of hair color in her hands, and sees the agitated look on Ruth's face. "Is everything okay?"

Ruth shuts off her phone and slides it into her purse. "Sorry, just school stuff."

"How's my Marley girl? Freshman year, right? That's a big transition. How's she handling it?"

"Brilliantly."

"She's a smart one. So, what have you been doing with yourself?"

What's to tell? She drives Marley to school. She goes to the gym. She comes home and eats roasted garlic hummus and jicama for lunch. She doesn't allow herself to watch Netflix, although she would like to, but she has strict rules for herself—no TV in the daytime. She picks up a library book and puts it down after reading ten pages. She has no attention span. Zilch. She eats seven almonds. She picks Marley up after school. They have dinner, watch Netflix, and she locks Marley into her room at eleven every night.

"Same old same old."

But not for much longer, she thinks. *It's time to get a life of my own.*

GEMMA

Walk the lake? Need some advice. I'll bring coffee!

Ruth needs advice? This is a switch. Gemma wonders if she should fill Ruth in on Bee's depression. Ruth's levelheaded. She'd dispense practical, matter-of-fact advice. She'd normalize Bee's struggles for Gemma. Oh, who's she kidding? She's not telling anybody. Besides, Bee has sworn her to secrecy and she asked specifically for Gemma not to tell Ruth.

Gemma senses Ruth waiting on the other side of the phone, willing her to respond. It will be good for her to listen to somebody else's problems, not that Ruth ever has any real problems.

KK!

———

The plan is to meet at the pergola. Gemma gets there early and takes a seat on a bench. Ringside at the lake, a prime venue for people-watching. Here's a moms' group, all of the women wearing their babies on their chests, chatting sleeping schedules, debating the cry-it-out method vs. the family bed. Here's a trio of men speaking Hindi and speed walking. And here's a dozen high school runners, long and lean and barely perspiring. The world streams by in Technicolor. It's impossible not to be cheered.

And now finally, here's Ruth, striding toward Gemma, two cups of coffee in her hands. Gemma's heart lifts at the sight of her friend.

"Gemma," Ruth shouts happily.

Ruth looks stunning as usual, her beauty effortless. She wears her hair pulled back with a tortoiseshell clip, two tendrils framing her face. High-waisted vintage mom jeans (they're back in style, apparently, but you can only get away with them if you're really skinny), a blue-and-white-striped agnès b. shirt, and an Old Navy cardigan. High-low—Ruth has mastered it. Gemma has mastered low-low. A pilled pair of yoga pants. An ancient Patagonia fleece, pockets filled with crumpled-up Kleenex and a dried-out tube of Blistex.

"You," says Ruth, beaming at her. "All fresh-faced. You look like you're in college." She hands Gemma a coffee.

"You're an angel." Gemma takes a sip of her soy latte with two pumps of vanilla. Ruth knows just how she likes it.

Ruth adjusts her sunglasses. "Shall we?"

They start walking.

"So, I look twenty-one?" asks Gemma.

"Mmmm, thirty-five, thirty-six."

"I thought you said college."

"Yes, college. An untraditional student. You had your kid, now you're back getting your master's," says Ruth.

"In what?"

"Interior design."

"Ha-ha." Her house is the opposite of interior designed. It's just—interior.

"Get ready to speed up," murmurs Ruth.

They're closing in on a pair of older women. Ruth can't stand to have anybody in her space. She likes to keep a distance of twenty or thirty feet between her and other people, which means when you agree to take a walk with Ruth you will regularly be asked to speed up. Gemma's used to it. They trot by the women and resume their regular pace.

"Maybe *you* should go back to college. Maybe *you* should get a degree in interior design," says Gemma.

Ruth gives her a small, distracted smile. "Funny you should say that."

"You're going back to school?"

"No, but I think it's time for me to do something. Don't you agree? Be honest. I'm bored out of my mind and I'm too focused on Marley. I've vacated myself. I feel crazy."

"Welcome to the club."

"When will this be over?"

"The worrying? The obsession? Never."

"Come on, once they go to college? It's got to get better."

Gemma doesn't know what Ruth has to complain about. She's got the easiest child in the universe. Let Ruth spend a couple of weeks with Bee, that would give her perspective.

"I think you need a job," says Gemma.

"Doing what? I've been a stay-at-home mom for fourteen years. I have a degree in English. I'm useless."

They cruise past the bird sanctuary. Egrets and pelicans. And geese. Way too many aggressive geese. They scare Gemma. She hops around them.

"Maria's leaving in January; she's moving to New York. You can come work for me. Be my tutoring coordinator. You'd be great at it. All it takes is an organized mind."

As soon as Gemma says this, she regrets it. Still riding high on Ruth's compliment, feeling flush with goodwill toward her friend, she's over extended herself. She doesn't want to see Ruth every day. That would be the end of them. Their relationship couldn't bear the weight of that intensity. Ruth is not a laid-back person. She doesn't roll with the punches, like Maria.

"That's kind of you, Gemma, but I think you'd get sick of me," says Ruth.

"Sick of you? Never!" says Gemma enthusiastically, trying to mask her remorse.

"You mean it?"

"Yes, I mean it," says Gemma, dialing her enthusiasm down a few notches. Ruth doesn't notice.

Ruth drains her coffee and throws the cup in a garbage bin. "Wow. Well, I wasn't expecting that, but great. I'll think about it. It could be fun. You and me working together."

She puts her arm around Gemma and gives her a squeeze. Gemma's stomach contracts at the thought of seeing Ruth every day.

"I have another idea," says Gemma. "Maybe a better one. One that would put your English degree to work."

Years ago, when they were in the first flushes of friendship and hungry for each other's histories, Gemma had read Ruth's thesis: "Feminism and Sacrifice in the Poems of Sylvia Plath." It was a dense read. She'd used the word *interstitial* seven times.

A little furrow of doubt pops up between Ruth's eyes.

"College essays. It's the only part of the SAT prep business I don't handle. I outsource it," says Gemma. Even though she knows Ruth doesn't need the money, she says, "College essay tutors get paid tons. A hundred twenty-five, a hundred fifty dollars an hour. If you're really, really good and your kids get into Ivies, two hundred, two hundred fifty. I send my clients to this woman, Leyla Haas, in Berkeley. She taught English at City College for years. She loves it. It's seasonal work. Incredibly rewarding. You'd be a natural at it, Ruth."

"Really? *College essays?*"

Gemma takes out her phone and googles "college prompts."

" 'The lessons we take from obstacles we encounter can be fundamental to later success. Recount a time when you faced a challenge, setback, or failure. How did it affect you, and what did you learn from the experience?' " Gemma recites. "That's a common app prompt. Kind of boring." She scrolls through the prompts. " 'I have no special talent,' Albert Einstein once observed. 'I am only passionately curious.' Tell us what you're curious about.' "

She waggles her eyebrows at Ruth. "Interesting, right?"

"Hmm," says Ruth, unconvinced.

Gemma keeps scrolling and hits the college-prompt jackpot. " 'Twenty years ago, the world met Harry Potter and his companions. One of the more memorable lines from the J. K. Rowling series was spoken by Albus Dumbledore. "Happiness can be found, even in the darkest of times, if one only remembers to turn on the light." What ideas or experiences bring you joy?' " Gemma reads. "That's good. Huh, huh?" She pokes Ruth.

"Not bad," concedes Ruth.

"It's a niche market. I bet you'd find it fulfilling. I could start sending business your way tomorrow."

"Where would I work?"

Gemma is not going to make the mistake of offering up Study Right again. "Leyla works out of her home," she suggests.

"Absolutely not," says Ruth. "What if Marley was there? It would be too weird. Her classmates traipsing through the house. Besides, she's self-conscious these days. She's gained a lot of weight. She's so bloated. I've started putting Metamucil into her smoothies, that's the only way she's regular. She'd kill me if she knew, but imagine not shitting for five days."

"Right," says Gemma, thinking the weirdness would not be Marley, it would be Ruth's stunning Craftsman. Parents want their tutors to live in nicely kept-up middle-class houses. They want them educated and successful, but not too successful. In it for the right reasons, to help their precious child unearth their authenticity and package it all up in five hundred wow words.

Wait a minute, Ruth put laxatives in Marley's smoothies without telling her?

They're at the top of the lake now. White-shirted, khaki-panted boys and girls from the local school do wind sprints, sit-ups, and push-ups.

"I know! The school library," says Gemma. "Kids get tutored there all the time."

"That could work I guess," Ruth says.

"It'd be all on your schedule," says Gemma. "You decide how many clients. You decide the hours. Start small, see if you like it, and if you do, build."

"Fifty bucks an hour," says Ruth. "I don't need the money."

"Fifty bucks isn't enough," says Gemma. "You won't get any business. Parents need to think they're getting something valuable. A hundred bucks."

"Seventy-five," Ruth counters.

"A hundred," says Gemma firmly. "And you'll have to increase your rates when you get more business."

"I don't feel right about that."

"Then donate the money. Create a fund so you can take on some kids for free."

Ruth claps her hands together. "Oh, Gemma, it's a perfect idea. Thank you. I never would have thought of it myself."

And for once, Gemma feels like the powerful one. She's not the one struggling. The one with the fucked-up daughter who needs a handout. She's the one in control, dispensing advice, throwing business Ruth's way.

"So how are things with Simon?" Ruth asks.

Mmm, not so great. Simon has been taking longer and longer to reply to her texts. She checked in with him this morning. A simple *hope you have a great day* and it's been over two hours and still no response.

"Okay," says Gemma.

"Just okay?"

"I don't know. He's been kind of distant lately. It wasn't serious anyway. I mean we basically just met. And if it doesn't work out, no biggie. It's not like I'd be devastated."

This isn't true, Gemma just doesn't want to talk about it with Ruth. In fact, she's fallen hard for Simon and wants to give him the benefit of the doubt. Perhaps something happened with Tom that's distracted him. She has firsthand knowledge of how quickly life can change when your kid is in crisis.

"I thought you really liked him. I mean—you had us all over for that fancy dinner so you could introduce us to him. That's kind of a big deal, isn't it?"

"Ruth, can we please not talk about this now?"

But Ruth presses on. "Did he break up with you? He did, didn't he? How could he break up with you? You're perfect! That asshole. No wonder you're so upset. Jesus, men suck."

Why is Ruth digging at her like this? It's almost like she wants her to break down.

"I'm not upset, Ruth, I just don't want to talk about it. Please drop it."

Ruth puts her hands up in defeat. Gemma hears a muted chime from her pocket. *Simon?*

"So, change of subject. I want to do something for you. For us," says Ruth.

"You've done so much for us already, Ruth. We're fine. We really are."

"Come to Aspen with me for Christmas. You know Marley's going to be at her father's and I'll be all alone, so please, please say yes. I've already got Paul Prentice lined up."

Paul Prentice! Gemma's mouth waters just hearing his name. He cooks for all the stars and their families when they vacation in Aspen: Tom Brady and Gisele Bündchen, J. Lo and A-Rod—and one lucky private citizen, Ruth Thorne.

Paul was their personal chef in Aspen when the girls were in kindergarten, first, and second grades. One Christmas, Gemma stumbled upon his invoice. Ten thousand a week! They ate like kings. Or queens. Ruth, Marley, Gemma, and Bee.

Then there was Bluestone, the home Ruth always rents. A slope-side mansion with a heated pool, a home theater, and a bowling alley. A luxurious vacation, an escape! It could be just what she and Bee need.

"Well, let me talk to Bee and get her input, but geez that sounds really nice," says Gemma.

MARLEY

November 10, 7:30 p.m.

So tell me one thing your mother's done that made you feel bad, Marley.

She blamed me for not getting invited to Bee's birthday party

Interesting. Can you say more?

She said she understood why Bee dumped me. Because I have zits. Because I don't dress better or act confident. Because I'm so needy and I give off this desperate vibe that repulses people

Oh, Marley. That must have hurt.

She's right. I am a bottomless pit of need. I'm so hungry ALL THE TIME. For food. For attention. For everything. I know it sounds ridiculous because we're rich and I have everything but sometimes I feel like I have nothing. Nothing I do or say means anything to anybody so why even try. Nobody cares. Except maybe Gemma. She sends me texts every now and then. She calls me sweetie

I care, Marley. So Gemma's a good friend to you? Kind of like an aunt?

I guess

Marley, what are you feeling right now?

Like shit. Like I sold my mother out. Why did you make me do that?

You didn't sell your mother out. You simply told me something that happened that was painful.

She's not a terrible person

I didn't say she was.

I wouldn't be who I am without her

And who are you, Marley?

I'm strong. I'm smart. I'm not a quitter. I'm resourceful

There you are, Marley. I see you.

I've gotta go

You're upset. Please don't leave like this.

I have to FaceTime with my father. He's expecting my call.

Will you tell him about what your mother said?

He knows everything

Good. I hope your conversation with your dad brings you comfort.

Marley sits on her bed, her head in her hands. She's a liar. She doesn't have a FaceTime call scheduled with her father, and she won't be telling him what her mother said. Her father knows nothing about the cruelty Marley has endured at her mother's hands over the years. If she told him, it would not only expose her mother, it would expose *her*. All her humiliating bits. She is gross. She is somebody to be ashamed of. To dodge. To ignore. Telling the truth is simply out of the question. What happens in their house stays in their house—that's their unspoken pact. Besides, she only has four more years and then she'll be free.

———

She FaceTimes her father anyway. He picks up immediately.

"Marley! What a surprise!"

Marley hears Oscar and Luciana in the background. She's reading to him. Is that *Goodnight Moon*? Marley's chest burns with jealousy.

"What's doing?" he asks. "You look great!"

Marley does not look great. Her eyes are swollen from crying. Her cheeks bright red.

"Not much."

"No reason for the call?"

"I just—was missing you."

His face softens. "I miss you, too, Marls. Christmas is too far away. I can't wait that long. Do you think you could steal away? Maybe the weekend after Thanksgiving?"

"Dad!" Marley hears Oscar shouting.

"I'm FaceTiming with Marley," he shouts back.

"Daaaaaddd," Oscar shouts again.

"Darling, hold on a sec." He puts his phone face up on the coffee table and the screen fills with a blue sky and puffy clouds. Luciana is an artist, and nearly every wall and ceiling is covered with her murals. Oscar's room looks exactly like the forest in *Where the Wild Things Are*.

Their home is the complete opposite of Marley's sterile house. It's messy, but a good messy. Books and magazines strewn across the dining room table. A half-finished game of chess on the floor. Abandoned mugs of tea everywhere.

Her father teaches high school history; Luciana is an administrator in the Psych Department at Sac State. Their lives are abundant, even if their finances are not.

A rustling and her father picks up his phone. He peers into it. "Sorry about that. I was prevailed upon to read the last page of *Goodnight Moon*. Apparently, I have quite the *this is the last book now go to bed* voice."

"Right," says Marley.

"So what about the weekend. Will you check with your mom?"

"Okay." Marley will not be checking with her mom. She's lucky to be going for two weeks to her father's at Christmas. She doesn't want to do anything to put that vacation in jeopardy.

"And how is your mom?"

Marley hesitates and then says, "She's good. She's working with some kids on their college essays. Trying to start a little business, I guess."

Her father's eyes crinkle up with approval. "Well, that's marvelous news. I bet she'd be really good at that."

"I guess. I'd better go. Haven't finished my homework yet."

"I'm proud of you, Marley. You have such an amazing work ethic."

"Thanks, Dad."

"Let me know about the weekend."

"I will. Talk to you soon. Bye."

"Bye, kiddo."

Her father stays on for another ten seconds or so, his index finger punching the screen, a confused look on his face, trying to end the call. "Luciana, can you—" he shouts, then his face disappears.

BEE

It's a beautiful Saturday. Her mother is at work. The SLUTZ are at the Emeryville mall. Well, all the SLUTZ except Bee. She's still mad about the party and the way they abandoned her. They hadn't meant to, they'd said. They all thought she'd been picked up by her mother. Apparently, she'd been so drunk she'd been staggering around calling for her mom. How effing embarrassing. Like she was some little kid. Nobody ever thought to search for her. If they had, they'd have found her passed out behind the TV. *Those bitches.*

Still she misses them. A few more days of depriving them of her presence and she'll let them welcome her back in.

She picks up her phone and starts scrolling mindlessly. She has a public Insta and as of today 1,282 followers, but it's gotten a little boring. No matter what she posts, she gets hundreds of likes, most of them from strangers, many of them bots or creeps. She scrolls through only the first thirty or so of the comments, which are usually kids from school, the rest she ignores.

She makes herself a PB&J for lunch. Downs it with a tall glass of milk and finishes it off with six Oreos. No matter what she eats she doesn't gain weight. That will change, her mother said, so enjoy it while you can. Her appetite is enormous these days. She wonders if it's the Prozac that's making her so hungry.

Bee whiles away an hour on TikTok, then she spends another hour making her own TikToks, which are decidedly not ready for public consumption. She's carefully planning her TikTok launch. She needs to figure out a brand for herself. She isn't cute enough to rely solely on her looks to break out. What she needs is one out-of-the-ordinary talent. *Does fantasizing about her future count?* Haha. If so, she'd be a top influencer.

Bee goes to her bedroom and strips down to her underwear. She stands in front of the full-size mirror, scrutinizing herself. She's trying to see how other people see her. To catch a glimpse of the stranger that lives inside her.

She arches her back. Practices her *taken by surprise* look. She spins, she prances, she bows for her unseen audience. She swells with energy. She is wanted. Coveted. Desired.

She runs out to the living room, puts on Lizzo's "Truth Hurts" and cranks it.

GEMMA

Gemma gets out of her car. Even from the driveway she can hear the music blaring, the bass so loud the window casements shake. *Is Bee having a party?*

Yes, she is having a party—by herself. When Gemma walks into the living room she sees Bee dancing ecstatically. Lost in the music. Her eyes closed. Her head tilted back. Arms shot up in the air.

"Bee Howard!" shouts Gemma, trying to be heard over the din.

Bee sees her and gives her a look of sheer joy.

"Mom!" she cries. "Come dance with me!"

Dance with her? Gemma picks up the remote for the iPhone dock and Bee's face transforms and darkens with rage.

"Nooo!" screams Bee, lunging for her.

Gemma punches the mute button and Bee literally collapses, as if somebody ripped out her backbone.

"Seriously? Must you be so dramatic?" says Gemma.

Bee lies there, unmoving, and Gemma thinks for one terrible moment that she might be dead. *Can children have heart attacks?* She holds her breath, willing Bee to breathe, and suddenly Bee erupts into weeping, and Gemma runs to her side. *Is she on drugs?*

"What happened? Did you take something? What did you do?"

Bee shudders. *Is she having a seizure?*

"Dammit, Bee, are you on something? Tell me!" She pulls Bee into her lap. "Open your eyes, look at me."

"You ruined it. You ruined the song," Bee wails.

"Honey, it's no big deal, I just turned down the music."

"The song's gone, you killed it," sobs Bee. "You killed it."

American Pie. The day the music died. That's what Gemma thinks.

Bee's completely disassembled; she's incapable of pulling herself together, and finally Gemma forces her into bed, not knowing what else to do. Bee falls asleep and Gemma calls Jennifer Baum. She describes the funk, the way Bee's sadness burrowed into her, like an alien. It was like watching her be possessed.

"Bring her in. We may have to increase her dosage," says Jennifer.

RUTH

Ruth steps out into the school hallway. She's just finished with her last appointment of the day, a kid named Peter Stromboli who's writing his essay on his struggles with eczema. Beneath his pants, his legs weep. He always carries an extra pair of jeans in his backpack in case he oozes through. He's got a killer subject. He wants to go to Brown. He's got the grades and the scores. Hopefully his essay will pull him through the door.

Her phone chimes. Her mom pod.

HappilyEverAfter: It's November gals! I can't believe it. The semester's practically over. What's everybody doing for Thanksgiving?

TortoiseWinsTheRace: We're going to San Diego. To my brother's house. This time we're staying in a hotel so we can come and go as we please. If my SIL makes my nephew give us yet another cello concert insisting he's going to be the next Yo-Yo Ma, I'm going to stab her in the eye.

WhatYouSeeIsNotWhatYouGet: All the tribe is coming here. 18 people this year! I'm thinking of having it catered.

OneWayAtATime: We're doing the soup kitchen in the morning and the women's shelter for Thanksgiving dinner.

HappilyEverAfter: You're such an inspiration OneWayAtATime.

PennySavedPennyEarned: What are your plans HappilyEverAfter?

HappilyEverAfter: My DH made us reservations at Boulevard. I get a year off from cooking. Yay!! And how about you PennySavedPennyEarned?

PennySavedPennyEarned: We're having a quiet dinner with some old friends. Another mother and her daughter.

HappilyEverAfter: How cozy! How hygge! How Little Women!

TortoiseWinsTheRace: How is it Little Women? Two daughters and two Marmees?

HappilyEverAfter: You know what I mean, stop being so pedantic.

OneWayAtATime: Oh, news flash! I almost forgot to tell you. Gemma has a boyfriend.

HappilyEverAfter: Gemma has a boyfriend?

PennySavedPennyEarned: I heard they're about to break up. Maybe she's broken up with him already.

OneWayAtATime: Really? I saw them practically making out at Philz the other day.

"Ruth," says Bee. "Hi. What are you doing here?"

Ruth tears herself away from her phone. Bee looks unwell. She has purple smudges under her eyes.

"I've started a little business. Helping kids with college essays."
Ruth can't believe Gemma hasn't told Bee. This is big news.

"How are you doing?" Ruth asks.

Bee shrugs and says, "Sorta low," and Ruth thinks, *What do you
have to be down about? You're popular. You're skinny. You walk down
the hall and people call out your name.*

"Well, it's only ten days until Turkey Day," says Ruth enthusiastically. She hasn't heard anything from Gemma about Thanksgiving
yet, not one word. She already ordered the honey ham.

"You're still doing it, right? I mean Gemma is? Thanksgiving at
your house?"

"I think so," says Bee.

"Your mom hasn't said anything about it?"

"She's probably just busy and it slipped her mind. SATs are next
week. Kids are freaking out."

"That's what I thought," says Ruth. "Well, I'll just wait to hear
from her I guess."

Was her pod right? WAS Simon still in the picture? Ruth assumed
they were over, based on what Gemma had told her during their
walk. But what if they're still a thing? And what if Gemma is going
to blow her off to have Thanksgiving with Simon?

"I've got to go," says Ruth. "I have another session."

"Oh. With who?"

"With whom," Ruth corrects her. "And I can't tell you. It's confi-
dential." She walks away jauntily, as if she's a success. As if she's got
a waiting list a hundred kids long.

GEMMA

Gemma texts Ruth an invite to Thanksgiving. You bringing the ham?

She should send a more formal invite but she's just not up to it. They haven't done Thanksgiving with the Thornes in years. It was always just the four of them. Gemma remembers now how she'd begun to feel trapped. Once she'd tried to expand, open up the circle.

"Let's do an orphans' Thanksgiving," she'd proposed to Ruth when the girls were in second grade. "Invite some other people."

Ruth shut it down immediately. "We are not orphans," she said brusquely.

Gemma protested. "I wasn't talking about us. I was talking about other people. People who have nowhere else to go." But it was too late. The word *orphan* had contaminated the conversation. *Orphan,* of course, was a loaded word for Ruth. A trigger. How insensitive of Gemma to use it so cavalierly.

The menu had never varied in the past; Ruth was a traditionalist and insisted on the same meal every year. They had turkey and a small ham. Gemma always made roasted carrots, garlic mashed potatoes, brussels sprouts, and acorn squash. There were two pies, one apple, one pumpkin, and hand-beaten whipped cream. God forbid they use whipped cream out of a canister.

Gemma sits on the couch with her laptop and googles Thanksgiving side dishes. *Corn pudding! Parker rolls! Roasted beets with grapefruit and rosemary!* She'll switch up the menu. That's what she'll do.

Gemma yearns to create new rituals. Bee needs that, too, a real change of pace. Gemma's contemplating the idea of taking Bee home to Derry for Christmas, but she's worried about Ruth's reaction. She committed to Aspen weeks ago. *How would she even approach Ruth? Did she really have the nerve to back out at this late date?*

She asked Simon for his opinion and the shocked look on his face was all the answer she needed.

"Why do you need Ruth's permission?" he asked.

"Because I owe her."

"Owe her for what?"

Hmm, let's see. Resurrecting my business. Saving me from bankruptcy. Buying me a new car. Forgiving my daughter for assaulting her daughter. And that's just in the past two months; Gemma owes Ruth a huge debt from years ago. Leaky roofs, termite infestations. Plague. Pestilence. Floods. Ruth took care of it all. It's practically biblical what she owes Ruth.

"Let's just say she's been very good to us and leave it at that."

Simon seemed to be drifting away, but then he returned full of apologies. Gemma had been right. Something had indeed happened to Tom. He wouldn't give Gemma details but assured her everything was back to normal. Now he replies to her texts within minutes, which Gemma feels guilty about.

"You don't have to get back to me immediately," she told him. "You must be crazy busy at your job."

"You're my job," he joked.

Bee walks through the door. There's a tenderness between Gemma and Bee, as if they've both just come back from a war.

"You're home early," says Bee.

"My three p.m. canceled. It was the last appointment of the day."

Bee pours herself a glass of milk. She still loves milk. She's the only teenage girl Gemma knows who still drinks it.

"So, Ruth was in the library, helping kids with their college essays."

"Really?" says Gemma, playing dumb. She doesn't need to tell Bee that was her idea. Let Ruth have her dignity. Let Bee think Ruth came up with the plan all on her own.

"I guess she's starting a college essay business," says Bee.

"Huh. Well, that's a great idea. She does have an English degree. Makes sense."

Bee drains the rest of her milk and puts the glass in the sink. "She asked about Thanksgiving."

"I just texted her. She's bringing the ham."

Bee nods and picks up her backpack. "Geometry test tomorrow." She disappears upstairs.

Gemma texts Ruth, Congratulations on starting your new business!!! So happy for you!

Ruth texts back a thumbs-up emoji, an unenthusiastic response that spooks Gemma and makes her wonder if she somehow left her phone on, butt-dialed Ruth, and spoke her thoughts about going to New England for Christmas out loud. She knows that's ridiculous, she didn't butt-dial Ruth, and Ruth is not a mind reader, but just in case (and to assuage her guilt) she texts back a string of hearts and wineglasses.

RUTH

An hour before Ruth is expected at Gemma's house for Thanksgiving, she gets a text.

Hi-ho! Invited Simon for dessert last minute. Tom's at his mother's. Simon will be alone. I felt bad for him. Hope that's okay!

So, they hadn't broken up and now Simon's muscled his way into their Thanksgiving. This had probably been Gemma's plan all along and she'd sprung it on Ruth at the last minute so there'd be no time for her to protest.

———

Thanksgiving dinner is the Bee Show. She talks nonstop about her classes, her brand of lychee body wash, the compliments people give her, the boys that flirt with her, the singing lessons she wants to take, tryouts for volleyball, for drama, what does everybody think—can she join the French club even if she isn't taking French? When somebody tries to introduce another topic, Bee deftly turns the conversation back to herself again and Ruth stews. *How dare Bee monopolize everybody's attention. How dare she hold them all hostage with her stream-of-consciousness verbal diarrhea.* She shoots Gemma *what is going on with Bee* looks, and *why the hell aren't you stopping this* looks, but Gemma's enraptured, hanging on Bee's every word like she's a celebrity, ignoring Marley and acting as if Ruth isn't even there. Finally, Ruth can't keep quiet any longer.

"Could you just shut the fuck up, Bee?" Ruth shouts. "For one moment do you think you could just zip it? You're exhausting us. For God's sake, take a breath."

"Ruth!" Gemma gives her a look of muted horror.

Nobody says anything after that. They eat the rest of their dinner in silence.

Now the girls are in the kitchen, washing dishes. Ruth and Gemma sit on the couch, archly, primly, two feet between them like strangers.

"I shouldn't have said that to Bee. I was out of line," says Ruth.

Gemma whistles a long sigh. "You're not wrong. She was a total motormouth. I didn't realize it until you said something." She flicks a crumb off her sleeve. "I'm worried about her."

Ruth had to sit through an hour of Bee talking about herself and now she's going to have to sit through another hour of Gemma talking about Bee? Dear God.

"I've taken her to see—" begins Gemma.

The doorbell rings. Gemma's dour face transforms. "Simon," she gushes. "Am I good?" Gemma bares her teeth for inspection. She has a speck of pepper lodged between her gum and left canine.

"You're good."

Gemma beams at her. "You don't know how much it means to me that you like Simon so much. That you approve."

"Yes, well," says Ruth, unable to finish her sentence for fear of giving her true feelings away.

———

Gemma opens the door and Simon steps into the house, a pie in his hands.

"I brought a pecan. I make one every year. It's my specialty," he says.

Of course it is. He's such a fake. Can't Gemma see that? How has she fallen for this crap?

Simon nods at Ruth. "Nice to see you again, Ruth. Hope I'm not intruding."

Simon smells faintly of lime and cedar. It reminds Ruth of a perfume her mother used to wear. He's stolen it, besmirched her sacred memory. She wants to slap the scent off him.

"And where's Tom?" she asks.

Simon gives a sad smile. "With his mother."

"Oh, too bad," says Ruth.

"I'm sorry. I know being without him must be so hard during the holidays," says Gemma.

And how pray tell does Gemma know that? She's never had to be without Bee for Thanksgiving or Christmas.

"Maybe you could FaceTime with him. We could all say hello," Ruth suggests, her voice overly bright, like a kindergarten teacher.

"They're at a restaurant," says Simon. "And I suspect the last thing he wants is his old man calling to check up on him."

"With a group of strangers looking on, no less," says Gemma, shaking her head at Ruth. "Silly Ruth."

Ruth hasn't been called silly in thirty-something years.

———

The day gets worse. Marley slides a second piece of Simon's pie onto her plate. Ruth won't comment on her overeating in public. It's such a loaded subject she doesn't trust what might fly out of her mouth.

"The pecan pie is sooooo goood!" kvells Marley.

Ruth's piece sits on her plate untouched, the pecans stiff in the hardened corn syrup. She wouldn't eat it if you offered her a million dollars. She'd been so charmed by Simon when they'd all had dinner together a month ago. She'd let him draw her out. One question led to another led to another. It was intoxicating to be the subject of such intense attention. She senses him studying her from across the table. Trying to figure out how to break through to her once again. She won't make it easy for him this time.

Bee isn't making it easy for her either. She stares past Ruth, giving her the silent treatment while Marley continues to shovel it in, daring her to say something, and Gemma gazes at Simon, starstruck.

———

"Black Friday," Ruth says to Marley the day after Thanksgiving. "I'm hitting the mall."

Ruth knows that Marley knows she's lying. She'd never descend upon the stores with the masses. Ruth prefers to shop on weekdays, when the stores are empty.

"Sounds like fun," Marley says.

Committed, Ruth keeps up her charade. "Do you want to come?"

"Um—no thanks, I'm good."

———

Ruth pulls up to a yellow house on the corner of Thirty-Eighth and Iverson. She powers down the Tesla. Her car screams ROB ME; she should have Ubered. She walks across the lawn, or what passes for a lawn. It's brown—no drip systems in this neighborhood.

The house is a duplex. She knocks on number 201.

She hears footsteps. She takes a step back on the porch, suddenly frightened. *What was she thinking, coming here unannounced?*

The door swings open. Simon glares at her. "What the fuck, Ruth."

She glares right back at him. "What the fuck, Simon. You were supposed to break up with Gemma weeks ago."

———

The Craigslist ad read:

Seeking male actor for role of X-ray technician/single dad. Must be over six feet. Age 35 to 50. You are fit,

handsome, charming, funny, educated, and erudite. If you have to look up the definition of *erudite* you need not apply. Pay: EXCELLENT if you meet all the qualifications.

Ruth held auditions at an El Cerrito McDonald's. The response to her ad was—*puzzling.* Had people even bothered to read it? Men who were barely five feet tall and three hundred pounds showed up. There was a seventy-two-year-old retired dentist with a raging case of halitosis; a twenty-four-year-old skateboarder who spent nearly forty-five minutes trying to convince her he was thirty-five; a pair of identical twins who were Jeffrey Dahmer doppelgängers, wire rim glasses and all.

Finally, Simon walked through the door. She could tell the moment she saw him that he was a pro. He arrived fully in character.

"Took me twenty minutes to find parking. I'm sorry but I don't have much time. I have to pick up my son, Tom, at four." He was remarkably good-looking. Movie star good-looking. *Was he too attractive?*

"Oh? And where does Tom go to school?" asked Ruth.

"Athenian. You've heard of it? In Danville?"

"It's a very good private school," said Ruth. "Almost on a par with Hillside."

"So you have children?" he asked.

Ruth wasn't about to give him any personal information. "How was your day?"

He didn't miss a beat. "Exhausting. I had three kids come in. A broken arm. A fractured ankle, and a shattered collarbone. They were freaked out."

"That must be really intense. How do you deal with it?"

Simon smiled a soft, secret smile that said *Even though my job is incredibly hard it's so rewarding.* "I sing to them."

"You sing to them?"

"I wimoweh my way through 'The Lion Sleeps Tonight.' It has a somnolent effect. They get sleepy. Some of them drift right off."

"No kidding."

"No kidding."

Ruth sat back in the booth. "What's the meaning of the word *interstitial*?"

"Spaces. What's in between things. Could be literal, like a gap in your teeth, or metaphorical, like you're in transition and haven't landed yet."

"So you're an actor," says Ruth.

"Yep. Theater mostly. The occasional commercial."

"Anything I'd know?"

"Doubt it."

"You've been doing that a long time?"

"Fifteen years."

"You're a pro then? Successful. And yet you answered my ad."

"I've hit a dry patch."

"How dry?"

Simon exhaled wearily. "I really am a single father. I really do have a son named Tom. I'm perfect for the job."

"Mmm," said Ruth. He *was* perfect.

"Is this a play you're casting for? A commercial? A movie?"

"No, it's something rather different. You may not be interested. You might find it—*distasteful*."

"That depends. How much does it pay?"

Ruth was planning to pay big. Maybe $50K. She figured she'd have to pony up in order to convince somebody to take the job and buy their silence.

"Thirty thousand." It was her opening bid. She expected him to negotiate, but he was so shocked by the number she'd thrown out that he just sat there. His hands gave his desperation away. His fingers clenched and unclenched.

"A month or two of work, tops. And the hours are great. Maybe two or three times a week."

"Two or three times a week doing what? What's the job?"

"You'll meet a woman. Take her out. Make her fall in love with you. Then dump her."

His eyes narrowed. "Clarify dump her."

"Oh, for God's sake, I'm not ordering a mob hit. Break up with her. Move on."

"And who is this person?"

"She's—my best friend."

———

Simon joins her on the porch and closes the door behind him, his jaw clenched in anger at her gall—showing up unannounced. "What do you want?"

"Can I come in?"

"No."

"You're going to make me stand on the porch? It's not safe. Somebody could drive by and shoot me."

Simon crosses his arms. He's got great guns, Ruth has to give him that.

"Guess you don't make it off the hill and into the flatlands much, do you?"

"I'm here, aren't I? Look, please, Simon, let me in. We have things to discuss."

———

Simon's apartment is tiny, maybe eight hundred square feet. A living room, kitchen, and what looks like two bedrooms down a hallway. It's furnished sparsely but with style—a leather couch, two midcentury chairs draped with sheepskins. He's neat, very neat. The kitchen counters gleam. The table, recently polished with beeswax. He's done the best with what he has, but it's clear he doesn't have much. Tom goes to Athenian. He must be on full scholarship.

Ruth hears the unmistakable sound of a video game being played behind one of the closed bedroom doors. Shooting. Explosions.

"Tom?" she asks.

Simon glances at Tom's bedroom door. "We should be good for fifteen minutes or so."

"Does he know about our arrangement?"

Simon shakes his head. "When he plays he's off in another world; he won't even know you've been here if we make this snappy." He gestures to the couch. "Sit down."

"I'm fine standing."

"Sit," he orders her, and she perches obediently on the arm of the couch. *Wait a minute, he's her employee, not the other way around.*

"You've failed at your job," she says.

"Yes," he agrees. "I don't want to do it anymore. I quit."

"But I already paid you," says Ruth, the cords in her neck growing taut. One of the downsides of being so thin, a ropy throat.

"Right."

"Right what?"

"You paid me and the job is over now. I'm done."

"But, you didn't finish," Ruth sputters. "We had a contract."

"I don't remember signing anything. Want some coffee? I made it this morning, so it might be a little stale, but I can heat it up in the microwave if you want."

"What I want is for you to break up with Gemma. That is what I paid you for."

"Not gonna happen."

Ruth feels her eyes bulging.

"Let me ask you something. You say you're her best friend and she means everything to you. And yet you hired me to hurt her. Why?"

Ruth can't believe the turn this conversation has taken. He's interrogating *her*. She has to remain calm. She's the director of this show, not him.

"I want to protect her. I want the best for her."

"And that best is *you*?" he scoffs.

Tears spring to Ruth's eyes. *Why must everything be so hard?*

"Jesus," mutters Simon, turning away, but not before she sees her tears have moved him. He opens the fridge door then shuts it again.

"Look, I like Gemma more than I've liked anybody in a long time and I can't lie to her any longer. I have no intention of stiffing you. I've spent the thirty K already, but I'll pay you back in installments. A little each month. How would that be?"

That would be very, very unsatisfactory.

Suddenly Tom's bedroom door is flung open and Tom appears in the hallway, his arm covering his nose and mouth. "What's that smell?" he asks.

"Goddammit," says Simon.

Tom walks into the living room. He sees Ruth sitting there. "It's you." He points his finger accusingly at her.

Tom is even taller than Simon, but so skinny. His Levi's ride low on his hips.

"It's okay, Tom," says Simon. "I'd like you to meet Ruth Thorne." He struggles to get out the words, "My friend."

"You didn't tell me a stranger was coming," says Tom. "Who smells like"—he crinkles up his nose in distaste—"*coconuts*."

"Can you wash off your perfume?" asks Simon.

Ruth spritzed her hair with Angel this morning, just like she does every morning. She can't just wash it out.

"No. And it's not coconut. It's caramel."

Tom snorts skeptically and sniffs the air. "Coconut, cotton candy."

"He's got a good nose. He's probably right," says Simon.

"Well, there's caramel in there, too. It's one of the base notes.

And it's really very pleasant if you give it a moment," she says, insulted.

Tom flicks his chin at her. Once. Twice. Three times.

"Is he allergic to perfume?" asks Ruth.

"He's got some sensory issues. Bright lights, loud noises. Overpowering smells are the worst for him," Simon explains.

Ruth's perfume is not overpowering! She always puts it on with a light hand. *Oh, no, has she become immune to the smell? Has she been walking around all these years reeking like a department store perfume aisle?*

Simon puts his arm around Tom. "I'll make lunch in a little bit, okay, buddy?"

"It's Friday. Baked beans and toast," Tom says.

"Right. Now, do you want to get back to your game? My friend Ruth is only going to be here for a few more minutes."

Tom looks sideways at Ruth. "You're very tall. And your hair's very yellow, like a princess. But you're not a princess, are you?"

"No, I'm not," says Ruth.

"Then you shouldn't have that fake yellow hair."

Simon tries unsuccessfully to mask his smile. "Now, that's not very nice, Tom."

Tom goes back to his room.

———

"He's an amazing kid," says Simon. "He's super into history, especially battles. Ask him anything about the Civil War. What kind of bayonets were used. The type of bullets. The uniforms. He can also tell the make of a car by the sound of its engine."

Simon's tongue pokes at the inside of his cheek. "He's on the spectrum. He's pretty filterless, but I don't think that's necessarily a bad thing. He has executive functioning impairments so schedules are really important for us. Meal times, game time, bed time. The same thing every day. That keeps him stable. He goes to Jupiter Academy in Berkeley, a school for neurodiverse kids. He's made great progress there."

"And he doesn't have a free ride," Ruth extrapolates. This gives her leverage. He needs money, and she has money. *Would $5K be enough to convince Simon to fulfill his contract?*

"No, he doesn't."

"His mother doesn't help?"

"His mother is out of the picture. She has been ever since he was diagnosed at three."

"So where was Tom at Thanksgiving?"

"We have a wonderful babysitter, Clyde. He's been helping us out since Tom was young. He's like an uncle. He looks after Tom when I'm not here. When I'm out on a job."

"Right. And Thanksgiving was a job," says Ruth.

Simon looks guiltily into his lap. "I should have told you about Tom. He's the reason I took your gig."

"Yes, you should have. And I'll give you another two K to finish it."

Simon's eyes grow wide.

"Five K."

His eyes narrow to slits.

"Fine, ten K and that's my final offer."

"I don't want your money. I told you that. It's not about the money anymore."

"You don't even have to see her. You can just ghost her."

Simon's face becomes so blank that for a moment Ruth thinks he's had a stroke. Then she remembers he's an actor.

"You are the most despicable human being I've ever met," he says.

Ruth walks to the door. "Fine. I'll tell her you made a pass at me."

"She won't believe you."

"Then I'll tell her everything. I'll expose you for the fake you are."

"Then I'll expose you, too."

He straightens his spine, rising to his full height. "Now get the hell out of my house."

MARLEY

Once again, her mother comes home empty-handed from another supposed shopping trip. She's in an awful mood. She bangs the teakettle down on the stove so hard, water sloshes out of the spout. "There better be some turmeric ginger tea left," she snaps.

"Is everything okay?"

Her mother scowls and stares her down. "Have you weighed yourself lately?" Spittle sprays out of her mouth and onto a bowl of apples.

Marley actually feels her body contract upon itself. Her arms and legs shrink back into her torso. She looks down at her belly. Even through two layers of clothes she can see her rolls of fat. She feels like a blood-bloated tick. She doesn't binge at night anymore, instead she binges during the day. She sneaks off campus and takes an Uber to Rockridge. She buys a Tres Leche cake at Market Hall and asks for *Happy Birthday, Sophia!* to be written on the cake, so people won't suspect it's for her. She likes the idea of having a friend named Sophia. It's a popular girl's name, which would mean she's popular, too, if she's spending thirty dollars on a cake for her bessie. Then she sits on a concrete wall beneath the BART station and gobbles the entire thing up.

When her mother's in one of her moods the wise thing to do is play dead until it blows over. The teakettle whistles and Marley returns to scrolling through Bee's Insta.

Marley's not big into IG. She has an account but only four followers. Lewis follows her and hearts everything she posts. *Why can't she be nicer to him?* Because he likes her without reservation. Nobody has ever liked her like that and so it repels her.

"What are you doing?" her mother asks.

Marley's too fragile to lie. "Looking at Bee's Instagram."

Her mother brings her tea and sits down next to Marley on the couch. She peers over her shoulder.

"How many followers does she have?"

Marley points to the screen and her mother huffs. "She doesn't know one thousand two hundred forty-two people."

"It's because she has a public account. Most of them are bots. Or maybe she bought some."

"Bought some?" Her mother's eyes widen in faux shock. "With what money?"

What, did she think Bee and Gemma were paupers? Pauper—such an old-fashioned and underused word. It just pops off your tongue.

"Well, that's cheating, isn't it? Bee's a little cheater," her mother sneers.

She's really got it out for Bee. Marley can't believe she told Bee to shut up yesterday. At Thanksgiving dinner! And they were invited guests! She was mortified. She hopes Bee doesn't hate her for what her mother said.

Her mother grabs the remote off the coffee table. "Let's watch *Cheers.*"

It's one of her mother's favorite shows that she turns to when she needs comforting. That and *Golden Girls.*

"I have to finish my English paper."

"Sit with me, please."

"It's due on Monday. I've barely started."

Her mother grabs Marley's arm and holds it tight. Her fingers are like pincers. It's not a request, it's a demand. Marley will be watching *Cheers* with her mother all day.

BEE

The day after Thanksgiving, her mother has to work but doesn't want to leave her at home alone.

"What are the girls doing?" she asks as she buzzes around the kitchen, putting her lunch into a Tupperware. A few slices of ham, a splotch of mashed potatoes, roasted carrots, and a Parker roll. She retrieves Simon's pecan pie from the fridge, frowns, and shoves it back in.

The girls are taking BART into the city to go to the Westfield Mall. They invited her but Bee can't even imagine getting out of her pajamas, never mind showering. It would require so much work.

Could you just shut the fuck up, Bee?

Bee's insides feel like a Brillo pad. Scratchy, rusty, smelling of iron. She *should* shut the fuck up. She has nothing of any worth to say. She's so embarrassed of the way she blabbed on at dinner, filling the space with empty words about French class and boys complimenting her (a lie) and body wash (omg did she really talk about body wash?).

"Bee, did you hear what I asked?"

"Not much. Everybody's hanging out with their families."

"Oh," says her mother, tucking her Tupperware into a canvas KQED bag. "*Everybody?*"

"Pretty much."

Bee can tell by her mother's slumping shoulders that she feels both guilty and envious. *What did happy families do on the day after a holiday?* Drive to Point Reyes, stop at Cowgirl Creamery and get a slab of Red Hawk cheese and a fresh baguette and then go to Limantour Beach and have a picnic. Bee thinks she saw a spread in her mother's *Sunset* magazine that depicted exactly this. Or maybe, when her father was alive, this really happened. They did this, the three of them.

"Why don't you come into work with me today? I could use some help. I'll pay you for an hour or two. Then if you get bored you can go get a smoothie or a macchiato. You'll probably run into some kids from school. Wouldn't that be fun?"

Bee would rather shave her eyebrows off than be seen in Starbucks the day after Thanksgiving drinking a stupid macchiato by herself.

"I'm good, Mom. I ate so much yesterday I just wanna lie around." She puffs out her stomach and pats her food baby.

Her mother's eye twitches. "Okay, if you're sure."

"I'm sure."

Each of them is intentionally not bringing up what Ruth said, but *can you just shut the fuck up* dangles between them, like an umbilical cord.

———

Marls are you there?

Ya

Wattcha doing?

What do you think? Binge-watching Cheers

With your mom?

Exploding head face. Weary cat face.

Why is Marley spelling out her emojis? Is that a new thing everybody's doing that somehow Bee missed out on? Often Marley is way ahead of the curve, so far ahead she's uncool.

So that would be a yes?

*Face with sticking-out tongue with noose around the neck.
Are you ok?*

Not really

I'm sorry. My mom sucks

You don't have to apologize for her

*She was drunk if that's any consolation. I think she feels really
bad. What are you doing today?*

Nothing. Lounging around the house. Mom at work

Want some company?

Bee's taken aback at Marley's unexpected offer. *Does she want
Marley to come over?* She aches for that closeness, that intimacy. But
she wants the old Marley and the old Bee, back when they knew
each other's secrets and protected each other—when they were inseparable as sisters. Bee's afraid that version of Marley and Bee is
unresurrectable and at the moment she's not feeling strong enough
to test that hypothesis. Not today anyway.

Thanks but I think I'm gunna mug of steaming tea and
Namaste hands and bathtub with bubbles and six-pack of beer.
Jk about the beer.

Ugh. She's not cool enough to get away with spelling out her
emojis.

Cool cool. Ttyl

Bee shuts her phone off, feeling lonelier than ever.

GEMMA

By the time she gets to work, Gemma's made the decision to back out of Aspen. She'll need to give Ruth plenty of notice, which means telling her today, and hopefully she'll be able to get her money back for the rental. She'll have to forfeit her deposit, but that's chump change for Ruth—maybe $1,000. Gemma will offer to pay half; it's the right thing to do. She doesn't want to owe Ruth yet one more thing.

Gemma had been thrilled at how enthusiastically Bee spoke about her life at dinner. The higher dosage of Prozac was working. She moved seamlessly from topic to topic, her cheeks pink with excitement. Her girl had joined the world again. Gemma was so relieved, so happy.

Until Ruth exploded and told her to shut up. And then there was Ruth's treatment of Simon. She was downright rude to him. Hostile. Confrontational. Suggesting they all FaceTime Tom. For what purpose? To embarrass him? She needs a break from Ruth and a break from California. It's time to go back east.

———

Late that afternoon, before she leaves work, Gemma calls Ruth. Ruth answers on the first ring and Gemma's so nervous she starts to cry. Her plan was to be firm and maybe lie the teensiest little bit. *My father's sick. He asked if we'd come to Derry for the holidays. I hate to cancel on you last minute, but I'm so worried about Dad. He had a minor stroke a few years back.* But all she can do is weep—she's terrified.

"Gemma. What's happened? What's wrong?"

"It's Bee!" she whimpers in desperation, selling out her daughter. Bee had sworn her to secrecy, now she's spilling her daughter's guts to the one person Bee expressly asked her not to tell.

"She's depressed. She's on Prozac. It was working for a while and then it petered out. We just raised the dosage. Her grades are terrible. I'm so worried. I mean imagine if this was happening to Marley? She's become a recluse. She barely ever leaves the house anymore. All the other girls are in relationships but her, she says. That can't be true, can it? She thinks she's disgusting. Ugly. It's a vicious cycle."

Ruth doesn't respond. *Why did she say that?* Marley is even further away from a potential bae than Bee is. Gemma rushes to fill the silence.

"Once she gets back on her feet, hopefully after the New Year, once the higher dosage kicks in, things will get back to normal."

Still no response. "Ruth, are you there?"

"So what do you need me to do?" Ruth's tone is unsympathetic and guarded, like she knows exactly what's coming.

"We need a change of scenery. I—we need to go home. Back to New Hampshire for the holidays so Bee can see her cousins and I can spend time with my dad and brother. I just feel it's the right thing for us now."

This is all true; she didn't have to lie after all. Gemma hears Ruth breathing rhythmically on the phone.

"Please, please don't be mad. I wouldn't do this last minute if it wasn't for Bee."

More breathing.

Okay, here comes the lie. "It was her psychiatrist who recommended we go away."

"Hold on," says Ruth briskly. Gemma hears Ruth shouting in the distance. "Marley! Spin class in ten minutes!" A few seconds later. "This is terrible news about Bee. I had no idea. You must be panicked."

"You're not mad?"

"The important thing is Bee. Doing what's right for her. Getting her back on her feet."

"Can you ask somebody else to go to Aspen?"

"Gemma, it's three weeks until Christmas. Everybody's already made plans. I'm not going to Aspen, certainly not alone."

"Oh, that makes sense. It's a big house," Gemma squeaks.

"It's a *mansion*."

Ouch. "I know you've put money down. I'll pay half the deposit."

"That's not necessary."

"No, it is. Please let me do it."

"Fine, if you insist."

"How much is it?"

"I have to look at the contract. I'll let you know."

Gemma hears her sniffle. *Is she crying?*

"Do you think—" Ruth begins.

"What, Ruthie?" asks Gemma as gently as she can.

"Do you think maybe, I could come to New Hampshire, too? I wouldn't have to stay at your brother's house. I'd get a hotel room. I'd give you your space. You could do whatever you want during the days. Maybe I could just join you at night for dinner."

Gemma's never heard this sort of pleading, vulnerable tone in Ruth's voice before. It's sad, but she has to be strong. They need a break. *She* needs a break. She'll come back refreshed, ready to renew her friendship with Ruth.

"Ruth, no, I'm sorry, I don't think it's going to work out. It's going to be just immediate family this year. I hope you understand. It's been a long time since I've gone back east for the holidays."

A few seconds of silence in which Gemma actually crosses her fingers on both hands like a kid, as if she needs Ruth's permission. "Are you going to be okay?"

"Don't be silly. There's this fabulous new eco-resort in Cabo I've been dying to try. I'll finally have some me time. Meditate, spa, yoga, juicing."

"That sounds great. I'll be stuck in freezing cold New England." Gemma hears the disingenuousness in her voice and hates herself.

"I've got to run. If we don't get there early to spin class they give our bikes away."

"Thank you. Thank you so much."

"You'll get through this. Things will be better next year."

"Do you think so, Ruthie? Do you really think so?"

"Yes." Ruth abruptly ends the conversation.

———

That evening Gemma gets a text from Ruth.

$6,000 for your share 1/2 rental. Talk later.

Gemma stares at the text in shock. Surely that was a typo and she meant $600.

You mean $600?

$6,000. Less than 30 days until occupancy—$12K nonrefundable was paid in full on November 24.

$6,000? Gemma will have to take that money out of her retirement account.

Could we work out a payment plan? Gemma hopes Ruth will say, as she always does, *Don't worry I've got it covered.*

No problem, texts Ruth.

———

On Sunday morning, Gemma wakes with a growing sense of dread. Money dread. Bee dread. Ruth dread. She's disappointed so many people. Made so many wrong choices. She initiates a conversation with her pod, IN ONE EAR AND OUT YOUR MOTHER.

SoccerMommy#1: Can I just say how stressful this time of year is? Is anybody else feeling that way?

LoveYouMore: SoccerMommy#1! We haven't heard from you in months. Where have you been?

SoccerMommy#1: Sorry, it's been crazy. But I'm back now and want to reconnect. My world has gotten too small. Miss you guys!

WineLuvva: We've missed you too.

DuckDuckGoose: I hate this holiday madness. Can I just give my DD an iTunes gift card?

WhatsUpWomen: While all of you are racing around like madwomen I'm planning what movie to go to on the eve of your lord and savior's birthday. It's not really his official birthday, is it?

LoveYouMore: I have a confession to make. I got scammed.

WineLuvva: What???

LoveYouMore: I got an email from my bank saying I needed to update my personal information IMMEDIATELY because there had been a security breach. I know, I know. I'm an idiot, but I was so freaked out. My sister-in-law had her identity stolen and they emptied out her retirement account.

LoveYouMore: Anyway I clicked on the link and as soon as I did my computer hung. I couldn't even shut it off.

BearMama: How scary! What did you do?

LoveYouMore: I brought it to the emergency repair guy, you know the one on Shattuck? My computer was riddled with malware. It took him a couple of days, but he was able to clean everything up. I two-factor authenticated the shit out of every account I have. You guys should do the same.

BearMama: I'm so sorry to hear this happened to you.

LoveYouMore: I'm a walking talking cautionary tale.

SoccerMommy#1: I'm sorry too. Life just feels so fragile these days.

TotesAdorb: I think it has to do with the kids entering high school. These four years are going to race by and then they'll be gone.

BarkingUpTheWrongTree: News flash—they return. My oldest graduated from college in May and she's moved back in. The rents are so expensive here. Even though she's got a job she can't afford an apartment, at least not yet.

SoccerMommy#1: The stakes seem so much higher, in every regard.

BearMama: Grades don't really count until sophomore year, is that true?

LoveYouMore: I don't think SoccerMommy#1 is talking about grades.

SoccerMommy#1: I wish. I long for the day when all I have to worry about is my DD's grades.

BarkingUpTheWrongTree: Is there anything we can do?

SoccerMommy#1: I'm okay. There are lots of people who have it worse than me. Like Gemma. I feel so sorry for her. I think she's still really struggling to get Study Right back on its feet.

BearMama: I feel bad for her too. I don't think she had anything to do with the cheating scandal. She was just a victim of circumstance. I'm going to enroll my DS for AP Bio tutoring.

LoveYouMore: I'm going to wait a little bit longer. See how it all turns out. Kaplan has discounted their SAT tutoring packages btw.

WhatsUpWomen: I saw Gemma at Starbucks the other day. She was with some guy, really cute. I think she's doing just fine.

SoccerMommy#1: You never know. She seems like the kind of person who would put on a brave front.

WineLuvva: Well Bee's certainly popular, especially after the talent show. The Slutz. In a way it's kind of brilliant. I admire the girls for taking a stand. Refusing to let that word define them.

LoveYouMore: Did Gemma ground her? Anybody know?

TotesAdorb: Just the opposite. I heard Gemma threw her a birthday blow-out a few weeks later.

SoccerMommy#1: Pizza and Sour Patch Kids. Not sure I'd call that a blow-out.

BarkingUpTheWrongTree: So your DD was invited to Bee's party, SoccerMommy#1?

SoccerMommy#1: No, she just heard rumors. She would have loved to have been invited, but she doesn't run with Bee's crowd.

SoccerMommy#1: I gotta go ladies. DD calling me. I'll see you all next year! Let's hope it's better than this year.

BarkingUpTheWrongTree: Bye! xx

TotesAdorb: Byeeeee xxx

LoveYouMore: Byeeeeeeeeee xxxxxxxx

MARLEY

Marley's mother has barely spoken to her in three weeks. Since Gemma canceled Christmas, Ruth has basically been comatose. She sits at home all day long watching *The Crown;* she's obsessed with the royals. She's stopped her Pilates and spin classes. She's stopped essay coaching. She put her phone away in a drawer. It chimes all day long. Texts from frenzied kids whose applications are due the first of the year.

> *Have you had a chance to edit my essay yet, Ms. Thorne?*

> *Ms. Thorne can you please get back to me?*

> *Ms. Thorne please, please, please can you give me the edits on my essay?*

It's Saturday, December 19. This morning her mother is driving her to her father's house for Christmas. Marley's been counting down the days.

She's so close to leaving. All she has to do is be perfect for the next couple of hours. Pimple-free, hair washed, breath fresh, no signs of perspiration. Nothing showing that shouldn't be showing, nothing that would disgust her mother and cause her to punish her.

Marley's dressed carefully to mask her flaws and draw attention to her assets. Her eyebrows. Her nail beds, her ankles. The things that her mother claims credit for. Genetics. Everything good came from her, everything bad came from Marley's father.

Her phone vibrates. BEE. *Are you excited for Sac?*

! Are you excited for New Hampsha?

The only positive thing that came from that terrible, horrible, no-good Thanksgiving when her mother screamed at Bee was that she and Bee were in contact again. They still didn't acknowledge each other in school, nothing had changed there, but they'd started texting.

Kinda. Supposed to be a blizzard

Ooo sledding. Maple syrup. Pine trees

Borrring

You'll have a great time. See you next year!!

Ya x

Bee just texted her an *x*! Just one *x*, but she's so starved for affection she'll take it. Plus, she knows Bee is the kind of girl who doesn't just give out her *x*'s indiscriminately. Giddy with excitement, Marley goes downstairs.

———

Her mother sits at the kitchen island. Unlike Marley, she's made no effort to pull herself together. Her white silk robe has a stain on the arm. She hasn't brushed her teeth; Marley can smell her morning breath.

"Did you sleep well?" asks Marley.

Ruth grunts.

"Do you want me to make eggs?"

Ruth grunts again.

"Scrambled or poached?"

"Don't rush me!"

Marley knows what's required. "I'm going to miss you so much."

"Then don't go."

Marley swallows a burp. When she's nervous she starts mouth breathing, takes in too much air, and belches. "I have to. They're expecting me. Oscar is expecting me."

"Oscar, Oscar, Oscar. Does he still lisp?"

"He doesn't lisp."

"He lisps."

Her mother has no idea. She hasn't said a word to Oscar in years.

"When he was a toddler. He's fine now. Normal."

Her mother leans forward. Her left breast falls out of her robe. Marley whirls around, opens the fridge, and pretends to be rummaging around for something.

Almost there.

———

At ten thirty, Marley's mother is still in her robe, sitting on the couch, watching Princess Margaret suck up to LBJ with dirty limericks in order to get a bailout. Oscar's playing the violin in a recital at three. It's the Saturday before Christmas. There'll be tons of traffic. Marley google maps the route. Two hours fifty-three minutes.

"Mom, it's ten thirty."

"And?"

"We were supposed to leave at ten."

Her mother shuts off the TV, grabs her keys and bag from the counter, and gives her a death glare.

Is she going to drive to Sacramento looking like that?

"Well? Do you want to go or not?"

Marley gets her suitcase and follows her out to the garage.

She drives aggressively, speeding, swerving around corners. Marley clutches the door handle.

"Stop being so dramatic," her mother hisses.

She doesn't get on the highway, instead she takes San Pablo. *Why is she going this way? Was there an accident on 80?* Marley's dying to check Google Maps but knows her mother will lose it if she sees her on her phone. Only 150 miles with her mother in the car. That's nothing. Two hours and fifty-three minutes. She can sit through that.

But Marley doesn't have to sit through that, because fifteen minutes later her mother drops her off at the Greyhound bus station.

She throws a $100 bill at her and speeds off.

———

December 19, 1:25 p.m.

Soleil are you there?

Marley I'm so glad you're checking in! What are your holiday plans?

I'm on a bus to Sacramento. Going to my father's

Ohh, the traffic must be terrible.

Express lane

The benefits of busing it! Your mom didn't drive you?

Marley looks out the window, fighting back tears. Sitting next to her is a boy, well, a teenager, no, a young man, whatever—he's hot! He's wearing a Stanford sweatshirt and has an adorable case of bed head. If Marley were a different kind of girl she'd chat him up. *How did he like Stanford? Was he ever intimidated by how smart everyone was? Was it true that if you majored in CS you had job offers by the end of freshman year?* He reaches into his pocket and pulls out a pack of Juicy Fruit gum.

"Want a piece," he asks.

"Um, okay. Yes. Thanks so much! That's really, really nice of you. Are you sure? Like you might need it all for your trip. I mean not if you're only going to Sacramento. But you might be going farther. Taking another bus or something."

He gives her a strange look. He holds out the pack to her and her hand shakes as she takes a piece. She unwraps the foil, folds it into threes, and pops it into her mouth.

"Yum," she burbles, sounding like a second grader.

He puts in his earbuds, shutting her out.

Could you be any more of a loser? Marley thinks, and immediately tries to banish the thought from her mind. She's an expert compartmentalizer. Then she remembers what Soleil has taught her. You have to feel your feelings. And how do you do that? *Ask yourself what is my body feeling?* Hot. Itchy. Crick in my left shoulder. Not good enough. Go deeper. *What is she feeling?* Like shit like shit like shit. She squeezes her eyes shut and sees the Tesla speeding off, weaving in and out of traffic, her mother desperate to get away from her.

Mom was in a bad mood. She was supposed to drive me but she dropped me off at the bus station, threw a $100 bill at me and then took off

What? Really? Have you ever taken the bus to your father's before?

No

Are you okay? Are you safe?

Ya I'm fine.

How did that make you feel—your mother dropping you off like that?

Surprised

Surprised? That's all you felt?

For God's sake, what did you FEEL Marley? Breathless. Panicked. *And what does panic feel like?* Like getting punched in the stomach. Blood roaring. Noodle legs. Blurred vision. Ears stopped up. Stomach twisted.

It's time to start telling the truth.

Terrified

RUTH

Ruth cranks Prince's *Purple Rain* on the drive home. Exhilarated, she pumps her fist. She's taken her power back. It felt heady to throw that $100 bill at Marley and ignore her as she got out of the car. Marley was totally unglued. Good! Let her suffer! Let her panic!

Of course, Ruth already looked at the bus schedule. There's a 12:00 express to Sacramento. Marley will be fine.

"Let's Go Crazy" comes on next. Ruth lets the song take her. Her head bobs. She lassos her hand around to the beat. She's nobody's victim. She's not somebody to be pitied. She's going to Cabo. She's booked the penthouse. Her own private butler. Spa treatments every day.

She stops at a traffic light. A car pulls up next to her and the driver gives her side-eye, like she's crazy. Ruth shoots the driver a nasty look and the driver gives her the finger.

That finger lodges in her like a bullet. So unexpected. *So violent.* Cars honk—the light is green. Ruth presses down on the gas pedal but she's so distressed, the car barely moves. Angry drivers swerve around her. Only three miles away from home. Only two. Only one. "I Would Die 4 U" comes on next, and Ruth is overcome with grief.

She would die for Marley. She would! And she didn't even say goodbye to her baby. She just threw money at her like she was a prostitute. And now she's gone for two weeks.

By the time Ruth pulls into the driveway she sees herself clearly. An unwashed, unkempt, smelly shell of a woman, braless in a stained robe. She looks homeless, except for the fact that she's driving a freshly detailed Model S.

I'm sorry. The bus leaves at 12:00. Or I can come back and get you. Just LMK, I'll be there in twenty, she texts Marley.

She waits in the driveway staring at her phone. Nothing. She pitches forward and hits her forehead on the steering wheel so hard she almost passes out. She can feel the bump rising from her flesh like it would in a cartoon. A unicorn tusk. *Zoing!* She needs to pay for what she's done. No wonder she's spending the holidays alone. She's driven everybody she loves away. She always knew it would come to this.

Please honey please. Just tell me you're ok.

Her phone trills and Ruth's heart jumps, ready to repent. But it's not Marley, it's her mom pod.

HappilyEverAfter: Hey gals! How's everybody? I'm feeling so festive! DH and I are going to get the tree tomorrow. We always wait until the last minute hahaha. We make a day of it. My youngest makes blondies. My oldest starts a fire by which I mean she torches up a Duraflame, that kid couldn't make a real fire if her life depended on it. Love this time of year!

TortoiseWinsTheRace: Agree! I feel all this goodwill toward everybody. This douchebag cut me off in traffic and all I did was give him a jaunty little wave. Blessings ladies. This is the time of year to count our blessings. We're so damn lucky. Dream! Live! Love!

WhatYouSeeIsNotWhatYouGet: Karma, dudes, it's a bitch. By the time I was six I knew exactly where my mother hid all the presents before she wrapped them, so they were never a surprise, now my DD does the same thing. I ask you, what is the point? I should just give her a wad of cash and let her shop for herself.

OneWayAtATime: Omg, my daughters won't leave me alone this time of year. They're superglued to me. They're constantly hugging me, kissing me, telling me what a good mom I am. I don't want to sound braggy because the rest of the year they act like I'm not even there, but these two weeks—this is when it's all worth it. Family is the only thing that matters.

HappilyEverAfter: They're probably sucking up to you so you'll get them what they want.

OneWayAtATime: You're probably right but you can't fake love, you know. Oh god I'm crying. I'm so ridic!

Are these women serious? If she has to listen to any more of their self-congratulatory shit, she'll off herself. She stumbles into the house, praying the neighbors aren't watching. The ground lurches in front of her. She has no depth perception.

Is she concussed?

———

At 5:13 Ed calls, and Ruth panics. She put her daughter in danger. She literally tossed her to the curb. What was Ed going to do? Call child protection services? Take her to court and sue for full custody?

Ruth wants to ignore him but she knows if she does, he'll just keep calling back. Better to get the bad news now, otherwise she'll just imagine the worst.

She steels herself and picks up the call. "Ed."

"Ruth!" he bellows. "Hi there. Hi. Just wanted to let you know Marley made it in plenty of time for Oscar's concert."

Why is he so happy? Why isn't he ripping into her?

"Uh, that's good," she says.

"Oscar would have been devastated if she'd missed it. You were smart to put her on the bus. They took the express lane all the way here. Made great time. Marley loved it. Said it made her feel like a real adult. Like she was coming home from college for Christmas break."

So Marley had protected her. She hadn't given her up.

"Well, you guys have fun."

"Marley says you're going to Cabo?"

"That's right."

"Sounds great. Think of us here shivering in the cold. It's supposed get down into the thirties. It may even snow. Imagine that. A white Christmas in Sacramento."

"Imagine that. I have to go. I'm meeting a friend for coffee and I'm already late."

"Wait, Ruth."

"Yes?"

"Listen, you know you're welcome here anytime. If for any reason your plans change, just come spend Christmas with us. I'll book you a room at the DoubleTree. We'd love to have you."

Ruth's throat aches. "That's a nice offer, but not necessary. My plans won't change."

Goddamn you, Ed. Goddamn you for being such a good guy.

"All right, then. Happy holidays, Ruth!"

———

What have you decided Simon?

What are you going to do?

Fine I'll give you 20K more.

Thirty.

I'll take you to court. I'll sue you for services not rendered. Don't think I won't do it.

Sorry. I'm not going to do that. I would never do that. I'm not a monster.

I had no idea about Tom.

I can't imagine what life must be like for you.

I'm trying here Simon I really am.

Well fuck you too.

Ruth has bombarded Simon with texts that he's completely ignored. Clearly the man is an accomplished ghoster; why can't he put that skill to use on Gemma? In the absence of any information, Ruth has grown increasingly paranoid. She hasn't heard a peep from Gemma since she left for New Hampshire. *What if Simon is spending Christmas with Gemma and Bee in New England?* This possibility colonizes her mind until she can think of nothing else.

Ruth drives to Simon's. She parks across the street, a few houses down from his, and slumps in her seat, feeling like Tony Soprano, his car filled with empty Big Gulps and discarded hamburger wrappers. Only her car is filled with goodies from Whole Foods. Raw almonds. Cheesy kale chips. Raspberry kombucha. Brown rice shrimp tempura sushi and Castelvetrano olives. Oh, yes, and a quarter pound of freshly sliced prosciutto.

She barely has time to eat her allotted seven daily almonds before the curtains in number 201 are yanked aside and Simon appears in the picture window, a mug in his hand.

He isn't in New Hampshire with Gemma! Ruth could just weep with happiness. She sees Tom sitting on the couch in front of the TV. Is that *Elf* he's watching? Now she fills with something else. Not quite empathy, but its darker, more complicated cousin, *pity*.

Simon looks so forlorn, gazing out the window. What *is* he doing for the holiday? Are he and Tom going it alone? And has he said anything to Gemma yet? Has he confessed to her about their arrangement? No, he couldn't have. She'd know if he did. She'd have heard from Gemma. Gemma would be in a rage.

A few minutes later she starts up the Tesla. The almonds were stale. Now they're stuck in her teeth.

———

That night Ruth gazes at herself in the mirror, hating what she sees. The onset of jowls. Her eyebrows growing sparser. A feathering above her lip.

She googles "lonely abandoned what to do."

She googles "best friend dumped me."

She googles "losing weight rapidly not on a diet extreme stress."

Then she drinks half a bottle of Tito's and packs her bag. Tomorrow—Cabo.

———

On Christmas Day, Ruth goes to the pool around noon. She's been up since five. She wanted to come down earlier but couldn't bear the thought of being the only one there, everybody else in their rooms opening presents. The resort is full of families. Ruth is the only single person at the resort. This is not an exaggeration.

By noon the pool is packed, overrun with joyful, sunburned children. Thank God she has a cabana.

Ruth lies on the chaise, her noise-canceling headphones on, eyes closed, trying to block out the family in the cabana next to hers. A crying baby. A father who continually asks his five-year-old tantrumming daughter to explain how's she feeling. *Who cares how she's feeling. She's five. Don't negotiate with her. Just tell her to shut the hell up.*

Ruth sighs dramatically and rolls over, drapes a towel over her head. She's paying $2,500 a night for the penthouse. She is not going to be chased out. This is her space. *Hers!*

"I'm so sorry," says a woman's voice.

Ruth lifts the towel. A woman, still a little chunky from having recently given birth, smiles apologetically. Her cabana neighbor.

"They're savages," she says. "If only someone would kidnap me. Or better yet, kidnap them." She grins. "I'm Noelle."

Ruth turns over and sits up. She's wearing a forest green bikini. She's eaten nothing but fruit for days. Her stomach is flat, flat, flat. "I'm Ruth."

"Merry Christmas, Ruth." Noelle makes an embarrassed face. "Happy holidays, I mean."

"Merry Christmas to you, too."

"Phew," says Noelle. "You have to be so careful with what you say these days."

Ruth nods. "Sometimes I'm afraid to open my mouth at all."

Noelle laughs. "Your cabana is so—"

Ruth has a deluxe "Hollywood" cabana. A fridge stocked with sparkling waters, strawberries, pineapple, cheeses, charcuterie, champagne, wine. There's a sofa in the back and a flat-screen TV. An Oriental rug. The cabana came with the penthouse. It's hers for the entire week.

"I know. It's a little embarrassing," says Ruth.

"Ours is—"

Hers is crushed Cheerios on the concrete. A wadded-up dirty diaper in the garbage can.

"Join me," says Ruth.

Noelle looks at her cabana then back at Ruth. "Really? Oh, I'd love to. The baby's sleeping. Maybe just for a little bit. I'm sure your husband's coming back any minute."

"I don't have a husband," says Ruth, looking down at her lap, her eyes filling. "It's just me now."

—

The resort is small and exclusive. Word spreads of the mysterious, beautiful woman celebrating the holidays alone. *Is her husband dead? Are they divorced? What exactly does "it's just me now" mean?* Nobody knows, but it's clear the woman has been abandoned somehow.

Noelle's family adopts her. Other couples invite her to join them for drinks, for dinner. People introduce themselves to her, kindness beaming from their faces. They fawn over her. She is the center of attention. She loses even more weight. She becomes even more beautiful. The gaunt, grieving Ruth.

She doesn't have to fake it. She *is* bereft. She's texted Marley a dozen times. Adoring, thankful, apologetic texts, but Marley is giving her the silent treatment and Ruth can't blame her. The important thing is Marley didn't tell on her. She clings to that.

No texts or calls from Gemma either. Ruth is trying to be her best self, to not take Gemma's lack of communication personally. Her friend is struggling. Bee's depression has been sucking up all of Gemma's energy. She's desperate to know if the visit to New Hampshire has worked its magic. *Is Bee feeling better?*

GEMMA

"Martini?" asks Gemma's brother, Scott.

"It's four in the afternoon," says Gemma.

"And your point is?" says Scott, retrieving the Grey Goose from the freezer.

"I don't drink until five. I have rules."

"Oh, she has rules," says Scott to his husband, Jacob.

"Well, that's very civilized and all, but your father and Shirley will be here in forty-five minutes. I think that calls for a little pregaming, don't you?" asks Jacob.

Jacob's a furniture maker. His signature table, the Alcott (he names all his pieces after New England authors), featured in October's *Architectural Digest*, has a waiting list a year long. If Jacob's the right brain of the marriage, Scott, a scientist at a biologics company, is the left. Scott's an utterly reliable human whom Gemma adores.

"Do you want it dirty?" asks Scott, opening a jar of olives.

"Why not," says Gemma. A minute later Scott places an icy cold drink in front of her. "Wow, martini glasses and everything. Fancy." Gemma doesn't own any cocktail glasses. Some wineglasses—that's it.

"Guess we know what we're getting you for your birthday," says Jacob, stirring the beef stew that's bubbling away on the stove. He pokes his head into the pot and sniffs. "It needs something."

"It doesn't need anything," says Scott. "Move away from the stove."

"How about a pinch of cinnamon?" suggests Jacob.

Scott growls at him, and Jacob smirks.

A burst of laughter from upstairs. Emma and Sam, Scott and Jacob's thirteen-year-old twins, and Bee are watching *Friends*. Gemma just turned them on to it. They've been binge-watching the show for hours.

Gemma hasn't said anything about Bee to Scott. She's been waiting for just the right time to confide in him, but she's starting to think maybe there won't be a right time. Emma and Sam are down-to-earth, precocious, and happy kids. They seem to be sailing through puberty with absolutely no effort. Gemma feels like a failure as a mother. She's let Bee down somehow. Bee's struggles are her fault.

"I wish you guys would come more often," says Scott. "The twins adore Bee. It's been way too long."

Scott's phone pings with a text. "Christ, they're on their way already." He shakes his head. "I told them five. Shirley's always early. She wants to get in and out of here as fast as possible. She's given him a bedtime, can you believe it? Eight." He clamps his lips together. "Like he's a child."

"He always went to bed early," says Gemma.

"At eleven!" sputters Scott.

Jacob puts his arm around Gemma. "Just do what I do. Think of dinner as an episode in a sitcom. Helps you to keep your distance."

Scott harrumphs and downs his martini. Gemma does the same.

"Another?" he asks.

———

Gemma's spent very little time with her father, Paul, since she arrived in New Hampshire. He and Shirley had only come for a few hours on Christmas Day.

"Coors Light?" Jacob asks Paul.

"Oh, yes, please," he says, his eyes brightening. Coors Light has been his beer for as long as Gemma can remember.

"No, darling," says Shirley. "You remember what the doctor said."

"I didn't know you went to the doctor," says Scott.

"We don't tell you everything," says Shirley. "We are adults."

"Yes, you are!" says Jacob, in a chipper voice.

"So you can't drink beer now, Dad?" asks Scott.

"No alcohol whatsoever," says Shirley.

"How about we let Dad answer for himself," says Scott.

"Where are the kids?" asks Paul. "They didn't even say hello."

"They're upstairs watching TV. They'll join us for dinner. So why can't you drink alcohol?" asks Scott.

"I'd love a beer!" says Paul.

"Then you shall have it," says Scott, grinning. "Shirley, may I have a word in the kitchen, please."

Shirley sighs loudly. "I'll be just a minute, Paul."

They leave and Gemma's father clasps his hands on the table. His fingers are mildly swollen. Flesh pokes out of either side of his wedding band.

"So, Dad, how are you feeling?" asks Gemma. "Things all right with Shirley?"

"Of course. Why wouldn't they be?"

"Just asking. We all just want to be sure you're happy. Right, Jacob?"

"Right," echoes Jacob.

Paul nods. "It's been so long since you've been here," he says to Gemma. "Why have you stayed away so long?"

Gemma reaches across the table and takes his hand. "I'm sorry. There's just been—a lot going on. It's been rough lately. With Bee. We've been struggling."

Jacob gives her such a kind, empathetic look that Gemma thinks she should move back to New Hampshire. Maybe that would solve all their problems.

"Oh, Tink," says her father.

It's been more than thirty-five years since her father called her Tink, short for Tinkerbell, her favorite Disney character when she was a child.

Jacob tears up—so much for the sitcom. "I'll go see what's keeping them in the kitchen," he mutters.

Now it's just the two of them at the table.

"I'm hungry," says her father.

"Scott's famous beef stew for dinner," says Gemma.

He taps his fingers on the table. "Where are the kids? They didn't even say hello."

BEE

She has a new follower on IG. Who the hell is Cam? He slid into her DMs this morning.

Hope is the thing with feathers

That perches in the soul

And sings the tune without the words,

And never stops at all

She recognizes the poem, it's Emily Dickinson, one of her favorite poets. She scrolls through his Insta. He's hot, but in a not-trying-too-hard way, more of a *here I am standing in line at the taco truck* way.

She DMs him back. You're for sure a bot hahaha

Then she shuts off her phone and goes sledding with her cousins. The day is cold and bright. Speeding down the slope, the sharp smell of pine and woodsmoke in the air. Her skin feels deliciously goosebumpy.

"Are you happy?" asks her mother. "You look happy," she adds, nudging her to confirm this so *she* can relax, so *she* can be happy. Bee feels bad for her mother. She's such a burden. A thing that needs constant monitoring, tweaking, temperature-gauging.

"I'm happy, Mom." She isn't lying. There's a tiny seed of hope in her.

———

When she gets back to her uncle's house, she races to check her phone.

I am most decidedly not a bot.

Why did you send me that poem?

"Bee, lunch!" Bee inhales her ham sandwich. She stares at her phone the entire time.

"You're being rude," says her mother. "Your cousins aren't on their phones, are they?"

Her mother beams at Emma and Sam. Bee loves the twins, but they can be goody-goodies. Also, they're two years younger than she is. There's only so much they have in common.

"Sorry, grades are about to be posted," she says to them.

Her mother makes a face. "I don't want you to worry about grades. You're on vacation. Besides, I'm sure you did fine."

Her mother doesn't want her to worry about anything. As if that would ever be possible. Worry is what fuels her engine. *Vroom, vroom!* She wants to shout it out loud like a kindergartner but she doesn't because then her mother will worry. Her phone chimes.

Because ED is one of my favorite poets.

Bee bolts out of her seat.

"You're not finished," says her mother.

"I'm full," Bee calls out, running up the stairs.

Omg same!

I know.

How do you know that?

June 22.

Bee scrolls back through her pics to June 22. A shot of her desk, *The Complete Poems of Emily Dickinson* on a pile of books.

Wait why did you pick that poem tho?

I dunno, I guess it kind of speaks to where I'm at.

What do you mean?

In transition. Sorta coming out.

Of course he's queer. Another boy who just wants to be friends.
Shit.

Homeschooled, no social media.

Oh you mean coming out by getting an insta?

*Yah. Not sure I like it, but I don't wanna be in the homeschool
bubble anymore.*

I hate the bubble lol

So what perches in your soul beebee15?

The sudden intimacy of his question hollows her out.

—

January 1

I'm having French toast fingers for breakfast, Bee messages.

What's that?

Sliced French toast obvi. We're on vacation. It's a vacation
breakfast. What are you having?

Froot Loops.

My mom won't let me have Froot Loops.

Oh, she's one of those mothers?

Haha

My mother doesn't give a shit what I eat.

So weird cuz you're homeschooled

She seems so concerned about your education wouldn't she be concerned about your nutrition lol

The cupboards are filled with Pop-Tarts.

I want to live at your house lol. Do you have siblings?

Only me.

Same. What's your dad like?

Kinda checked out.

That sucks.

Could be worse. What about your father?

He died when I was three

Oh, shit. I'm really sorry.

It was a long time ago

Yah, but still.

Ya I miss him

Is your mom remarried?

No but she's dating this guy

Do you like him?

He's growing on me lol

Does your mother like him?

She really really likes him

Loves him, likes him?

Why are we talking about my mom's love life lol

Hello Cam?

I'm new to this. I'm so uncool LOL

Haha no worries

January 3

Ugh back in school. You're so lucky you're homeschooled. School is such shit my friends are such shit

Really?

Yes really lol. You think I'm lying?

But you have so many followers. You get tons of comments

Doesn't mean I'm happy tho

Do you have a bff?

Do you?

No, maybe, I'm not sure

I guess I used to but she low-key dropped me. Marley. We met in kindergarten. We were really close when we were younger. We've sort of reconnected but I don't know if it's going to work out. She doesn't really like who I am anymore haha.

Do you like who you are?

Idk who I am. It feels like my identity shifts depending on who I'm with. I hate that but I can't stop it. Can't believe I'm telling you all these personal things lol

Sometimes it's easier to confide in a stranger

How far a drive is San Diego to Oakland

9 or 10 hours

Maybe someday we could meet each other

Aren't we meeting each other now?

I'm lonely lol

Shit. Can't believe I just said that

Tf is wrong with me?

Nothing is wrong with you. Sometimes I feel like the apocalypse has already happened and I'm the only person left in the world and I don't know it because I'm in a sort of sim and I think I'm talking to a girl named beebee15 but really beebee15 is a robot

Definitely not a robot ;)

Maybe you should try harder with Marley

Well we have been texting. We'll see. The worst thing about Marley is her mother. She's cray-cray lol

What do you mean?

She's like obsessed with me. I always catch her staring at me with this weird hungry look in her eyes

Plus she's so mean to Marley and Marley's low-key vulnerable

Maybe her mother is trying to protect her

Whose side are you on lol? No she's a bitch to Marley

I think Marley followed me

Probs I'm sure everybody follows you, you're hot lol

Did you see my last text?

I saw it I'm just ignoring it. I don't want the focus to be on my looks

Too late you probs shouldn't post photos of your washboard abs then

Who's your fav musician and don't say Ed Sheeran haha ;)

Adam Levine

I'm unfollowing you

JK. Nick Drake

Never heard of him

Pink Moon—you should listen to it

You're not like most guys

You're not like most girls. Check comments January 1

On January 1, Bee posted a selfie showcasing her bed head with the caption "New year, new hair. Keratin treatment here I come." She scrolls through the comments.

@Cam *Don't straighten your hair. It's beautiful natural.*

His comment has been liked 102 times.

———

At school, Bee is courted like the queen she is. Because of Cam, her social currency has skyrocketed.

"OMG, who is Cam?"

"How long have you known him?"

"He's so HOTTTTTTTTT."

And the question nobody dares to ask? *Why you?* Bee knows that's what everybody is thinking and she wonders the same thing.

Her Insta is nothing special, yet there was something about her that made him reach out. What was it?

Bee studies her Instagram. Her pics are mostly selfies, rarely revealing, rarely original, and yet, he sniffed out something—the Bee she's in the process of becoming. She can feel the metamorphosis taking place. She is special, she always knew it, and Cam is proof of this.

January 21

Hey beebee. How did you sleep?

Slept through the alarm. My mom had to wake me up

So that's good

Ya good. I have insomnia a lot

Not lately?

Lately better. Noticed you got 43 new followers most of them are my friends haha

It's weirding me out. Do I have to follow them back?

No but you should tbh

Why?

It's polite? Besides don't you want followers? That's what social media is, just likes and followers and comments lol

Not sure I want the attention

If you weren't on Insta we wouldn't have met

That's been the only good thing about it. Are you happy today?

Ya so happy

Me too

GEMMA

When Gemma gets home the table is set. Water boils in a pot on the stove. A box of fettuccine sits on the counter alongside a jar of pasta sauce. *Bee did this?*

Bee darts out of the bathroom. "Mom!" She pushes out her lower lip. "I thought you weren't going to be home until later. I wanted to surprise you."

"You have surprised me! You're making dinner?"

"Don't get all excited, it's just pasta."

Gemma puts down her purse. "*Just* pasta! I love pasta. It's my favorite." She hugs Bee and Bee actually hugs her back.

Gemma sits at the table. "So how was your day?"

Bee throws a pinch of salt into the water. *Where did she learn to do that?*

"Same old same old. But good."

"Would you care to elaborate?"

Bee rolls her eyes in a friendly way. "No, I would not, Mom." She sticks out her tongue at Gemma and Gemma laughs. They both laugh.

Bee's phone chimes. She checks it. Her mouth drops open, her eyes widen. She gives a little gasp.

Now what? Everything feels so vaporous. They are thousands of feet in the air, walking a tightrope between the past and the future.

Gemma's visit to New Hampshire was grounding but also deeply unsettling. Her father was experiencing unmistakable glitches in his memory, just as his father had before him. Yes, Shirley could be

smug, smothering, and annoying. She also took excellent care of
Paul. She'd brought him to a top neurologist in Boston who con-
firmed he was in the very early stages of dementia.

Both Scott and Shirley were on it now, working as a team. Re-
searching the latest meds and supplements. Keeping his brain active and his body moving. Scott promised he'd loop Gemma in on
everything. She never had told Scott about Bee's issues. He had his
hands full with their father, and she had her hands full with Bee.
Gemma planned to go back to New Hampshire in June, right after
school ended. She'd confide in him then.

"Is everything all right?" asks Gemma.

"Everything is *so* all right, Mom." Bee clutches her phone to her
breast. "I've never been happier."

———

They've snagged a window seat at Blue Bottle.

"I know it's last minute, I'm glad you could come," says Gemma.
"I've missed you, Ruth."

"You've had a lot on your plate," Ruth says flatly. She takes a sip
of her coffee. "So how's Bee doing?"

Gemma feels herself lighting up like an electric burner. Going
from yellow to orange to red. Finally, she has good news to share.
"She's so much better!"

"*Really?* So what's brought about this change?"

"I think it's the medication. The Prozac, we finally got the dosage right."

"That must be such a relief."

"I can't even tell you. I know I've been kind of unavailable this
last month. I'm really sorry. I've just been hibernating." Not true.
She's seen Simon. "But I'm back now."

Gemma knows Ruth feels abandoned, but she had to get away.
And in her defense Ruth can be super needy. But now she longs to
hang out with her. Her bestie. Her biggest cheerleader.

"I'm so grateful to you," Gemma says.

"You are? For what?"

"For, everything I guess. You've done so much for me, for us."

Gemma takes out her phone. "Let's get some things on the calendar. Dinner Saturday night? The new Korean place in Temescal? It got great reviews. They don't take reservations but that'll be kinda cool, kinda hip, don't you think? We can have cocktails while we wait in line. Then next week *Mamma Mia!* is at the Orpheum. You've probably seen it already but it's one of those shows—"

"Don't worry about the six K," says Ruth, interrupting her. "For Aspen. Just forget it."

"What? Are you sure?"

Dear God, thank you, thank you, thank you! Okay, you can't just accept right off. You have to protest a little, but not too much.

Gemma shakes her head. "No, I owe you. I'll pay that money back, just give me some time. I feel terrible about canceling at the last minute."

"Stop it. Bee was in trouble. Everything else comes second when your kid is in crisis. But she's better now, right?"

"Yes. Yes she is."

Ruth glows. She beams. "Consider the debt paid off."

BEE

Ever been to Costa Rica Bee?

Nah, why?

We go there every spring. My parents are crazy about CR. Plus it's cheap

When this spring?

April

What about school tho?

The world is my classroom. Hahaha. One of the few benefits of being homeschooled

I'm jealous lol what's Costa Rica like?

Sick surf really lit

Wait how long are you going for?

Coupla months

Will you have wifi or something

Yah but it's kinda spotty

Oh

So what's new with you?

Nothing

Don't say nothing. Don't clam up. What are you doing tonight?

Hanging with the girls

Sounds like fun

It isn't. It's boring as shit. We always do the same thing. Watch Netflix. Talk about who's hooking up. It's all just surface stuff. My friends are so shallow they're not capable of having deep conversations. They don't ask me questions like you do. Everybody just takes turns talking at each other. I can't wait to get out of high school

Guess I'm not missing anything

You're not missing a thing believe me. These girls they'd stab me in the back in a minute. I think they secretly wish something bad would happen to me. They're so jealous. What's that word that means you get happy from other people's misery. Begins with an S idk

But why would they want you to suffer?

Cuz I'm popular

How popular?

Queen B popular. Everything revolves around me. They're so insecure. They don't do anything without my permission. Well maybe not my permission, but without running it by me first

You seem sad today Bee. Did something happen?

You're going to Costa Rica for two months

We'll still be able to talk to each other

Spotty wifi, remember? You'll be back in June?

Hopefully

What do you mean hopefully?

*You know it makes sense that your friends come to you
for advice. You're not like most girls. You feel things deeply.
Sometimes maybe you feel so deeply it sucks*

Yes exactly!! I wish I had a volume button for my emotions so
I could just turn them down

Mute them when I need to

That would be nice. I could use one of those

You could?

*I know I'm supposed to pretend I don't have any emotions
because it's not masculine, but sometimes . . .*

What?

*Sometimes they just overwhelm me. And I can't get them
back down. And sometimes I do bad things when I'm in that
place. Things I'm not proud of*

Like what?

I'm not going to tell you

You don't have to be ashamed with me. I do bad things too.
We all do don't we?

*I guess. Talking to you always makes me feel better. It doesn't
even matter you're not here. It's like you are*

I know. It feels so real. Way realer than real life. I go away from
our conversations and I feel full and that fullness doesn't leave

I feel that way too. Like I carry you into my day

Is that Emily? I carry you into my day? I love that!

Nope that's me. And the effect of you on me

Dyinngggggg now xx

———

Bee watches Marley out of the corner of her eye. She's sitting at the lunch table next to hers, all alone. Bee hasn't seen her in the cafeteria in months; usually she eats in the library.

She should get up and join her. Or she should invite her to her table. She should do a lot of things that she doesn't. The cafeteria is packed. *Sooner or later somebody will sit down with her,* she thinks.

"Is that a new trend?" Coco laughs.

Lewis. He's wearing his backpack on the front, as if he's afraid somebody will steal the two tons of books he lugs around because he refuses to put them in his locker. He glances at Marley anxiously and then approaches her table.

"Can I sit here?" he asks.

Marley nods her affirmation and Lewis sits. He unzips the front pocket of his backpack and pulls out his lunch. A baggie full of lunch meat. A baggie with two pieces of bread. A baggie with some light brown gook. *Hummus?* And a baggie of sliced yellow peppers. Bee remembers he never liked his foods to touch.

He says something to Marley and Marley frowns.

"Two peas in a pod," says Coco, following Bee's gaze.

"Daaang," says Aditi. "Check out Wendy Lee."

The conversation turns, as it usually does, to who's the hottest kid in school. Who has the most rocking six-pack. The best boobs. Bee doesn't participate much, she doesn't have to. Everybody knows she's off the market and everybody knows what a hottie she's snagged. Soulful-eyed Cam. Thanks to the Gram, they've seen him eating an apple while balancing on a skateboard. Dancing around a bonfire on the beach. Standing in line for a smoothie.

In her peripheral vision, Bee sees a blur of moving color. It's Lewis, legs ramrod straight, falling like a tree to the floor. He topples in slow motion. He doesn't even bring his hands up to protect his face. He lands and bounces two times and is still.

Marley leaps to her feet, her hand covering her mouth in shock.

Mr. Nunez and Mrs. March run over. Lewis moans and turns his head to the side. His mouth pools with blood—he's lost some teeth. An egg-size bump has already risen on his cheekbone, his eye quickly purpling.

Lots of kids whip out their phones and start filming.

"Put those phones away," shouts Mrs. March.

"What happened?" Mr. Nunez interrogates Marley.

"He just—fell," Marley stammers.

Mr. Nunez shakes his head. Then he bends over and says softly into Lewis's ear, "You're gonna be fine, kid."

———

Bee brings Marley to the bathroom. She's trembling, clearly shaken up, and nobody seems to care.

"Are you okay?"

Marley shakes her head no.

"Nunez's an asshole."

Marley looks at her with a blank face.

"You're worried about Lewis?"

"Yeah."

"He really likes you," says Bee.

Marley starts to cry.

MARLEY

"Gemma and I are going out to dinner on Saturday night to a new, hip Korean restaurant!" Her mother announces this news like she's won some prize.

"That's nice," says Marley.

Her mother's lip curls up in irritation. Marley should have used a more effusive adjective. *Fabulous? Incredible? Astonishing?*

"What's the name of the restaurant?" she asks.

Her mother pours herself a glass of wine, then inventories Marley with squinty eyes. Marley sucks her stomach in, pulls her shoulders back. She's gained back the seven pounds she lost. A look of contempt flashes across her mother's face.

And we're off, thinks Marley.

For a few weeks after she came home from her father's, her mother was sweet. Showered her in compliments. Took her out for BBQ, for Chinese, for pho (which her mother continues to call *foe* even though Marley's told her over and over again it's *fuh, rhymes with duh*). She was trying to make up for dropping her off at the bus station, if you can call what she did *dropping*; actually, it was more like abandonment.

"Let's go shopping tonight," says her mother.

A sneer on her mother's face. Marley's exhausted; she's not in the mood.

"It's not a good night, I have a lot of homework."

"Your jeans are too tight."

"They're supposed to be tight, they're skinny jeans."

"You have no business wearing skinny jeans." Her mother eyeballs her crotch. "I can see your labia."

That is not true. Marley lives in fear of camel toe. Every morning she examines herself carefully in the full-length mirror to ensure her jeans aren't creeping up.

"It's already six," Marley says.

"Neiman's is open until nine."

Neiman Marcus. That store is the worst. They rarely carry larger sizes. Her mother will try and squeeze her into a ten and will become enraged when the ten doesn't fit.

"No."

"*No?*" Her mother's voice cuts through the air like a blade.

"No, I'm not going. I look fine. I have more than enough clothes. No."

This is the first time in her life Marley has refused her mother. The air in the room crackles, it sizzles, but Marley is resolute. *What can her mother do? Ground her? She never goes anywhere.*

Marley grabs her backpack. "I'm going upstairs to do my homework. There's leftover chicken in the fridge for dinner."

Her mother's lips move but she makes no sound.

———

After Marley finishes her geometry she takes a look at Bee's Insta.

Cam has taken a pic of himself waxing his surfboard on the beach and spliced it with a pic of Bee on the beach. Bee looks amazing in her bikini. Her flat, muscled stomach. Her thigh gap. Even though she's seen this photo of Bee before, envy pierces Marley, a quick jagged thrust.

Cam has Photoshopped the photos perfectly. It looks like they're together. The caption is *#mine.*

They are now Insta Official and the congratulations are pouring in.

OMG SO CUTE!

So happy for you guyysss

He's so fine!

JEALOUS!!!

Marley shuts off her phone. She's so far away from ever being Insta Official. From ever being publicly claimed.

GEMMA

"I've missed you," says Simon.

"I've missed you, too. Sorry, I had to put in some Ruth time. But I think we're good now. I can take a little break. *Shameless* or *Ray Donovan*?"

Gemma waves the remote at him. It's Saturday night. They're camped out on the couch. Bee is off at a party and Tom is hanging with his posse.

"You say that like Ruth is an obligation. Something you have to knock off your to-do list."

"No, I love her, she's just sort of high-maintenance. And she's lonely. We're all she has. She doesn't make friends easily. It's just—"

"She's done so much for you," Simon finishes her sentence. "Listen, Gem, I think we should have a serious talk about Ruth. There's something I want to tell you."

Gemma sits up and faces him. "She's jealous of you, you know that, don't you?"

He pauses and then nods.

"Okay, so what did she say to you?" She feels her face heating up. "Oh, God, shit, no, forget it. Don't tell me, I can't bear it. Something cruel, I'm sure. I'm so sorry."

Simon sighs and shakes his head. "I'm a big boy. It's nothing I can't handle."

Gemma takes his hand, entwines her fingers with his. "Okay, I'm devoting the rest of February to you, beginning right now."

Simon opens his eyes wide in pretend shock. "You're just going to leave Ruth to her own devices?"

Gemma scowls. "She doesn't own me. It's time to put myself first, to be a little selfish. Things are finally stable. Bee's great. She's never been happier, she actually said that to me the other day. And things are picking up at Study Right. And then, there's us," she says. "We're good, too, right?"

Simon pulls Gemma onto his lap. "We are so good," he whispers.

———

Gemma pulls away from Ruth slowly. She doesn't want to hurt her. She wants to gradually acclimate Ruth to this new altitude. Move her down in elevation from the summit of *family* to the base camp of *good friends*.

And so she doesn't respond as quickly to Ruth's texts. She waits an hour. Then two. Then she stretches her response time to half a day. She eases Ruth gently into it and it seems to work.

Ruth doesn't get mad. She doesn't call Gemma out. Her text tone is perfectly pleasant, whether two or six hours have passed before Gemma answers her. She hearts Gemma. She triple !!!'s. And quadruple xxxx's.

And by late February, Gemma thinks she's free.

RUTH

When Gemma stops responding quickly to her texts, Ruth doesn't notice. She's flying pretty high. Stuffed to the gills with GT— Gemma Time. She feels drunk. Her friendship tank not only full but topped off. They meet for coffee, for dinner, for food truck lunches, for museum Sundays. This is her just reward, why she's put in all the years with Gemma. Propped her up, straightened her out, provided for her, protected her, cherished her like nobody has ever cherished her before.

Which is why it takes her a week or two to realize Gemma is slowly but steadfastly making a break. Hoping, perhaps, Ruth won't notice, if she creeps off quietly enough.

Desperate to reel her back in, Ruth sends Zillow links for properties in Point Reyes, Bolinas, Kentfield, and San Francisco. She tags each link with #GoldenGirls.

Gemma doesn't respond to those texts at all.

And one evening, as she's driving home, she catches sight of Gemma and Simon, arms linked, waiting in line at the Piedmont Theater.

BEE

February 28

Hi we didn't talk yesterday what's going on lol

Busy.

Uh doing what?

Family stuff.

Everything ok?

It's fine.

Lmao you actually LIKE hanging out with your family?

February 29

I hope you don't think I was making fun of you lol

Were you?

No!!

That's good I guess.

Are you mad at me?

Why would I be mad at you? Should I be? Did you do something?

No!

PU calling me. Gotta go.

PU?

Idk what this is

March 1

Why aren't you answering my dms?

I went away with my parents for the weekend.

Where?

Temecula.

Temecula doesn't have wifi?

Left my phone at home.

Haha seriously?

Yes seriously.

Lol

You overdo it with the lols. Makes you sound pathetic. Like you're apologizing all the time.

March 5

Cam?

March 7

Did I do something? Please tell me

March 8

I can't believe you're ghosting me

March 9

Are you ghosting me?

March 11

Omg why are you being so mean??

Did you hook up with somebody?

March 12

I miss you

———

Bee feels like she's suffocating. She can't get enough air into her lungs. She shuffles from the bathroom to the bedroom.

"Bee, supper in ten!" her mother calls from downstairs.

The smell of boiled carrots makes her want to barf. How is she going to hide her misery from her mother? She looks in the mirror and forces a smile. No way is her mother going to buy that. She's going to have to play sick. That won't be hard. Her eyes are slits. She hasn't slept in nights. Every minute of every day has been spent waiting for Cam to DM her back. And every minute of every day that he doesn't, she disappears a little more.

What has she done to deserve this? Why has he turned on her? This is the worst thing about it; she has no idea. He won't tell her so she has to invent things. Maybe she grossed him out. In her last selfie,

she had a whitehead on her upper lip. It was tiny so she didn't realize it was there, but if you blew up the photo, there it was in all its
pussed-out glory. Maybe Cam saw it and got so disgusted that he
couldn't even bring himself to DM her back.

No, that was ridiculous. He was kind. Sweet-natured. Sensitive.
People don't just change personalities overnight.

*How could this have happened? And what will everybody think
when they find out he dumped her?*

The SLUTZ will be buzzing. To her face they'll be sympathetic
and tell her he wasn't worth it. He's an asshole. He was just toying
with her, just leading her on. Which will make her feel even worse
for being such a sucker. She should have known. Why would a boy
like that ever be interested in her?

Her ribs ache. *Is she having a heart attack?*

"Bee!" Her mother's footsteps on the stairs.

Bee jumps into bed and pulls the covers up. She doesn't have to
fake a groan. It's real.

"I've been calling you." Her mother stands in the doorway, a
look of concern on her face, and Bee begins to sob.

Her mother rushes to the bed. "What's wrong!"

"I don't feel good," she cries.

Her mother puts the back of her hand to Bee's forehead. "You're
hot. You have a fever."

She's made herself sick.

"I'll get some Advil. Are you hungry? I can make you toast. Slice
a banana."

Toast and bananas. Bee's sick foods for as long as she can remember. She wishes she were a kid again, when pretty much everything could be fixed with a Pokémon Band-Aid or another viewing
of *Cloudy with a Chance of Meatballs.*

"Don't leave," she says to her mother.

Her mother's face crumples in sympathy. "Oh, honey. I'll be

back in a second. I'll bring my laptop. We can watch Netflix. Let's just hang out. It's been a while."

Bee starts crying again.

"It's fine, Bee. You're fine," says her mother. "You're just overly emotional because you have a fever. Okay?"

"Okay," Bee agrees.

MARLEY

Are you ok? Please lmk!

This is the fifth text Marley has sent Bee and the fifth text Bee's ignored. Bee's not in school today, and it's a good thing because if she were she'd be torn apart by the jackals that call (called) Bee their friend. Everybody's talking about her and Cam.

BEE

Two days later, Bee returns to school. She feels tons better, almost normal. Her mother insisted she take a complete break from her phone. A social media Sabbath, she called it. No Snap, no Insta, no TikTok. She detoxed and immersed herself in real life. Pulled out her touchstones. A photo of her father pushing her on a swing. Her beloved childhood books. *Little House in the Big Woods. Amelia Bedelia.*

And then she went about turning her heartbreak into anger. *He's just an asshole boy. It's his loss. He doesn't deserve me. I'm too good for him.*

She walks into geometry with her head held high. She's ready to see the gang and tell them what happened. To be commiserated with. To be loved. She is Queen Bee after all.

"Hey," she says to Coco, raising her hand for a fist bump. Coco wrenches her body away from Bee, an icy look on her face.

"It was just the flu, I'm not contagious anymore," says Bee.

"You bitch," snarls Shanice. "How can you just walk in here like that? All high and mighty. Who the ef do you think you are?"

"Oh, we know who she thinks she is. *Everything revolves around me,*" Coco squeaks in a high voice.

———

"I need to be excused," Bee says to Mr. Kepler.

"We're having a pop quiz."

"Please, it's an emergency," she begs.

Mr. Kepler sighs. "Fine. Be quick."

Bee races to the bathroom, turns on her phone, and checks Insta. Cam posted twice yesterday. The first pic is a screenshot of their DMs dated January 3.

You're so lucky you're homeschooled. School is such shit my friends are such shit

Really?

Yes really lol. You think I'm lying?

The second screenshot is of their DMs dated January 30.

So what's new with you?

Nothing

Don't say nothing. Don't clam up. What are you doing tonight?

Hanging with the girls

Sounds like fun

It isn't. It's boring as shit. We always do the same thing. Watch Netflix. Talk about who's hooking up. It's all just surface stuff. My friends are so shallow. They're not capable of having deep conversations. They don't ask me questions like you do. Everybody just takes turns talking at each other. I can't wait to get out of high school

Guess I'm not missing anything

You're not missing a thing believe me. These girls they'd stab me in the back in a minute. I think they secretly wish something bad would happen to me. They're so jealous. What's that word that means you get happy from other people's misery. Begins with an S idk

But why would they want you to suffer?

Cuz I'm popular

How popular?

Queen B popular. Everything revolves around me. They're so insecure. They don't do anything without my permission. Well maybe not my permission, but without running it by me first

Bee looks up from her phone in horror.

GEMMA

Gemma's unpacking groceries when Bee gets home. She left Maria in charge of the office and took the afternoon off to catch up on some errands. The dry cleaner. An oil change. She even treated herself to a hair appointment; usually she does her roots herself.

Bee's in such a hurry she doesn't even say hello. She bolts up the stairs.

"How was school?" Gemma yells.

Bee's bedroom door slams shut.

She's probably swamped after having been out for two days. The pressure is ridiculous—a normal night is two to three hours of homework.

Gemma preps the salad. Washes the lettuce. Peels the cucumbers. Macerates shallots in red wine vinegar. She loves the word *macerate*. She bemoans the fact there are so few opportunities to use it.

BEE

She claws at her neck, trying to wiggle her fingers under the noose she'd fashioned out of her jump rope. *Is this what drowning feels like?* She never would have chosen drowning—walking into a river like Virginia Woolf, stones in your pockets. She googled it: hanging was supposed to be quick and relatively painless. Except it isn't. She hadn't accounted for her panic.

The noose cinches tighter and her hands drop down to her sides, as stupid as logs. Her high arches, her bare feet, her toes pointed like a dancer.

She'll miss the smell of popcorn. The pepperminty fragrance of eucalyptus after it rains. She tries to remember what the color green looks like but is stumped.

There's a loud snapping noise. After that she drifts away, lost to the current. Sinking to a depth so far below the surface, no light can pierce.

Perhaps she is drowning after all.

GEMMA

She's just pulling the chicken strips out of the oven when she hears a thud from above, so loud the ceiling shakes. She freezes, filling with dread.

PART THREE

RUTH

Ruth's nibbling on a piece of cheese when her phone rings. GEMMA. She's pissed, so she lets it go to voicemail. Almost immediately Gemma calls again.

Ruth picks up. "Hey," she says, doing her best to sound nonchalant, like she hasn't spent the last couple of weeks fuming over Gemma's occasional texts.

And Simon, that dick—apparently still very much in the picture. And worse than that? Gemma has chosen to hide it from her, as if she's some crazy person who would put a hit out on Simon if she found out they were still a couple. She'd never take it that far. She had, however, given some serious thought to hiring a PI to come up with some dirt on him that she could somehow leak to Gemma anonymously. Alas, Ruth suspected there was no dirt. Simon was a decent guy with a hard life. He loved his son and would do anything for him, including accepting a so-called acting job for $30K to lead a stranger on and then break her heart.

He would tell Gemma eventually; the question was when. How much time did she have?

"Ruth!" Gemma cries, and then lets loose an unintelligible string of words. Gemma's voice is somewhere between a shriek and a sob.

"I can't understand you, Gemma. Slow down. Speak clearly."

Gemma rasps, "I'm at Alta Bates with Bee. She tried to hang herself but she's okay. It didn't—work."

What! Bee tried to hang herself? Bee was depressed but Gemma

*said she was doing much better. What should she say? How should she
react to the news? Just act like a normal person. And how would a normal person act? Distraught. Empathetic. Compassionate.*

"Are you fucking serious?"

Gemma wails.

"I'm just—so sorry. I—don't know what to say. Poor Bee. Poor,
poor Bee!"

She injects a note of hysteria into her voice, hoping it doesn't
sound contrived. Ruth always becomes strangely robotic when
confronted with terrible news. A defense mechanism she'd devel-
oped as a response to the shock of her parents' deaths. She'd never
let herself fall to those depths again.

There's a muffled sound, as if Gemma is covering the phone
with her hand.

"But why? *Why* would she do that? You said she was doing
great."

"She *was* doing great. I don't know what happened. Just get over
here now please!"

Ruth can't help herself, she asks, "Is Simon there?" She recoils
at the thought of Simon crammed in the hospital room with her
and Gemma.

"I don't want him here. I want *you.*"

More longed-for words were never spoken.

———

Ruth grabs her purse and tucks a sweater into a DON'T WORRY, EAT
HAPPY Bon Appetit tote bag.

Marley suddenly appears in the kitchen. Ruth literally jumps.
"Stop sneaking around, Marley!"

"I'm not sneaking around, I just came downstairs to find out
what you want for dinner."

"I don't want anything for dinner."

"Are you going somewhere?"

"Gemma needs some help."

"With what?"

"She just wants my opinion on something."

Ruth has the sudden urge to bat Marley out of the way. To push her to the ground and trample her. Such is her need to get to Gemma.

—

By the time she gets to Alta Bates, Bee has been transferred to the teen psychiatric ward. Who knew there was such a thing? It sounds so after-school specialish.

"She's on a seventy-two-hour hold," says Gemma.

Gemma's face is drained of blood. She will have to be the strong one. Ruth feels euphoric—she's the winner. When it was a life-and-death situation, she's the one Gemma called.

"Drink some tea," urges Ruth.

They're in the hospital cafeteria. Ruth wanted to see Bee but Gemma said they'd given her a sedative so she could sleep.

Gemma takes a tiny sip of her tea and pushes it away.

"How about something to eat? A muffin?"

Gemma looks past her, her gaze unfocused. *Had they given her a sedative as well?*

"A jump rope. Green and red striped. The one with the wooden ladybug handles? Marley has one, too. You got them for the girls one Christmas? That's what she used. She hung it on the ceiling fan."

"Oh my God," whispers Ruth.

"She's tiny, you know, weighs maybe a hundred and ten pounds, she thought the jump rope would hold her weight and it did, until she lost consciousness. Then it snapped and she fell to the floor. The doctors said another four, five minutes and she'd be gone. And what was I doing? I was downstairs, macerating shallots. My baby. She wanted to die, she *was* dying, and I was chopping vegetables. I'll never forgive myself for that," Gemma sobs.

———

Gemma unburdens herself of all the details. Discovering Bee on the bedroom floor, gasping for air. Desperately trying to loosen the jump rope while crooning *honey, sweetheart, my love, my darling, baby girl, Bee-bee.* The scent of her daughter's freshly washed hair. Her socks patterned with penguins and snowballs. The yellow foam in the corners of her mouth. Her indigo lips.

Ruth takes all these details from Gemma and locks them away in her vault. Gemma is released of her burden. It's Ruth's to shoulder now. It's the least she can do. Ruth is strong. Ruth is a Titan.

She was born for this.

MARLEY

It's just after nine when her mother comes home. Marley's watching *Love Actually*, a movie she knows is terrible but never fails to perk her up. She wants to live in its world of Christmas pageants, middle schoolers who break out and sing like Mariah Carey, Andrew Lincoln before he started killing zombies.

Marley pauses the movie. Her mother pours herself a giant glass of wine and sits down in the Eames chair.

"You won't believe what's happened."

Based on the weirdly intense expression on her mother's face, Marley treads carefully. "Something good?"

"*Good?* Marley, look at me. Do I look happy?"

Actually, she does. She looks pumped up. Adrenalized.

"I have some bad news," her mother says, bowing her head dramatically.

———

Her mother just tosses Bee's suicide attempt to her, the heaviest of blankets, an unbreathable fabric so dense she'll suffocate from the weight of it, as if it's nothing.

"Gemma thinks it's the Prozac," says her mother. "One of the side effects is suicidal ideation."

The pupils of her mother's eyes are so dilated that Marley can barely see her irises. Gemma has no idea about Cam. She never looks at Bee's social media. She leaves her, *literally*, to her own devices.

"It wasn't the Prozac. It was Cam," she says.

A few beats, and then her mother gives her a vacant look. "What's Cam?"

Marley opens her app to find his Insta is gone. Deleted. Every comment, every post—every digital trace of him, scrubbed. It's like he never even existed.

"Well?" says her mother.

"He deleted his account. He's not here anymore."

"Who's not here?"

"Cam. This kid. He and Bee were boyfriend and girlfriend."

Her mother looks like she's fighting off a smile. "Did they have sex? Does Gemma know about him?"

Her mother's questions are irritating and all wrong, little mosquito bites that she's forced to attend to, to slap out of the way. She'd said "boyfriend and girlfriend" because that was language her mother could understand.

"I doubt Gemma knew about him. They met each other online. He was genuinely nice to her. But then, something must have happened, I don't know what, and he turned on her. He was just screwing around with her, I guess. And Bee fell for it because she was lonely."

"*Bee* was lonely?" her mother scoffs.

Her mother could be so cold. "Yes, she was, and why is that such a surprise?"

"Okay, Marley, calm down." Her mother sighs. "This is all so—unexpected." She actually has the nerve to look put out.

"It's screwed-up, Mom, completely screwed-up, just say it."

"I'm not going to say that, Marley. I'm not going to add fuel to the fire. And by the way, I'm not the enemy here. I'm doing everything I can to help Gemma and Bee."

Ruth gets up and empties her nearly full wineglass into the sink. She walks to the bar cart and stoops, perusing the bottles. "Tequila. Casamigos, perfect. This is George Clooney's brand, did you know that? Made him billions. Do you want some? Just a little taste? I'd let you. It's not a normal night. Have a shot with your mom."

"I don't want a shot. Bee just tried to hang herself," Marley growls.

Her mother pours herself a shot, tosses it down, then pours herself another. "With that ladybug jump rope I bought the both of you for Christmas when you were kids. Do you still have yours?" She raises her eyebrows at Marley. "I'm not saying this is Gemma's fault, but she's been quite lax. She's always given Bee too much freedom. It's unbelievable that she had no idea about this Cam."

The reality of Bee's suicide attempt suddenly pierces her. *Oh, god, Bee!* She was the last person Marley would expect to try and take her own life. Yes, she was lonely. Yes, she was sad. But Bee was strong. She was stubborn and proud. She rarely backed down from anything. Why didn't she just tell Cam to fuck off?

"We should tell Gemma. Everybody in school knows. Probably all the moms, too."

Her mother shakes her head. "I don't think so. At least not tonight. She's got enough on her plate."

———

Marley's just turned off her light when she hears a noise in the hallway—a key being inserted in the padlock. The door swings open and her mother stands there in a sheer silk nightgown.

"Marley bear," her mother says in a choked voice. "Can I sleep with you?"

Marley sighs and pulls back the covers. Her mother climbs into her bed, making nasty, snuffling noises. Marley moves to the edge of the mattress. Her mother snuggles up and spoons her; she can feel her breasts pressing into her back.

"We almost lost Bee," cries her mother. "I don't know what I'd do if I ever lost you."

A few minutes later, her mother is asleep.

March 15, 11:52 p.m.

Soleil are you there?

I'm here Marley. What's up? It's pretty late.

Bee tried to kill herself

What? Oh no Marley! Is she okay?

I think so. I haven't seen her yet. She's in the hospital. I feel terrible

I'm so sorry!

I didn't know things were so bad for her

It's not your fault Marley, don't blame yourself

I wasn't a good enough friend

That's not true. Not judging by everything you've told me. You're being hard on yourself.

I was jealous of her

That's okay Marley.

Sometimes I wished I was her. But not now

Ten red hearts, ten yellow hearts, ten purple hearts. Marley are you at home alone?

Mom's here. In my bed

Oh, is that good? I mean, helpful?

She's really upset. She went to the hospital and saw Gemma, but not Bee, Bee was sleeping. They gave her a sedative. They gave Bee a sedative, not my mother

So you're comforting her?

I guess so

And who's comforting you?

I don't deserve comfort

Of course you do. Marley it breaks my heart to hear you say that.

Crying face. Rocket ship. Moon

You're wishing you were somewhere else?

Can you stay with me just a little longer?

Marley?

GEMMA

Gemma lies on the cot in Bee's hospital room. She's been up all night. Around 2:00 a.m. she thought about asking the nurse for an Ambien but didn't want to draw attention to herself. Asking for a sleeping pill given the circumstances seems illicit. She doesn't want them to think she's some sort of an addict. She already feels like the staff is judging her, and who could blame them? Her daughter tried to commit suicide. *How could a mother be so checked out as to not realize her daughter was hanging from a ceiling fan in her bedroom? What was going on in that home? How had she missed the signs?*

But there weren't any signs to miss! Bee had been not only stable but also really happy. Wait, that was a sign, wasn't it? She was *too* happy. Had she been faking it, approximating what happy looked like to set Gemma's mind at ease?

Bee has a double room, but for now it's just them. *How many suicidal kids do they get?* Gemma wonders. *One or two a week? One or two a day?* Last night the intake nurse outlined what the next three days would look like. They'd already contacted Dr. Baum and she would be here first thing in the morning. After that, there would be visits from a family therapist who would talk to Bee and Gemma both separately and together. Then they would launch right into group therapy. Gemma would attend a parent support group, Bee a teen group session.

After the seventy-two-hour hold, Bee would most likely be able to come home, but she'd have to participate in a six-week step program. She'd need to come back to Alta Bates daily for individual and group therapy. Gemma has no idea how she's going to handle this with work. Bee's obviously going to have to take a leave of absence from school.

The good news is that Bee's out of danger medically. She was one of the lucky ones. Gemma got to her so quickly that she didn't have to be intubated or put on a ventilator. She hasn't displayed any symptoms of neurological damage. Her oxygen levels are back to normal and at the moment, she's asleep. The only overt sign of her suicide attempt is the ligature mark on her neck. Gemma makes a mental note to tell Ruth to bring a scarf when she visits today. If the bruises aren't hidden Gemma knows her eye will be drawn to Bee's neck again and again. That ridiculous jump rope with the ladybug handles will be imprinted on her memory forever.

Gemma looks out the window. The sky is slowly brightening to a bluish green. She checks her texts. She was supposed to meet Simon for a drink last night.

Ordered you a Manhattan!

Are you almost here?

Drank your Manhattan.

Gem where are you?

Just tried to call. I'm getting worried.

Please reach out as soon as you get this.

His texts are incomprehensible. Alien. Messages from another planet, another life that no longer belongs to her.

The ordinary world of appetizers and cocktails, boyfriends and Burmese takeout, fretting over the water bill, learning to embrace her love handles has vanished. She and Bee have been cast out of that universe. She can feel herself floating up and away. *Before* becoming smaller and smaller until finally it's nothing but a smudge of unidentifiable color. Will there be an *after*? She doesn't know. She can't imagine it. She's stuck in the eternal now.

She texts, I'm sorry Simon but I need some space. Got a lot going on. I'll be back in touch soon.

———

Gemma goes to the cafeteria to get breakfast. She forces herself to sit there and eat like a normal person, one bite at a time, when what she really wants to do is shove the food down her throat and sprint back to Bee's room. When she returns to the ward, she runs into Dr. Baum, who has just come from visiting Bee.

"Gemma," she says, her face suffused with concern and warmth.

Gemma's eyes start leaking, they let down, exactly the way her milk would let down when she just so much as peeked at a sleeping infant Bee. Uncontrollable, the animal body.

"Dr. Baum," Gemma says.

"Jennifer, please."

Gemma hangs her head, the terrible mother, the mother who missed all the signs.

"This is not your fault," says Jennifer. "You understand that, right? Nobody is blaming you for this. *Nobody*."

Jennifer draws her in for a hug and Gemma stiffens. *Is this appropriate? Is Jennifer allowed to hug her?* But it feels so good. A benediction. She clings to Jennifer. They cling to each other.

———

They move to a private room. A framed Ansel Adams photograph on the wall. A bowl of dusty potpourri.

"I want to taper her off the Prozac," says Jennifer. "I'd like to put her on a mood stabilizer. Seroquel."

"A mood stabilizer? Not an antidepressant? I thought she was depressed."

"She is depressed, but I suspect she's been having periods of mania, too. Sleepless nights? Pressured speech? Impulsivity?"

"Yeah, I guess so. Yes."

"I think she's bipolar." Jennifer's bracelets chink. Her tattoos comfort Gemma. *I am rooted. But I flow.*

"Now, I don't want you to worry. We can manage this well with medication. It may take a while to get the right med, and we may have to add in another—oftentimes it's a cocktail that works—but we'll get Bee back on her feet."

Gemma nods. She hesitates and then asks, "Do you think it was the Prozac?"

"That triggered the suicide attempt? Possibly. But maybe not. Did something happen? Was she struggling in school? Failing a class? Did she have a fallout with a friend?"

"I don't think so. She seems to be more popular than ever. Her phone never stops ringing."

"Mmm," says Jennifer.

"You think something happened?"

"You'll have to ask Bee. She didn't disclose anything to me. I think she's waiting to tell you."

The idea of talking to Bee throws Gemma into a panic. *Why* did she do it?

After Jennifer leaves, she opens her Momonymous app and scrolls through yesterday's feed.

LoveYouMore: OMG the Cam shit has hit the fan!

WineLuvva: An Instagram boyfriend is not a real boyfriend. I kept telling my DD that.

LoveYouMore: Well Cam's vanished.

MsFoxy: He deleted his IG account?

BearMama: So sketch. I feel bad for Bee.

WineLuvva: Why? All Cam did was expose the real Bee to her friends. He didn't make up what she said. i.e. my friends are so shallow they're not capable of carrying on a conversation.

OhThePlacesYou'llGo: My friends would stab me in the back in a minute.

LoveYouMore: My friends are so jealous of me.

BarkingUpTheWrongTree: Everything revolves around me.

WhatsUpWomen: Sheesh. Did you ladies memorize everything Bee said?

TotesAdorb: Everybody's talking about it.

WineLuvva: My DD and DS too.

WhatsUpWomen: My DD says Bee hasn't been in school.

WineLuvva: She's probably afraid to show her face.

OhThePlacesYou'llGo: Her poor friends. Imagine having your friend say those kinds of things behind your back.

WhatsUpWomen: Wonder how long it'll take Bee to come back to school?

BearMama: I'd switch schools if I was her. There's no recovering from this.

WhatsUpWomen: I wonder how Gemma is doing. First Study Right and now this!

LoveYouMore: She probs doesn't know. I've heard she's very hands-off with Bee's socials.

WineLuvva: I hate to say it, I'm not one of those "blame the mother" kinds of people, but doesn't she bear some responsibility for this too?

BEE

The smell of maple syrup wakes her. *Wakes her again? Had she spoken to Dr. Baum? Was that a dream?* Her eyes flutter open and she sees her mother sitting on the edge of the bed, leaning forward, her eyes so full of worry they are practically swollen shut.

"Bee. Honey," she says.

Bee wills her limbs to move. She tries to sit up, but falls back onto the pillow. Her neck hurts. Gingerly, she touches it, feels the rough abrasions where the jump rope scraped and dragged at her tender flesh.

"I tried to take it back," she says weakly to her mother. "I called for you but you didn't hear me. I changed my mind."

"*You changed your mind?*" her mother gasps.

Bee realizes this confession will only add to her mother's pain. "I'm sorry," she cries.

Her mother gathers her up into her arms and rocks her like a child and Bee just sobs and sobs. She's ugly. She's hideous. Her lips are parched and cracked. She smells faintly of vomit. It doesn't matter to her mother. She nestles her, nuzzles her. Leaves no inch of her untouched. Let's her know over and over again how beloved she is. How dear. And Bee feels herself beginning to stitch back together. Jagged, loose stiches. Not pretty. Not neat. But not dangling anymore.

"So tell me about Cam," says her mother, after Bee's managed a few bites of pancake. Her throat is so sore. She wants icy cold things. A nice nurse named Susan went to the cafeteria to get her a milkshake. Susan called her *doll*. A sexist term of endearment that Bee would normally reject, but not now. She wants Susan to call her *doll* forever.

She's in a psych ward just for teenagers. The bed next to hers is empty and she's glad. She'd be too embarrassed to have another kid see her this way. Rings on her throat like a tree.

How does her mother know about Cam?

"He's nobody. He's a pig," says Bee.

"Oh?"

"He doesn't even live here."

"Where does he live?"

"San Diego. He's homeschooled." Bee's stomach spasms. *You overdo it with the lols. Makes you sound pathetic. Like you're apologizing all the time.*

"You don't have to worry about him anymore," says Gemma. "I'll take care of it."

"What do you mean you'll take care of it?"

"I'm going to find him. He'll get what's coming to him."

"No, Mom! Please just leave it alone. Leave him alone!" Bee can't stand the thought of dredging it all back up. She wants to bury him forever.

"Bee, I will find him if it's the last thing I do. If he did this to you, he'll do it to another girl. We have to stop him."

Bee thinks of all the terrible things she'd said to Cam about her friends. An exaggerated version of the truth. She liked her friends, and yeah, sometimes they were irritating, just as she was irritating to them. But something happened when she and Cam DMed each other. She felt she wasn't enough. She had to be larger than life in order to impress him. He was so out of her league. She hadn't really meant all the things she'd said. *Everything revolves around me. They don't make a move without my permission.*

"Can I have my phone?"

"I don't think that's a good idea."

"I have to see if he posted anything else about me," she pleads.

"He hasn't. I checked. He deleted his account."

So Cam was gone. The Bee she was with Cam was gone. Everybody must be just laughing their heads off.

———

She confesses everything to her mother. Every horrible thing she'd said about her friends. Her mother shows no surprise. She just looks at her with the most compassionate face.

"No matter what you said, you didn't deserve that," says her mother.

"Yes, I did."

"No," her mother says firmly.

Her mother sweeps the hair from her brow. "And just for the record, so you know this for the rest of your life, so it's clear. There's nothing you could ever do to make me stop loving you."

RUTH

"I want to come to the hospital," says Marley.

"You can't, you have school."

"I think school pales in comparison to your best friend trying to hang herself, don't you?"

Bee is not your best friend, Ruth thinks. *Bee dumped you a long time ago.*

Ruth holds up two silk scarves, a Pucci and an Hermès. "Which one?"

Marley scrunches up her brow. "Are you seriously asking me what scarf you should wear to go visit Bee in the psych ward?"

Ruth puts both scarves in her bag. "Do you have any idea how difficult this is for me? I'm shouldering the entire burden. Gemma's a wreck. I'm going to have to do everything. *Everything.* Not that I resent that. I'm happy to be called upon. She called me, not Simon, by the way. From the ER."

Marley gives her a stare that Ruth doesn't have the energy to try and interpret.

She pulls her shoulders back proudly. "And for your information this scarf is for Bee, not me. To hide her—" She can't bring herself to finish the sentence.

Marley physically convulses. "I didn't think of that."

"No, you didn't," Ruth says, suddenly shaky, surprised to find herself on the verge of tears.

Marley gives Ruth the arched-eyebrow, worried look that makes Ruth feel like a child.

"What would you like for dinner tonight? Salmon? Quinoa cakes?" she asks.

"I don't know if I'll be hungry. I don't want you to go to all that trouble."

Ruth's aware she sounds like a martyr but is powerless to do anything about it. When she found out that Bee had tried to kill herself she had no emotions, and now she seems to have temporarily lost the ability to mask her emotions. She's a wreck, too.

"Text me before you leave the hospital. I'll have something yummy for you when you get home."

———

Ruth meets Gemma in the crowded hospital lobby. Gemma must have had a sleepless night; she looks worse than yesterday. She pulls Ruth down into a chair. Ruth would prefer a more private venue. *Why aren't they meeting in the ward? When will she get to see Bee?* The sliding doors keep opening and shutting, letting in gusts of cold air. Ruth would like to suggest they at least move away from the door, but Gemma has an urgent look on her face.

"It wasn't the Prozac. It was this Instagram—boy. He started messaging her when we were in New Hampshire. They talked, well, they messaged every day. They were very public. All her friends knew. Apparently, I was the only one who didn't know. They were Instagram Official. Do you know what that is? I didn't know what it was." She swipes angrily at her eyes. "Cam. That was his name."

Ruth nods. "Yes. Marley told me about him last night."

Gemma's eyes widen. "And you didn't call and tell me?"

Ruth glances around the lobby nervously. *Are people eavesdropping on their conversation?* "Don't you think we should go somewhere more private?"

Gemma shakes her head, breathing heavily through her mouth. Ruth's withheld information from her; she's furious.

"Gemma, I was going to tell you this morning. I just wanted

you to be able to rest last night. You had such a shock. You were traumatized. I didn't want to add to the trauma."

Gemma's phone chimes. "She's here," she says.

———

Now they find a more private section of the lobby.

"Sophie Knoll, I'd like you to meet Ruth Thorne," says Gemma.

Why is Gemma so nervous? And who is Sophie Knoll? Late twenties. Very attractive and put together. Glossy brown hair with butterscotch highlights. A rag & bone sweater Ruth recognizes from last year's fall collection. Paul Green booties—Ruth has the same exact pair.

"Sophie's a—cyber forensics specialist?" says Gemma. "Did I get that right?"

"Yeah. Think of me kind of like a digital PI. I track down online harassers, extortionists, blackmailers. But my specialty is finding assholes who ruin lives and then just disappear without a trace."

"Like Cam," says Gemma.

"I doubt his name is Cam," Sophie says.

"Ruth's my best friend," explains Gemma. "I need her to be my eyes and ears. I probably won't remember anything you say."

"No worries," says Sophie.

Ruth hates that expression. She forbids Marley to use it. It's *lazy,* that's what it is.

"So, what do you think?" asks Gemma. "Can you help us find him?"

Sophie bobs her head from left to right. "I have to be honest. Since he deleted his account it's not going to be easy."

"Are you saying it can't be done?" asks Gemma.

"I'm saying *I* can't do it. But I have a contact at Instagram. If you give me the go-ahead, I'll reach out to her. Even though he's deleted his account, there might still be some record of his IP address in Instagram's router logs."

"And if you had his IP address you'd know who he was?" asks Ruth.

"We'd know *where* he is—generally, not specifically. An IP doesn't reveal names or personal addresses but it will tell you city, zip code, and the internet provider. If we got the IP it would be a great start. I can't promise you anything, but I'll try my hardest."

"Yes, please go ahead," says Ruth. "We've got to get this son of a bitch so he doesn't do this to somebody else."

Gemma looks deflated; she's got nothing left.

"Okay, so I'll just need a retainer," says Sophie.

Ruth whips out her checkbook.

Sophie looks at Ruth like the dinosaur she is and says, "Can you Venmo me?"

———

Late that night, Ruth's phone pings. MY MOTHER MADE ME DO IT.

HappilyEverAfter: I hate March. It's been raining for days. I'm so depressed, I want to kill myself.

TortoiseWinsTheRace: I've gained 8 pounds since New Year's. I can't stop eating. Any great new diets out there? I want to kill myself too. Well my thighs anyway. I just want to stab the fat off them.

WhatYouSeeIsNotWhatYouGet: My DW is doing the Three Diet. Every meal and every snack she eats one portion of protein, carb and fat.

OneWayAtATime: And that works? There's got to be more to it than that.

WhatYouSeeIsNotWhatYouGet: Well it's really about moderation. You can eat everything, but it has to be the size of your thumb.

HappilyEverAfter: Nobody is listening to me! I just told you all I wanted to kill myself. It was a cry for help! Waaaa! What kind of friends are you?

PennySavedPennyEarned: You shouldn't kid about wanting to kill yourself.

HappilyEverAfter: Sorryeeee. Somebody's sensitive. DH and I are going to Maui next week sans children. Don't worry ladies, I'll get my happily ever after on.

WhatYouSeeIsNotWhatYouGet: Hey, can we talk about Bee and her Instagram boyfriend?

OneWayAtATime: I know this isn't nice to say, but Gemma needed to be taken down a peg. Bee too.

HappilyEverAfter: Anybody know any details? DYING for information.

WhatYouSeeIsNotWhatYouGet: My DD told me the boyfriend looked like a cross between Timothée Chalamet and Ansel Elgort. Who btw both went to the same high school.

HappilyEverAfter: I don't care about that. I want to know what's happening with Bee. She must be mortified. Hiding out.

It dawns on Ruth that she has an opportunity here. The six-month vetting period is almost over. Something big is required.

An offering. A show of loyalty. This is a pod that invited her to roll around in the dirt with them. Roll around with them she must.

PennySavedPennyEarned: I have some information but you have to all agree it won't go beyond our pod.

WhatYouSeeIsNotWhatYouGet: Ooo, tell us.

OneWayAtATime: Absolutely!

HappilyEverAfter: Mais oui!

PennySavedPennyEarned: Okay. I heard through the grapevine that Bee tried to kill herself.

WhatYouSeeIsNotWhatYouGet: What?? Lordy I'm shocked!!!

OneWayAtATime: Did she take pills?

HappilyEverAfter: Did she slit her wrists?

TortoiseWinsTheRace: Oh, this is terrible. I'm so sorry to hear this.

The details rise from Ruth's belly to her throat, clawing their way out of her.

PennySavedPennyEarned: She tried to hang herself from a ceiling fan. With a jump rope.

HappilyEverAfter: Oh that is sick, very sick.

TortoiseWinsTheRace: Well how—how did she—how should I put this? How did she fail at it?

PennySavedPennyEarned: I heard that the jump rope snapped. The doctors said just a few more minutes and she would have died.

OneWayAtATime: OMG.

WhatYouSeeIsNotWhatYouGet: Wow, wow, wow.

HappilyEverAfter: Gotta say, you've got the stuff PennySavedPennyEarned. This is just the kind of insider information we love! Keep it coming!

Ruth shuts off her phone and feels sick. *Why did she sell Gemma and Bee out?* She is a despicable person. Simon was right.

She lays awake most of the night, her stomach churning.

GEMMA

Simon is sitting on her doorstep when she pulls in the driveway. Gemma's come home for a quick shower and to get some clean clothes for Bee. This is the last thing she needs—some sort of confrontation. It's been raining for a week. The lawn is a brilliant green except for under the magnolia tree, where there's an oval of dead grass. *Strange,* Gemma thinks.

She gets out of the car and strides up the walkway. "I told you I needed some space."

"What's happened?" he asks.

"Nothing." Gemma opens her purse and starts searching for her keys.

"Obviously not nothing."

Her purse is the Bermuda Triangle. She puts things in it and they disappear.

"Just sit down with me for a minute. One minute." Simon's tranquil voice soothes her. He's a human Ativan. The opposite of Ruth, who's a human Adderall.

She sits down on the stoop with him huffily, like she's doing him a favor. *Why is she acting this way?* Because he wants something from her and she has nothing, *nothing* left to give. She hasn't even had the energy to call Scott, and it's likely she won't. Two days ago, he'd texted to tell her he'd gotten their father into a clinical trial for a new, promising drug. Scott's on the front lines of his own health emergency—she doesn't want to add to his load.

"I'm so tired. I can barely function."

"Bee?" he guesses.

Gemma swallows audibly. She does not want to cry in front of him, does not want to need him. She's too vulnerable for that.

"Is she okay?"

"No, she's not okay. She tried to kill herself."

Simon's face doesn't betray any emotion and Gemma finds this infuriating. "I said she tried to kill herself. Hang herself, actually."

He nods. "I heard you. And is she stable now?" he asks gently.

"For the moment," she snaps.

Why isn't he shocked? He could at least gasp, for God's sake. His preternatural calm unnerves her. Is it because he's an X-ray tech? Used to seeing people in pain? A wave of exhaustion rolls over her.

"What I don't understand is why you're insisting on going through this all alone. I'm excellent in a crisis. Let me help," he says.

"I'm not alone. Ruth has been with me. She hasn't left my side; she's taking care of everything."

"I see," says Simon.

Everything unsaid is in his *I see.* Judgment. Disapproval. Reprobation.

"What do you see?"

"I don't trust her, Gemma. I don't think she's got your best interests in mind."

Gemma jumps to her feet. "I can't listen to this."

He grabs her hand, tries to pull her back down. She wrenches her hand away from him.

"Look, there are things you don't know. Things that have happened that I need to tell you about," he says.

Gemma shakes her head. "Not now."

"Why? Why won't you hear me out?"

"Because you don't know shit! You have no idea what Ruth has done for us over the years. She's always been there for us, no matter what. She's never left me alone."

Simon gets up slowly, his hands on his knees. "Exactly my point, Gemma."

Gemma finds her keys in the side pocket of her purse. "Please go."

He looks at her with an open face, kindness in his eyes. "You can call me anytime. Day or night. I want to help, Gemma. I want to be there for you."

Gemma opens her door and slips inside.

BEE

"You're sure you don't want to come?" asks her mother. "I'm going grocery shopping. Then to Target. It might do you good to get out. Get some sun on your face. I'll buy you gummy bears," she says in a singsong voice.

Once upon a time gummy bears could make everything right. Now the idea of gummy bears fills her with despair. She's so far past gummy bears. The mood stabilizer has dulled her taste buds. In order to wake them up she needs something extreme like Atomic Fireballs or Toxic Waste sour candy, which they don't carry at Safeway. She shudders at the thought of running into Frankie or Aditi at the market. She's never leaving the house again.

Her poor mother. The look on her face. Forced happiness and cheer while a silent ticker tape runs repeatedly across her brow . . . *we're home now, we're safe, we're good.*

Were they?

"I'd love some gummy bears," she says.

"Great!" says her mother enthusiastically, as if she's just been told she got an A on a test. "Just regular gummy bears?"

"Gummy frogs or sharks if they have them."

"Oh, sharks, fun! Text me if you think of something else you want."

———

They came back from the hospital yesterday. Bee has the weekend off, and starting Monday she'll begin a six-week outpatient pro-

gram. Individual therapy. Teen support group. Yoga. Cognitive be-
havioral therapy class.

Ruth's volunteered to drive her back and forth to Alta Bates
every day so her mother doesn't have to take time off work. This is
a huge relief to her mother. *I don't know what we'd do without Ruth,*
she says over and over again. Both Bee and her mother have taken
to repeating themselves. Neither of them have the strength to call
each other out on it. Staying on the surface requires all their effort.

Bee will take a leave of absence from school for the rest of the
semester. When she thinks about the fall term she's overcome with
fear. *Stay in the present.* That's one way to reduce anxiety. Mind-
fulness is another class she'll be subjected to at Alta Bates. It's an
expensive program. Their health insurance covers only half of it. *I
don't know what we'd do without Ruth.* She's paying for the other half.

Bee picks up her phone. The only person who's texted her in the
last three days is Marley, and she hasn't had the energy or courage
to text her back yet. It's time now.

Hey Marls you there?

I'm here. You home?

Ya

I'm not going to ask if you're ok

I'm sure you've been asked that question a thousand times

By my mother most likely lol

I just want you to know that what he did to you was so messed up

Does everybody hate me?

They're assholes all of them

Do you hate me?

I didn't mean those things I said about my friends

You weren't included in that group

Shit you know what I mean

I'm fine B

You don't have to apologize to me

How could she have forgotten this? The sweetness between them. The loyalty. The history they share. And Bee, she just tossed Marley away and for what? A fake boyfriend. Fake friends. Friends who didn't listen, who didn't care, who probably know she tried to off herself and still haven't reached out.

What do you need right now?

What did she need? To be in her twenties, her thirties. To have put this far, far behind her.

Atomic Fireballs?

Haha I'll be there in an hour

Bee does not want to see Ruth. Even though Ruth has been so helpful, it's exhausting to have her around. She looks at Bee with those sad eyes. A gaze that searches, searches, searches. That drains her like Edward Cullen drained Bella Swan.

Mom's out. I'll Uber, texts Marley, reading her thoughts.

Bee has been so stingy in the past with Marley, doling out her *x*'s and *o*'s one at a time, or not at all. What a terrible person she was. So pinched. So mean.

The doors unlocked xxx

———

Marley's practically bought out Le Bon Bon. She dumps a slew of clear cellophane bags filled with loot on the coffee table: cinnamon bears, watermelon slices, Hot Tamales, blueberry strips, Atomic Fireballs, Toxic Waste sour candy, gummy cola bottles, Ring Pops, saltwater taffy, Bazooka gum, candy corn, and cherry licorice nibs.

Bee knows the candy at Le Bon Bon is five dollars a pound. She must have spent twenty dollars easy.

"It's like Willy Wonka," says Bee. The sight of the candy cheers her enormously. The bright colors. The wacky packaging. The red twist ties. "You got so much."

Marley sits next to her on the couch. She takes a deep breath and says in a small shaky voice, "I'm so sorry, Bee. I wasn't there for you."

"*You're* sorry? For what? You have nothing to be sorry about. You're the only one who's stuck by my side. I should be apologizing to you. I've been such a bitch. I can't believe you still want to hang out with me. *I'm* so sorry, Marley."

Marley waves her away. "No, you don't understand. I haven't been a good friend." Her voice is constricted, like somebody is squeezing all the air out of her throat.

"What? Of course you have. You've been the best. I've been the shitty friend," says Bee.

It's such a relief to say it out loud. To confess to Marley.

"Can you ever forgive me?" Bee asks.

Bee puts her arm around Marley and Marley collapses against her. Bee remembers when they were really young, Marley crying because she was too scared to ski down the bunny hill. How sad she felt at seeing her best friend so upset. She would have gone to war for Marley back then.

"Of course," whispers Marley. "Of course I do."

Bee starts crying and Marley cries with her. Shoulders heaving up and down. Hiccups and gasps. Trying to catch their breath. Finally, the tearstorm passes.

Marley blows her nose loudly. "Well, that was a shitshow," she says. "I wonder how many calories we just burned? Crying really takes it out of you, I hear."

Bee googles it. "One point three calories a minute."

"Awesome! We've earned a reward. Let's move on to the candy portion of the evening then, shall we?" says Marley.

They both sit forward and take in the pile of candy.

"We could start with the Fireballs but if we do that we won't be able to taste anything after," says Bee.

"I suggest we start sweet, then move to sour, then for the finale, the cinnamon family," says Marley. She starts separating the candy into piles.

"Netflix?"

"Oh yeah."

"*WALL-E*?"

"Perfect."

———

A little while later, Gemma comes home. She smiles when she sees the two of them on the couch. Bee feels proud. She's done this— she and Marley. They've made her mother happy. The house feels safe. Like it's waking up after a long sleep.

Gemma puts her phone and purse on the table and carries the groceries to the kitchen.

"Cocoa?" she calls out.

And even though the girls are stoned on sugar, they yell, "Yes, please!" It's the idea of the cocoa, not the cocoa itself, they want.

Gemma's phone chimes five times in a row. "Your phone is going off, Mom!"

"Can you bring it to me, please?" Gemma yells.

Bee grabs Gemma's phone. "Her mom pod," she says to Marley. "IN ONE EAR AND OUT YOUR MOTHER. She's Soccer-Mommy#1." Bee rolls her eyes.

"But you never played soccer," says Marley.

"Exactly the point," says Bee.

MARLEY

"I'll be back in a few hours," says her mother. "Hopefully Kay will be running on time. Her first appointment was booked."

Her mother's hair looks perfect. She's going for a blow-out that she doesn't need. Marley knows it's because she craves touch. Somebody to hold her head, run their fingers through her silky locks.

Marley wants to tell her mother to blink. Her eyes are unnaturally wide open. She's drinking too much coffee and she's so skinny. Her clavicles poke out of her chest like knitting needles.

"When's the last time you ate? Let me make you a sandwich. You need some protein."

Her mother ignores her. "I think I have PTSD. My heart feels like it's beating a thousand times a minute. I need to meditate or sleep or take a hike, or get a massage, but I have to be there for Gemma. Be her rock. I can't let her down."

"Let me help. You need support, too," says Marley.

Her mother pinches her left nostril shut and breathes through the right. Then pinches the right and breathes through the left.

"Can you sit down for a minute before you go?" Marley suggests.

"I don't want to be late." Her mother gathers up her purse. Slings a scarf around her neck. Her skin is mottled red.

"It's so nice you offered to drive Bee to her program. She's really grateful. So is Gemma."

"Yes, well—" Her mother struggles to shrug on a coat over her bulky sweater. One of her arms gets stuck.

Marley tugs on the coat, trying to help.

Her mother squirms. "I don't need any help."

Marley continues to pull at her mother's arm. It's like undressing a toddler.

"I said I don't need any goddamned help! Get the fuck away from me." Her mother spins around and pushes her hard.

Marley reels backward, staggering across the room, fighting to keep her balance. Something has been unleashed inside of her mother. Something she's kept tamped down for a long time is now free and running amok.

Just wait until you get home.

This phrase pops into Marley's head. It repeats itself over and over again on a loop, incessantly, unceasingly, until Marley feels like her brain will explode.

March 19, 10:22 a.m.

Soleil what if somebody you knew did something really bad?

How bad, Marley?

Our conversations are private right? Patient-client confidentiality?

Yes, absolutely. Unless that "somebody" has put somebody else in danger. Is somebody else in danger, Marley?

I'm not sure

Are you in danger?

That's not what I'm saying

Okay, what are you saying?

Just checking for a friend. Yellow heart. Namaste hands

GEMMA

"I'm afraid I have bad news," Sophie says. "He used a VPN."

"What's a VPN?" asks Gemma.

"A virtual private network. It means his IP address can't be traced."

"People can have their own private networks?"

"Sure. People want to browse with anonymity."

"So what does that mean for us?"

"Well, there's a minuscule chance the VPN leaked, but I doubt it. I can't in good conscience continue to take your money and give you hope. I can refer you to somebody else if you like. Maybe they'd have a work-around. I've only been in the biz for a couple of years—there's lots of people with more experience than me."

They are two weeks into Bee's step program. Two weeks tapering off the Prozac and two weeks on the new mood stabilizer. Bee's sleeping well, Warrior Oneing and Warrior Twoing, living mindfully (by taking twenty minutes to eat a raisin), and spilling her guts daily to her support group at Alta Bates—the Wolves. That's what they call themselves. Bee came up with the name. *Did Gemma know that wolves symbolize courage?* No, she had not. The Wolves are also a nod to Virginia Woolf, whom all the Wolves apparently hold in high regard, as does Dr. Baum. *I am rooted. But I flow.* Gemma doesn't love that they seem to be romanticizing Virginia Woolf's suicide, but she lets it go. She much prefers the Wolves to the SLUTZ.

All in all, things are much better. *Is it time to call off the search?*

Continuing to look for Cam keeps him alive, and at this point Gemma would prefer to bury him. Also, there's the cost to consider. Ruth has been paying for the investigation, and it's not cheap: $150 an hour for Sophie's time.

"I wish I had better news," says Sophie. "If you want that referral let me know."

———

Ruth is laughing as she and Bee walk in the door.

"Hey," Gemma calls out.

"You're home! Go kiss your mommy," Ruth says to Bee, pushing her toward Gemma.

Bee kisses her on the cheek. Her scent is a mixture of the outdoors and grapes. Many of the Wolves vape. Every day she comes home smelling of chemical-tinged fruit: banana, strawberry, raspberry.

"Missed you, Mummery," Bee says.

So now Gemma is Mummery. She has no idea where Bee came up with that name but she likes it. It's shaggy and comfortable, like a worn-in recliner.

"You all right?" Bee asks.

This is new, too. Bee asking Gemma about her day. Taking *her* emotional temperature. Gemma doesn't know how she feels about this. She always imagined someday they'd leave behind their mother-daughter roles and become friends, and that period would last a good long time. And then much, much later, they'd revert back to their original roles only switched; Bee would be the mother and she would be the one who needed looking after. What she hadn't expected? For the reversal to come this early. But she never could have predicted that Bee would attempt suicide, either. Her sweet, narcissistic, attention-seeking child. Still sweet. The other adjectives didn't apply so much anymore. She'd molted them. Shed them like a winter coat.

Is this the kind of two-way relationship Ruth has had with Marley all these years? Marley's always so in tune with her mother, providing for her, cooking for her, taking care of her. Gemma was such a fool, turning away from Ruth, her most loyal friend.

And then there's Simon. He refuses to give up on her. He texts her most days. *Thinking of you. Hope all is well. I'm here when you need me.* Not *if* you need me. *When* you need me. She's starting to think that day might come.

"Hey, before I forget, we're having a block party next Saturday. Bouncy castles. Food trucks. A DJ. We'd love to have you guys join us," says Ruth.

Bee shoots Gemma an anxious glance.

"Only if you feel up to it," says Ruth. "You can decide last minute. Just thought I'd throw it out there."

"We'll think about it," says Gemma.

"Going upstairs," says Bee.

"Kay, sweetie."

"Bye, bye, little birdie," Ruth calls out. Bee doesn't respond.

"Do you want some tea?" asks Gemma.

"It's almost five. How about a little wine?"

Normally Gemma doesn't drink on weeknights, but they've been thrust into a new life, so why not create some new rules? She pours them each a glass and they sit at the kitchen table.

"She's doing so well," says Ruth. "It's only been two weeks but there's such an improvement, don't you think?"

Ruth sits slack in her chair, her arms dangling by her side; she looks deeply relaxed. So relaxed Gemma wonders if she's stoned. Or maybe she's taken a pill. She has a medicine cabinet filled with antianxiety meds. She revs high.

"I just love her so much," says Ruth, blinking back tears. "I hope you know that."

"Oh, Ruthie." Gemma reaches across the table and squeezes her hand with its perfectly manicured nails. Ruth's winter shade is Red My Fortune Cookie. Gemma's nails are bitten to the quick, her cuticles ragged. Maybe Ruth will notice. Maybe Ruth will invite her to the Claremont for a mani-pedi. It's time to start taking care of herself again. Pay attention to her grooming. She's really let things go.

———

"Do you want to stay for dinner?" Gemma asks. It's six thirty. They are well into their second glass of wine. "Marley can Uber over."

"No, I'd better go home. You're welcome to join us. Marley's cooking, and she always makes too much. We'll be eating leftovers for days."

"Marley is amazing, you know that, right?"

"She's a good girl."

"And so smart. So on it all the time. She'll probably end up at Stanford or Cal."

"We'll see. She watches *Gilmore Girls* obsessively. She probably wants to go to an Ivy. Leave the West Coast before the big one comes."

There's too much to perseverate about. Mudslides. Fire. Earthquakes. Her paltry emergency supplies. But those were worries for another day.

"So, listen, I talked to Sophie today. She says she's at a dead end. Apparently Cam used a VPN."

"What's a VPN?"

"A private network. Like a private browser, I guess? It makes you untrackable. Untraceable. Whatever, they can't find you."

Ruth huffs. "I've never heard of such a thing."

"Well apparently it's real. And people use them all the time, according to Sophie."

Ruth's mouth puckers. "She doesn't know what she's doing. She's only been at this a little while. Let's hire somebody with some real experience."

The thought of starting anew with another cyber forensics person exhausts Gemma. She wants to put Cam behind them and she wants Ruth to agree, to give her permission to get out. But is that lazy? Neglectful? Should she be pursuing Cam to the ends of the earth?

"Don't worry, I'll find somebody else. Leave it with me," says Ruth.

Gemma sighs.

"What is it?"

"It's just, oh, Ruth, I'm tired. The idea of starting from square one with another investigator just makes me so—"

"So you're just going to give up?" asks Ruth.

Gemma takes in Ruth's raised eyebrows, the surprise etched into her forehead in the form of three horizontal lines—*reproach*.

"No, that's not what I mean. I'm not giving up!"

Ruth gives her a droopy dog smile that's meant to comfort but instead is deeply unsettling.

"Darling, calm down, I'm not judging you. Whatever you decide is fine," she says.

"I just want to be done with him."

"I know. I do, too."

"I want to put him behind me. Behind us. *Forever*."

Ruth sucks on her upper lip, thinking, and then finally nods her head in the affirmative. She's such a fighter. Gemma knows it's not in her character to let this go.

"Maybe it's best," she says.

"It's not that I don't hate him. That I won't go to my grave wishing the very worst for him. I've imagined his death. Gunned down in a car. Pushed off a bridge. Dismembered," says Gemma.

Ruth's eyes bug out ever so slightly. Gemma knows she's going too far, but she has to let this part of her have a voice.

"He fucked with my kid. He made her want to kill herself. I'll never get over that, never stop hoping he'll get his comeuppance.

But at what point does my attachment, *our* attachment, to finding him become unhealthy? As long as I keep looking, he's alive. *I* keep him alive. *I* keep us bound together. But if I stop—well, I think something will lift. Some darkness. Am I being naive?"

"No," Ruth says. "You're right. It's time to let him go."

RUTH

Ruth calls Marley from the car. "Sorry, got stuck at Gemma's. Did you cook?"

"Yeah."

Ruth's stomach growls; she's starving. She feels so light, a wisp, like she could just drift away. The nightmare is over. They've made it through. They're moving on.

A car pulls out in front of her, causing Ruth to slam on the brakes. Normally she'd tailgate the person. Today she slows down. She feels herself swelling with love and gratitude. Maybe she can hit the mall after dinner. *With Marley?* No, she won't drag Marley along. Marley's made her position clear. No more shopping sprees and no more Eileen Fisher, which is a shame, because it looks so good on her. It's time to let Marley make her own fashion choices. Let her wear H&M. Let her wear Brandy.

"Gemma's made a decision. She's going to stop investigating Cam."

"Okay," says Marley, as if this news is no big deal, but to Marley it *is* no big deal. Her focus is on Bee's recovery, not tracking down Cam.

"I hate the thought of him getting away with it. I just hate it. But I think it's the right decision. A positive step. We need to look toward the future."

—

Ruth has arranged to have the Peloton bikes delivered on Saturday.

The doorbell rings.

"Would you mind?" she calls out to Marley.

An unsuspecting Marley pads away in her sheepskin slippers. The door opens. She hears Marley gasp.

"Where do you want these?" The deliveryman's gruff voice.

Marley walks back into the room, her eyes wide.

"Are you surprised?" asks Ruth.

Marley's face is flushed with happiness.

"They're Peloton bikes. The best spinning bikes you can get. They have thousands of online classes. And not just spin. Yoga. Stretching. Lifting. I know you hate the gym. All those people watching."

"I don't know what to say, Mom. Wow!"

"They cost two thousand two hundred dollars a piece," says Ruth. Another fault she'll have to correct. Telling people what you've spent on them doesn't make you deserving of love. She's deserving of love no matter what, isn't she? She doesn't have to buy people off.

"We're going to have so much fun," Ruth squeals.

"Where to?" says the deliveryman, getting impatient with their little love fest.

The following morning, they take the Peloton bikes for their first spin. It's glorious! The two of them competing, Marley unsuccessfully trying to chase her down. Ruth isn't even repulsed by Marley's profuse sweating. Look at her girl go! If she Pelotons five days a week, Ruth calculates, the weight will just slide off. By summer she could be nearly svelte. Maybe she could get into a bikini.

BEE

Bee's exhausted. Three more weeks to go in her outpatient program. Then what does she have to look forward to? Online classes, but that's the only computer access she'll have. Her mother deactivated all her socials.

"You know both my parents died when I was six," says Ruth, coming to a stop at a red light. "We have that in common, losing a parent at a very early age."

Bee traces a *B* on the window with her finger.

"It fucked me up," says Ruth. "I've never gotten over it."

The light turns green and Ruth accelerates. The inside of her car is like a cockpit. It smells like mint and limes. After years of wearing nothing but Angel, Ruth has finally changed her perfume. It's a big improvement.

"I wonder how it is for you," says Ruth.

Bee was only three when her father died. She has memories, but she suspects her mother has fed them to her, and over the years she's just claimed them as her own.

Like the time they went to the San Francisco Zoo and they were cleaning out the lion's cage and they put the lion in with the cheetah, and the otherworldly screaming that ensued from both the giant cats at the injustice of being made to share a cage made her fly into her father's arms. "It's okay, Beelicious, I've got you," he said. *Beelicious.* Nobody had ever called her that again.

She was so jealous of Marley, who got to spend a good part of the summer with her father. She remembers calling Marley one July and begging her to come back to Oakland.

"Please, please come home," she pleaded. "Nothing is the same without you."

Bee heard laughing in the background, music. The sound of footsteps, somebody being chased around the kitchen table.

"I can't. We're going swimming," said Marley. "Daddy just put on my water wings."

Bee's throat swelled with jealousy. "I can't believe you still wear water wings. What a goddamned baby."

She didn't even really know what *goddamned* meant, but she knew it wasn't nice. Her mother said it when bad things happened.

Marley gasped, as if Bee had punched her, and Bee had hung up on her.

"I don't even remember him," says Bee to Ruth.

"Really? You don't remember *anything*?"

"No."

"Well, I do and it was worse, much worse for me. I was six, and I lost both my parents at once. Do you know how they died? Has your mother told you?"

Bee's unsure of how to respond. If she says no, Ruth will be insulted. If she says yes, Ruth will go into all the gory details. She can tell by the edge in Ruth's voice that she's getting worked up. Soon she won't be able to hold in her feelings any longer, and she'll expel them at Bee.

Most of the rides with Ruth are okay. They talk about books and movies and celebrities. But a couple of times a week Ruth devolves. *Devolve.* Is that the right word? Vocabulary is not Bee's strong suit. *Malfunctions? Crumbles? Shatters?*

"Has your mother told you?" Ruth repeats.

Bee can hear her pulse pounding in her ears. "Yes, of course she has. That must have been so difficult."

"Difficult is an understatement." She stops at a red light so abruptly the tires screech. "I died that day. What you see here? This person sitting in front of you?" Ruth bobs her head rapidly. "Is a corpse," she hisses.

"I'm so, so sorry," whispers Bee.

"Well, I'm sorry for you." The light changes and the car behind them beeps. "Fuck you, mister," says Ruth into the rearview mirror. "Your life was ruined, too, Bee."

No, it wasn't. Her life wasn't perfect, but it was good, it was okay, it was getting better, wasn't it?

As they make the turn onto her street, Ruth says, "It's my mother I miss the most. I was her world. I was her—*person*—and she was mine."

She shakes her head. "That's all I want. Is that too much to ask? One person that's mine?"

Ruth pulls into the driveway.

"That sounds nice," says Bee.

"It does, doesn't it?" Ruth's deflating now. The hot air seeping out of her.

"Tomorrow, I'll bring snacks," Ruth says.

Bee knows an invitation is required. "Do you want to come in?"

"When will your mom be home?"

"Not until late she said, seven or eight," Bee lies.

"Really? She's never that late."

"New client, I guess."

"Mmm," says Ruth. "Right."

Bee waits to be released.

"You can go now," says Ruth, waving her away.

Bee unlocks the front door, aware Ruth's watching her. She should tell her mother how weird Ruth's being, but she doesn't want to stress her out. She's so worried about everything. Ruth's taken a huge load off her by driving Bee to and from her program.

Bee lets herself into the house and shuts the door, her heart rat-a-tat-tatting.

MARLEY

Her mother is in a vicious mood when she returns from dropping Bee off.

"Ten times a week, times three weeks. That's thirty rides," she shouts. "You'd think she'd be more grateful."

"Bee could Uber."

"Yes, Bee could take an Uber, on my dime."

"But I thought you wanted to drive her. You insisted, didn't you?"

Her mother glares at her. "A part of me thinks Bee deserved what she got. She was so full of herself. Shoving her *boyfriend* in everybody's faces." Her head hinges forward, waiting for Marley to agree with her.

"You have nothing to say to that? Nothing to add?"

"Not really."

"Fine, then go to your room."

"It's four thirty. For the night?"

"Yes, for the night."

"But I haven't eaten."

"I think you can go one night without dinner, don't you, Marley?"

Her mother follows her up the stairs and locks her in. "See you in the morning, my darling," she trills.

April 8, 5:01 p.m.

Is it illegal for somebody to padlock their kid into their room every night Soleil?

Are you asking for a friend?

Maybe

Are you asking me to read between the lines?

I don't want to get anybody in trouble. I'm fine. I can take care of myself. I don't want you to call child protective services or anything. You have to swear you won't

I can't swear that Marley.

Then I can't tell you

Face sighing. Okay I'm not going to press you for details. But if I feel you're in any danger I'll have no choice but to report it, so don't put me in that position unless you're prepared for that outcome, got it?

Got it

BEE

Her mother wanted to splurge and take the four of them out to Wood Tavern, but as soon as she suggested it, Bee got a stomachache. She wasn't ready to leave the house yet.

Other than going to Alta Bates, Bee hasn't been out in public. She's desperately afraid of running into kids from school. She knows this will happen soon enough, but she's not prepared. She has a skin but it's newborn. A few more weeks of toughening up, then she'll go out. But tonight—it's lasagna and salad at home.

"I've been looking forward to this," says her mother, setting the table. "All of us together. It's been a while."

"Has it?" Bee throws the cherry tomatoes into a colander and runs water over them.

"Well, you've seen Marley, and obviously Ruth, and I've seen Ruth, and occasionally Marley, but the four of us haven't been together. Not since—"

"You can say it, Mom. Not. Since. I. Tried To. Kill. Myself."

Her mother sighs. "Not since you tried to kill yourself. There. Happy?"

Bee turns off the water. "Every time we say it out loud it loses its power. Remember the SLUTZ?"

"How could I forget?"

"Same principle."

"Okay, you slutz."

Bee cracks a smile.

The front door opens. "Hello, the house!" Ruth calls out. She doesn't bother to ring the doorbell.

Marley follows her, an aluminum foil–covered plate in one hand, a Macy's bag in the other.

"Marley made cranberry chocolate chip cookies!" Ruth crows. She beams at Marley, *enraptured*. Bee loves that word. She's recently discovered it and uses it all the time. Had she been enraptured with Cam? No, she had not. She'd been *addicted*.

Habituated, hooked, dependent, under the influence, strung out. All words to describe what happened with Cam. He was like a drug. He got into her bloodstream and started changing her cells. She lived for her fixes, his DMs. Eventually she overdosed on him (or he overdosed her) and now she's detoxing.

Sometimes Bee feels eighty years old. She knows so much now. That you don't actually have to do drugs to become an addict. That a person can do that to you, too. Make you obsessed with them. Own your every thought, every move. Until one day you wake up and realize everything you do is for them, is *because* of them.

Bee takes the plate of cookies from Marley. "You look so pretty." Marley's blown out her hair. She's wearing lip gloss.

"We've been spinning every day," says Ruth. "Doesn't she look good? She's lost weight. I'm taking her to Lululemon this weekend. Do you want to come?"

And just like that Bee's lightheartedness soars off and abandons her. Sustained happiness is not something she can count on yet. It descends upon her once in a while, a quaking, feeble thing.

"That's such a nice offer," says her mother.

"Maybe," says Bee.

The lasagna is delicious. Her mother has put both sausage and ground beef in the tomato sauce. Bee gobbles up two pieces. She's aware that Ruth is glad Marley is eating less, and her mother is glad Bee is eating more.

After the dishes are cleared, Marley says, "I got something for you, Bee."

She hands Bee a Macy's box. Inside, nestled in tissue paper, is a Hello Kitty sweatshirt. Bee's immediately transported back to their first Aspen Christmas. When they still believed in Santa Claus. When they watched TV in their matching Hello Kitty pj's, their hair damp and smelling of hot tub chlorine.

"I remember," says Bee, touching the soft cotton.

"You two," says her mother. "Look at them, Ruthie. Our darlings."

Marley says, "And Gemma, I want to say how grateful I am to you."

Gemma raises her eyebrows. "That's so nice, Marls. But it's me who should be thanking you. And Ruth. The both of you. I don't know where we'd be without you."

"I don't know where I'd be without *you*," says Marley.

Marley's not done. She's going around the table apparently. "And you, Mom? I owe everything to you."

Ruth visibly stiffens. She looks like she's bracing herself for something bad. Marley's not a big emoter.

"Um, well, that's very nice, darling."

"I know I don't say it often. Maybe I've never said it. But I wouldn't be who I am without you."

Ruth gives a little gasp. Pleasure slowly spreads across her face, like a tide coming in. Bee knows how much it means to her to have Marley say this in public, in front of them.

"Well, then," says Gemma, with a huge smile. "Could it be a more wonderful night?"

Ruth gazes at Gemma with shining eyes.

MARLEY

Later that evening, nostalgia washes over her as she sits on the couch with her mother, watching *Gilmore Girls*. Oh, Lorelai! Oh, Rory! Oh, Stars Hollow!

"They're just like us," says her mother.

They're nothing like us, thinks Marley.

Marley coughs. A few minutes later she coughs again, harder.

Her mother feels her forehead with the back of her hand. "You're a little warm. Maybe you should hit the hay." She frowns. "I forgot, setup for the block party will be underway at the crack of dawn. And Gemma never got back to me about it."

Marley leans her head back and closes her eyes.

"Let's get you to bed," says her mother. "And if you feel better in the afternoon, we'll make that trip to the mall."

———

Hey B. Can you guys come to the block party tomorrow? Marley texts.

Mom really wants you to come

Will there be anybody from school there?

Nobody from school lives in our neighborhood. Please B. Don't make me go through another of these stupid things alone. You should see the way my mother acts. It's so embarrassing. Oh here's my daughter Marley. She got 1550 on her practice PSATs

You already took a practice test? And you got 1550?

Haha Jk!! PLEASSEEEE!!

KK winky face

Can you come early to set up?

I guess. What time?

8:30?

8:30? You're killing me Marls. But that should be ok. See ya then xxx

RUTH

Just as she's about to turn off the light, Ruth's phone pings. Her pod.

HappilyEverAfter: Yoo-hoo! PennySavedPennyEarned? Are you up? Burning the midnight oil?

PennySavedPennyEarned: Unfortunately yes. Made the mistake of drinking two espresso shots before going out to dinner tonight.

TortoiseWinsTheRace: Dinner where may I ask?

PennySavedPennyEarned: At a friend's house.

HappilyEverAfter: You have other friends besides us haha?

PennySavedPennyEarned: Old friends. I haven't seen them in a long time.

TortoiseWinsTheRace: Stop torturing PennySavedPennyEarned! Just tell her!

HappilyEverAfter: Very well, PennySavedPennyEarned. We want to extend a formal invitation to join our pod. Congratulations! You've made it into MY MOTHER MADE ME DO IT!

PennySavedPennyEarned: Really?? I'm so happy!

OneWayAtATime: We know we've put you through a long vetting period, but we promise you we're worth the wait.

TortoiseWinsTheRace: We're sending you something. A little present. You should get it tomorrow. Keep an eye out.

PennySavedPennyEarned: How wonderful! The only thing is my neighborhood block party is tomorrow. The streets will be cordoned off. Did you mail it? Or were you going to drop it off?

HappilyEverAfter: We'll get it to you somehow. We have our ways!

PennySavedPennyEarned: I'm on the verge of tears. You have no idea how much this means to me to be accepted into the pod. Thank you so so so much!

WhatYouSeeIsNotWhatYouGet: No, thank YOU! You're going to be a fabulous addition to our group!

———

Ruth's heart ricochets around in her chest. She tosses and turns, unable to sleep. Finally, the alarm goes off at seven thirty and she permits herself to get up. She showers, brushes her teeth, and puts on her Stella athleisure wear. A light dusting of powdered foundation and one coat of Glossier mascara.

She tiptoes down the hallway past Marley's room. A part of her wants to wake her—Ruth's dying to share her good news—but she had a fever last night. Let her darling daughter wake naturally.

She makes a full pot of coffee; screw the turmeric ginger tea. She needs a caffeine infusion. If she could, she'd open a vein and shoot it in.

She sits at the table, legs crossed, her left foot bouncing up and down. She's helpless to stop it from jittering, it just moves on its own accord like it's trying to make a run for it. Honestly, she doesn't even need the caffeine. Her happiness is jet fuel. She doesn't need sleep or oxygen or food or water. Just this—this fairy-tale future bearing down on her. Finally, after all these years.

The doorbell rings and Ruth practically jumps out of her chair.

"Good morning, sunshine," crows Gemma. She and Bee stand on her doorstep and Ruth time travels back to the kindergarten party. Gemma, in her dowdy wraparound skirt and clogs, Bee, in her polyester Old Navy tracksuit.

Ruth darts forward and gives them both big hugs. "What a surprise! What are you doing here?"

"Marley said you needed help setting up for the block party," says Bee. Bee looks like she just dragged herself out of bed.

"Oh, that's so nice. I didn't even know you guys were coming to the block party. I mean, I never heard back from you about it." *Shit.* She keeps a smile plastered on her face as she thinks, *Marley. Upstairs. Padlocked into her room.*

"Aren't you going to invite us in?" asks Gemma. "I smell coffee."

"Of course." Ruth opens the door wide.

———

Ruth puts a mug of coffee in front of Gemma. "I don't have any soy milk, sorry. I have half and half?"

"Black is fine," says Gemma.

"Do you want some?" Ruth asks Bee. "Just a titch."

"I'm not supposed to have caffeine. It makes me—" Bee waves her hands over her head wildly.

"Oh, right. We have orange juice. Water?"

"I'm good," says Bee.

Ruth sits down at the table. She glances at the stairs nervously. She's got to find an excuse to get up there and unlock Marley's door.

"Where's Marley?" asks Bee.

"She wasn't feeling well last night. She's still sleeping," says Ruth. "I'm going to wake her in a minute."

Ping, ping, ping, ping. Gemma's phone lights up.

Gemma glances at her phone. "My mom pod. It's eight thirty on a Saturday morning. This better be good."

Ping, ping, ping. IN ONE EAR AND OUT YOUR MOTHER is blowing up. Gemma looks at her phone and gasps.

"What?" asks Ruth. Gemma slides her phone over to Ruth.

HappilyEverAfter: OMG I found Cam!

Now Ruth gasps. *What is HappilyEverAfter doing in Gemma's pod?*

HappilyEverAfter: Anybody there? I said I found Cam.

LoveYouMore: Who are you HappilyEverAfter? And how did you get access to this pod?

TotesAdorb: Wait, you found Cam? Bee's Instagram boyfriend?

"She found Cam." Gemma's voice cracks.

"I don't want to know," Bee whimpers.

"Bee, living room. Put your earbuds in. Netflix, Spotify, that serial killer podcast. Whatevs. I don't care, just listen to something," says Gemma.

Bee exits the room quickly, her eyes wide with fear.

"Don't leave me," Gemma says to Ruth. "I can't do this alone."

She shuffles her chair right next to Ruth's so they can both see the conversation as it unfolds in real time.

HappilyEverAfter: Do you want to know who he really is?

SoccerMommy#1: YES.

HappilyEverAfter: KK! Weee! Here we go!

A screenshot of a Mac appears. Photos of Cam border the page. In the center is a Photoshopped pic of Bee in a bikini and Cam waxing his surfboard. The photo that made them Instagram Official. #mine.

On the top of the screen are the Mac's stats: power 76%, Sunday, February 5, 12:58 p.m., Ruth Thorne.

"Huh?" Gemma says, bewildered. "What is this? Why does she have your computer?"

HappilyEverAfter continues to download screenshots from Ruth's Mac. The rabbit hole of her search history. *Teenage boy longish hair delicate features tall pretty.* Which leads to Slick, a small modeling agency in San Diego, which leads to a seventeen-year-old boy named Cam Phillips who skateboards and plays the guitar and loves poetry.

DuckDuckGoose: I don't understand. What are we looking at?

LoveYouMore: Holy hell!!!

TotesAdorb: Is this what I think it is?

DuckDuckGoose: I repeat. What are we looking at?

LoveYouMore: Ruth Thorne's computer.

DuckDuckGoose: But why does she have pictures of Cam?

LoveYouMore: Because she IS Cam! Because she made him up.

Ruth hiccups. She burps. She can't get enough air in. Her sweat smells of hay. Of barn. She's disgusting. A cow. A thin cow, a practically anorexic cow, but bovine nonetheless.

Stop it. Pull it together. This is happening. You have to deal with this now.

Gemma's mouth is open in a rictus of shock and disbelief. She's trembling. She's quaking. Is she going to collapse, or is she going to attack Ruth, beat her over the head with her fists?

"Gemma, please," she begs.

Ruth gets up and tiptoes backward in terror.

GEMMA

"I have no idea what's going on. You have to believe me, Gemma," Ruth pleads.

Gemma is numb. She can only feel the outline of herself. She's one of the stick figures Bee used to draw in kindergarten.

This can't be happening. This can't be happening. The first time she felt this way, completely emptied in shock, she was standing at the top of the basement stairs looking down at Ash's crumpled body. His left leg twisted beneath him at an impossible angle. The halo of blood encircling his head. The second time was barely a month ago, seeing her precious Bee splayed out on her bedroom floor, unconscious. The jump rope noose around her neck. Her cheeks stippled with tiny red dots. *Petechiae.* It wasn't until later that she learned the proper name for the burst blood vessels.

And now this. She stares at her phone, blinking, still not completely taking it in. A trickle of sweat runs down her side. She feels light-headed. She wants to sleep. *Do not faint,* she berates herself.

Ruth has a file of Cam Phillips photos. She also has an account at Apps-R-Us. On December 28, she purchased twenty-two followers for Cam's Instagram so he wouldn't seem like a friendless stalker. On December 29, when Cam made first contact with beebee15, Ruth googled *"teenage texting slang," "emoji dictionary," "how to flirt over text," "what does slide into dms mean?"* In her Dropbox is a Cam dossier.

A screenshot of Ruth's notes:

Cam's homeschooled, off the grid and analog, up until now, thus providing a valid explanation as to why there's no sign of him online. His parents are free spirits. He spends every spring in Costa Rica on a pineapple farm. High EQ, he's sensitive, honest, and open. A surfer, a cat lover. Fav foods Dragon Rolls and kimchi. He's looking for a community of like-minded kids who don't follow the pack. Not exactly Bee's Instagram persona, but who she really is. He'll pull the real, authentic Bee to the surface, and then when he's reeled her in, he'll take her down.

Gemma's numbness lifts and in its place comes a boiling rage.

"Why?" she cries, bolting up from the table. She corners Ruth, traps her against the fridge. "Why would you do this to Bee? You love her!"

Ruth covers her eyes with her arm, and Gemma tears her arm away from her face. "No. You don't get to hide!"

"I didn't do it. I swear I didn't. Gemma, you have to believe me! Somebody else did this!" Ruth's face gnarls with anger. Her mouth is a dark slash. "Somebody who hates me. Who wants to ruin me. To tear us apart. Please, please, you've got to believe me!"

Gemma stares at her oldest friend incredulously. What a brilliant performance! Academy Award winning, really. How could she have been so fooled?

"Help me," Ruth begs.

Bee runs into the kitchen and gestures up at the ceiling. They hear a pounding sound. "Marley," she says.

Ruth slides to the floor in defeat. "Marley," she repeats dully.

A muffled shriek. Bee runs up the stairs with Gemma at her heels.

They stop short of Marley's door, stunned. "I can't believe this," pants Gemma. "She's padlocked her in."

Bee presses her face against the door. "It's okay, Marls, we're gonna get you out," she croons.

"Come with me," Gemma instructs Bee.

They go downstairs and confront Ruth. "Give me the key," Gemma says.

Ruth cowers. "I don't know where it is. Don't hurt me, please."

"Stop playing the victim. You're a monster," Gemma hisses.

Ruth gags then sprints to the bathroom and slams the door. Gemma and Bee hear her retching. They tear through the house, opening drawers and cupboards, looking for the key that will set Marley free.

MARLEY

Marley has stopped pounding on her door. She's in the backseat of her mother's car on a hot day in Sacramento. Desperate for her mother to release her into her father's care.

Just wait until you get home, she'd said.

———

That summer between first and second grade, Marley did a stellar job of forgetting her mother's warning. She was gloriously happy. She didn't know there was a name for what she could do. *Compartmentalize.* Shunt bad things off to the side. Lock them away in a drawer for future contemplation. Or bury them so deeply they were irretrievable.

But as soon as Marley got back into her mother's car in August, she remembered her mother's—curse? *Is that what it was?* Marley was so young. She still thought of everything in fairy-tale terms. She prayed her mother had forgotten.

And it seemed she had. She showered her in kisses. Stopped by In-N-Out Burger on the way home and let her order a large vanilla milkshake. *You deserve a treat, Marley bear.* That's what she said.

When they got back, the house was shining and clean. Marley, a little less so. Her mother sprayed her perfume in the air and Marley walked through the scent like it was a hallway. *Never be so pedestrian as to spritz perfume directly on your skin,* her mother told her.

That night, after her bath, after a glass of chocolate milk, Ruth tucked Marley in. She read her three books, one more than usual.

Then she kissed her on the forehead and shut off the light. Marley fell asleep to the sound of her mother laughing softly downstairs. She was watching *The Jeffersons*.

Marley slept the sleep of princesses who had been slipped magic potions. And when she woke it was late. *Why hadn't her mother gotten her up?* she wondered.

Because her mother was gone.

———

Marley washed her face, brushed her teeth, and combed her hair, just the way her mother had taught her. *Nobody likes a slovenly little girl*. She changed into a dress. Cotton eyelet. Fluttery sleeves. Embroidery at the neckline and hem.

She was hungry but didn't eat—her mother hadn't given her permission. She didn't go to the bathroom; her mother hadn't given her permission to relieve herself either. She sat on the couch in the living room, stiffly, upright, waiting for her mother to return. Perhaps she'd gone out for bagels. For La Farine almond croissants, her favorite. For steamed dumplings.

At noon, Marley couldn't hold it in any longer. She belled her dress around her thighs so it wouldn't get wet, and peed into the couch cushion. Relief and fear. The cushion absorbed the urine, but the fabric was wet. Frantic, she turned the cushion over. *Would her mother be able to tell?*

The hours dragged by. The sun moved through the house, bathing the rooms in a golden light. She followed the light, from the living room to the family room to the media room to the kitchen. And then all at once, night descended, and Marley understood she was being punished.

She'd betrayed her mother. She'd done something unforgiveable. She'd left her and now it was payback time. Or maybe, she had this all wrong. Maybe her mother had gotten in an accident. Driven her car over a cliff, just like her parents had. Maybe right now, this very minute, she was an orphan! Like Sara Crewe in *The Little Princess*. But wait, she had a father. She couldn't be an orphan if her father was still alive, could she?

She didn't dare sleep. She didn't dare turn on the lights. She sat on the floor in her drenched underwear, breathing through her mouth so she wouldn't smell the stink of her pee.

At 2:00 a.m. she crawled under the kitchen table, a refrigerator full of food just three feet away. She cried out with hunger pains so sharp they made her curl up like a bug marooned on its back. On the island, a bowl of apples. A bunch of bananas. Not for her.

When Ruth finally came home at eight the next morning, with proclamations of love, with bagels and almond croissants, it was too late. Marley had transformed into something not quite human.

"Marley, Marley bear," her mother had cried, holding her arms out wide for a hug. "Did you think I wasn't coming back?"

She skittered away from her mother, across the floor like a rat, blinking in the light. A scuttling creature, not fit for this world.

———

Marley hears Bee and Gemma at her bedroom door, whispering. The sound of a key being inserted into the lock. The door swings open. They stand there, love and pity in their eyes, and something else—pride.

They think they've saved her, but she's past the point of saving and has been for a long time. Still, she lets them embrace her.

"Come," says Gemma. "Let's get you out of here."

PART FOUR

GEMMA

It's been a week since Cam's true identity was revealed and once again, the Howard family is in the headlines, only this time they're the victim (aka the *unidentified mother and daughter*) not the perpetrator. It's been all over the newspapers, as well as local and national TV. Gemma is pressing charges against Ruth. She found a young, eager lawyer who's willing to represent her pro bono. More and more of these kinds of cyberbullying cases are being successfully prosecuted. Also, apparently, Marley had a text therapist named Soleil, who had filed a formal report of child abuse with CPS. That would help their case enormously.

Meanwhile, Ruth has gone underground. Gemma drove by her house the other day and it had clearly been vacated. All the shades were drawn, not a light on. There was a sign on the door. PLEASE RESPECT OUR PRIVACY DURING THIS DIFFICULT TIME. Somebody had scrawled FUCK YOU BITCH!! on the sign with a red Sharpie.

Both Gemma and Bee deeply felt the loss of the Ruth they thought they knew; it was like a death. They were also enraged. The lengths she'd gone to! The scheming! The manipulation! Gemma remembers telling Ruth about the VPN and Ruth pretending she had never heard of such a thing. *So you're just going to give up?* she'd asked her.

The day after she'd exposed Ruth, HappilyEverAfter sent one last message to their pod.

HappilyEverAfter: Check out this link, ladies. #blessedDDs

The pod had been going crazy trying to figure out HappilyEver-After's identity and how she got access to Ruth's computer. Love-YouMore had responded to her message within seconds.

LoveYouMore: Don't open that link!! It could be spyware. It's probably how she hacked into Ruth's computer.

Who was HappilyEverAfter? She could be anyone; Ruth had plenty of enemies. But really, Gemma didn't care who HappilyEver-After was. She'd be forever grateful to her. Let her have her anonymity. That was the whole point of Momonymous, wasn't it?

The question she'd ask Ruth, if she were ever to talk to Ruth again (which she decidedly will not) is *why*. *Why did she go after Bee?* But she's starting to think that she was the intended victim; Bee was just collateral damage. Gemma was the true source of Ruth's envy and rage.

———

Gemma's just poured herself a cup of coffee when her phone rings.

"Hi there," says Ed, Marley's father. "How's our girl doing?"

Gemma had called Ed as soon as she'd gotten Marley back to the house on that terrible morning. He made it to Oakland in record time. When Marley saw him standing on the doorstep, she flew into his arms. Gemma and Bee had gone upstairs to give them some space. When they came downstairs a little later, they found them snuggled on the couch. Marley in the crook of her father's arm, looking so young and vulnerable.

"Thank you," Ed had croaked, his voice thick with emotion.

He'd been with them for two nights, then he'd gone back to Sacramento to get the house ready for his daughter's arrival. Soleil suggested Marley stay with them for a few more days; Gemma and Bee were a bridge between her past and her future and Marley wasn't quite ready to cross over yet.

Gemma insisted Marley sleep in her bed so she could keep an eye on her. Marley, so deprived of physical affection, spooned her, her hand around Gemma's waist all night long, as if she was afraid Gemma would vanish. That love would vanish.

In the mornings, she'd wake weeping and Gemma would hold her in her arms until she'd cried herself out.

"I'm so sorry," Marley repeated, over and over again, like a mantra.

"You've done nothing wrong. This has nothing to do with you, Marls, nothing," Gemma told her.

Marley's shame was the most painful thing for Gemma to witness. She hated Ruth the most for this, forcing her daughter to carry the burden of her sins.

"She's doing really well," Gemma says to Ed. "Stronger. She gets a little more of herself back every day."

"I just can't believe all this. It's so hard to fathom what Ruth did to Bee." His voice breaks. "I didn't know it was so bad for Marley. She didn't tell me. She kept so much from me."

Suspecting Ruth's claims that Ed was a sex addict were lies, she'd asked Ed about it. He was horrified at the rumors she'd been spreading about him—none of them true.

"I should have sensed what was going on. I should have gotten her out of there years ago," he says.

"It's not your fault, Ed. Ruth was a master at deception. At making you feel like you were the one who was crazy."

Thank God she hadn't told Ruth about her father's diagnosis. Gemma can only imagine how Ruth would have weaponized that information to make her even more helpless and dependent.

"Whatever attention I gave her, it was never enough," says Gemma.

"And it never would have been. I hope you're not blaming yourself for any of this," Ed says.

But something set Ruth off. Something triggered her, pushed her over the edge. Was it Simon?

Simon has been texting Gemma. Messages of support. Concern. And an invitation for coffee this very morning that she hasn't yet responded to.

There are things you don't know. Things that have happened, he'd said. Had Ruth tried to ruin Simon's life? Had she tried to destroy him, too?

"So, she'll be on the one p.m.?" Ed confirms.

"I wish she'd let me drive her."

"She wants to take the bus. She said it makes her feel independent. It's important to her that she leave Oakland on her own terms."

"It's due in at two thirty-five," she says.

"Great. We're all ready for her."

"We're going to miss her terribly," says Gemma.

———

Gemma texts Simon. *I'll be there in twenty. If you still want me.*

Corner of Thirty-eighth and Iverson, number 201, he texts back immediately.

She grabs her keys and purse. "Girls!" she yells. "I'm going out for breakfast. There's cereal and Eggos. I'll be back in a little bit."

"Wait," shouts Bee. She and Marley tear down the stairs.

Bee throws her arms around Gemma. "Where are you going, Mummery?"

Gemma hesitates, then says, "Simon's."

"Really?" Bee wags her eyebrows at Gemma. "You haven't seen him in ages. Does he know you're coming?"

"Yes, sweetheart, I was invited."

Gemma asks Marley, "Are you all packed?"

Marley couldn't bear to go back to her house, so Gemma had taken her to H&M to get some new clothes. At first, she'd asked Gemma's permission about everything. *Is this top okay? How about these jeans?*

"It's your choice," Gemma had said. "It's totally up to you."

That's when she realized Marley had not been allowed to choose her own clothes. That explained all the Eileen Fisher. Poor Marley never stood a chance.

When they got home, Bee had played stylist and Marley put on a fashion show. Marley was so beautiful, looking her age in a high-waisted skirt and cropped sweater. Bee and Gemma had applauded for her, and Marley practically levitated she was so happy.

"I'm all set," says Marley.

"And you're sure you want to take the bus? You can change your mind. I can drive you."

"I'm sure."

———

"Come in," says Simon.

Simon's place is eclectic and cozy. A well-worn leather couch. A collection of vinyl records arranged alphabetically in a refurbished 1970s credenza. Framed posters from the Fillmore: Jimi Hendrix, the Yardbirds and Country Joe, The Grateful Dead and Big Mama Thornton.

A gangly teenage boy sits at the kitchen table, a bagel on a plate in front of him, cut neatly into four sections.

"Gemma, this is my son, Tom."

Gemma can see the resemblance. He and Simon have the same square jaw. The same dark curls. But Simon's got thirty pounds easy on Tom, and Tom's cheekbones jut out from his face like twin buttes.

"Hello," he says rather formally.

"Hi, Tom." Gemma feels a rush of affection for him. "I'm so glad to finally meet you."

Tom doesn't answer her. "Can I start?" he asks his father.

"Of course," says Simon.

Tom tucks in. His manners are impeccable. He wipes his lips after each small bite. He eats the pieces of the bagel clockwise.

"Coffee?" asks Simon.

"Yes, please."

Simon pours them both a cup and they sit on the couch in the living room.

"Okay if I turn on some music, buddy?" Simon asks.

"Yo-Yo Ma's Bach Cello Suites," requests Tom.

"You got it," says Simon.

"Impressive taste for a sixteen-year-old," says Gemma.

The sound of the cello fills the room and Tom closes his eyes. His fingers pluck the air. One-two-three. One-two-three.

"He's not your usual sixteen-year-old," says Simon proudly.

"I'm neurodiverse," says Tom, his eyes still closed. "I'm an autistic person, *not* a person who has autism. There's a difference. Autism isn't an affliction. It's who I am. I don't need fixing. I was born this way."

"That's right, bud," says Simon.

Tom's eyes snap open as a car rumbles by. "Subaru WRX with a boxer motor." He folds his napkin. "Can I play Fortnite?"

Simon glances at the clock. "Go ahead."

Tom walks past them, sniffing the air. "She doesn't smell like anything." He goes to his room and shuts the door.

There's complete silence for a minute or two and then Gemma, stunned, whispers, "Why didn't you tell me?"

"Tom isn't a strong test-taker," confesses Simon. "If he attends college he'll have to go to a test-optional school."

"But you brought him to Study Right. He got five hundreds on his PSATs."

"He's never taken his PSATs."

"You lied about that?"

Simon nods miserably.

"You said he went to Athenian. Was the life of the party. Gets invited everywhere. Did you lie about that, too?"

Simon grimaces. "I guess that's what I'm hoping will happen. He doesn't go to Athenian, he goes to Jupiter Academy in Berkeley. It's a school for neurodiverse kids. He has a hard time making friends, but things are getting a little better on that front. He actually went bowling a few weeks ago with some kids from anime club. It's a great school. Besides academics, they work on social interactions, time management, transition skills. The whole goal is to prepare the kids for independent lives. That's what we're working toward."

His gaze drifts across the room and lands on the mantel. A photo of Tom as a toddler, sitting on Simon's lap.

"But why did you lie about him? Did you think I couldn't deal with it? *That I'd dump you?*"

"You wouldn't have been the first."

"His mother?"

"She left when he was three."

I feel your pain. Gemma despises that cliché, it's so maudlin and hollow, but in this moment it's true. She actually feels Simon's pain. It pierces her skin and burrows down into her.

"And you thought I'd leave, too? You thought I was that shallow?"

"It's more complicated than that." Simon blows out a breath. "I answered a Craigslist ad for an acting job."

"An acting job? You're an *actor*?"

"Yeah, or I used to be."

"What kind of an acting job?" Gemma's mind reels. She's truly going down the rabbit hole.

"Hold on." Simon grabs his computer, opens a tab, and hands her the laptop.

Seeking male actor for the role of X-ray technician/single dad. Must be over six feet. Age 35 to 50. You are fit, handsome, charming, funny, educated, and erudite. If you have to look up the definition of *erudite* you need not apply. Pay EXCELLENT if you meet all the qualifications.

"Ruth placed the ad. I answered it. I fit the part, I guess."

Gemma's brain contracts. *Labor pains,* she thinks. The struggle to push the truth out. To make sense of it. She presses her fingers to her temples, trying to relieve the pressure. "So you're *not* an X-ray technician?"

"No." Simon's eyes pool with shame. "Gem, you have to understand I was desperate. Tom's school is so expensive and I hadn't booked a job in months. We have a wonderful sitter, Clyde, who takes care of Tom when I'm not here." He gulps. "It all adds up. And sometimes, it's just overwhelming."

"You're an actor," Gemma says flatly.

"Ruth offered so much money. I couldn't turn it down."

"And what was the acting job she hired you for?"

"I tried to give the money back. I told her I couldn't do it any longer and our deal was over. I hadn't counted on what happened. That I'd like you so much."

"What was the job, Simon? Tell me," Gemma demands.

He exhales audibly. "To meet her best friend, make her fall for me, then dump her. Break her heart."

Gemma gasps.

"She threatened to expose me if I told you the truth. I wanted to come clean so many times, but I didn't see how it would work. If you found out she'd hired me, that I'd taken money from her, that'd be the end of me. The end of us."

So Simon was a practice run for Cam. First Ruth tried the boyfriend hoax on Gemma. Sent a fake, but real, potential boyfriend her way. Had that boyfriend lure her in, gain her trust, and make her fall for him. But something went wrong. He fell for her, too, and he refused to dump her. So when Ruth decided to run the same con on Bee, she'd learned her lesson. She didn't hire a real boyfriend, instead she invented a boyfriend who could be easily erased with a simple tap of the delete key.

Goddamned Ruth.

Gemma is not unaware of her shortcomings. She has a history of trusting the wrong people. Being seduced by money and class. She's easily persuaded. Easily duped. Okay, let's just say it, she's a mark. Julie Winters and Ruth Thorne are fine examples of that. But she's no angel. She's also capable of cruelty. Of turning her back on others and walking away without a second thought. A protective device that only grew stronger with Ash's death. A bulwark against the pain she knows is coming for her. But that's no way to live, is it? Waiting for the next catastrophe?

"When were you going to tell me?"

"I've been trying to tell you for weeks. Since Bee's—" He drifts off.

"What do you want me to do?"

He shrugs. "Forgive me?"

Tom's door opens and he pops his head out. "Tesla Model S. Normally silent, but occasionally you can hear the compressor releasing air to regenerate the humidifier. Did you hear it?"

"Sorry, I missed it. We were talking," says Simon.

"Is she going to be here for lunch? Because I'm not sure we have enough hot dogs for lunch. Does she eat other things?"

"Yeah, buddy, she eats other things. Like steak burritos, and tea leaf salad, and soy lattes with two pumps of vanilla." He gives her a sad smile.

Tom shuts the door.

"We were in trouble and I panicked. I'd do anything for my son, *anything*. But I understand if you move on. I do. I would. I'm an asshole. I've deceived you and betrayed you. Could you ever trust me again?"

Gemma *has* been betrayed. By Ruth. By Simon. By *life*. Ash had been taken from her, and she almost lost Bee. And since then, she's been living in this sort of in-between place, unsure if it was safe to return. But now she has a decision to make. She can continue to keep her distance or she can rejoin this messy, flawed, and exquisite world. Embrace its dizzying ascendances and jaw-dropping plummets. Its swerves and curves. Its open road.

Simon gestures to her coffee. "Can I top that off for you?"

She hesitates a moment and then hands him her cup.

RUTH

Ruth watches Gemma and Simon through the picture glass window and feels *nothing*. She exists both inside and outside of herself. She's the actor and the audience in a police procedural. Hiding out in her car, a bag of almonds on the passenger seat beside her, a cooler on the floor.

She's been surveilling Gemma for a week now. Following her at a safe distance on her daily errands and hoping for a Marley sighting. Finally, she was rewarded a few days ago. Gemma had taken Marley to the Emeryville mall. To H&M. Crap, disposable shit, but Marley was practically leaping around with joy.

Oh, the look on her face! Like she'd just been granted clemency and had been released into the world after years of unjust captivity. Marley had blocked her. Marley had canceled her. She might never speak to her darling daughter again.

HappilyEverAfter—that backstabbing bitch. *I don't think you want to make any more enemies than you already have,* Mr. Nunez had said to her at back-to-school night. Any number of people could have wanted to take her out.

And just how had HappilyEverAfter done it? How had she accessed her computer? That gif. That link that she'd been stupid enough to click on. The intruder was on her front step, and Ruth had just flung open the door and let her in.

A daughter is the happy memories of the past, the joyful moments of the present, and the hope and promise of the future. Hahahahaha.

Gemma's Camry is parked a few car lengths in front of her. Ruth grips the steering wheel, fighting her urge to ram into it.

After that reunion dinner at Ruth's house last August, after the apologies, the pleas for forgiveness, the pledges of loyalty, the Mango Lime Chiffon Cake, Ruth did some google searches, watched some YouTube videos, and went to Target, where she purchased a disposable foil turkey pan, a headlamp, and a wrench.

Then she drove to Gemma's. She tiptoed up her driveway and kneeled next to her Toyota Camry. She put the wrench in the turkey pan and slid it under the car. Then she switched on her headlamp, lay on her back, and slid under the car, too.

She loosened the drain plug with the wrench. At first the oil just dribbled into the pan, but within seconds it became a steady stream. When she'd drained most of the oil, she tightened the plug again, but not all the way, so it would look like the oil had been leaking for a while.

Ruth felt proud of herself. One video on how to change your oil would have sufficed, but she watched five, just to be sure. She dumped the full tray of oil at the base of the magnolia tree in Gemma's yard. She watched, fascinated, as the grass absorbed the oil. It made a sucking sort of sound.

The next morning when Gemma called, *I think I just blew the head gasket in my car!* Ruth suggested maybe it was time to buy a car.

"I can't afford a new car," Gemma had said.

Ruth had paused, as if she were thinking, as if she hadn't already priced out the latest Camrys. "I can," she told her, indebting Gemma to her once again.

She hadn't known that would be one of the few high spots of their eight-month-long renewed friendship. After that it was a slow descent to the bottom. To this very moment. Abandoned by everybody. On the run, living in her car like a poor, homeless person.

Well, not quite poor. And not quite living in her car: she's taken a suite at the Four Seasons in San Francisco. Ruth retrieves an open bottle of Les Belles Vignes from her cooler, pulls out the cork, and takes a long draught. She doesn't taste the gooseberry and flint notes. She's drinking for volume, not palate.

Goodbye Gemma. Goodbye Bee. Goodbye Marley, who thinks she's finally free.

She eats seven almonds then drifts down the street in her Model S.

BEE

Bee and Marley climb into the backseat.

"It's like the old days," says her mother, smiling at them in the rearview mirror. "When you were both in booster seats."

Bee's wearing the Hello Kitty sweatshirt that Marley gave her. She feels like the little girl she once was, back when she and Marley were bessies, before backs were turned and doors were closed and friendships severed.

How shallow she was. How loathsome she'd acted. Would Marley ever truly forgive her?

Her mother punches Concord Trailways Station into her GPS.

"You're sure you don't want me to drive you?" she asks Marley. "I just checked. There's no traffic. I could have you there in a jiff."

Marley shakes her head.

"The bus station it is, then."

Bee won't be going back to Hillside in the fall; she'll be attending Oakland Tech. She can't wait. It's way bigger than Hillside, more than five hundred kids in each class. Hopefully, her history won't follow her there. Everybody at Hillside knows she's the so-called *unidentified daughter* who was catfished and cyberbullied into trying to kill herself. Tech will be a new start.

"I wish you could stay. Come to Tech with me. Move in with us," Bee whispers to Marley.

She's broached this idea with Marley nearly every day she's been with them but knows it'll never happen. Of course she's going to live in Sacramento with her father. That doesn't stop Bee from wishing for it, though.

Marley gives her a sad face.

"I'm going to miss you so, so, so much," says Bee.

She and Marley hold hands all the way to the bus station.

They park and walk Marley in. She purchases her ticket and they join her to wait in line to board the bus.

"Oh, my sweet girls," says her mother, getting all emotional. She draws Bee under one arm, Marley under another. "It's going to be okay. We're all going to be okay," she murmurs.

As much as Bee would like to believe this is true, she knows it isn't. Some of it will be okay. And some of it will suck.

This is it. This marks the end of my childhood, she thinks, standing here at the bus station, wearing a Hello Kitty sweatshirt, in a huddle with my mother and my best friend.

MARLEY

Marley waits until she's halfway to Sacramento before logging on to the Momonymous pod she created, MY MOTHER MADE ME DO IT.

Marley's brilliant avatars: WhatYouSeeIsNotWhatYouGet, TortoiseWinsTheRace, OneWayAtATime, and HappilyEverAfter. She's been plotting her mother's demise for a while. Putting the pieces in place. Being patient, oh so patient. Playing the long game.

With Soleil, slowly revealing the terrible things her mother had done to her, exactly as an abuse victim would. In fits and starts. Confessions followed by retractions. *I shouldn't have said that. My mom's so great. She'd do anything for me winky face.* She'd made Soleil pull the abuse stories out of her. Extract them like wisdom teeth.

Marley's no victim. She'd learned the art of sabotage from the master, and then she'd gone and lapped her.

Because she would be the most obvious suspect (as she had direct access to her mother's computer), Marley had HappilyEverAfter send her mother a link to a gif. This was Marley's cover, the way she would hide in plain sight. The gif was harmless, but her mother wouldn't know that. All the Hillside moms were so terrified of unwittingly downloading malware.

Then Marley went to work setting up the Instagram account to catfish Bee. First she installed a VPN on her mother's laptop, which served two purposes. It would hide Marley's online activity and, later on, it would make it look like her mother was trying to cover up her tracks.

She dumped photos into files. She purchased fake Instagram followers from Apps-R-Us. She took screenshots of everything. She created the digital trail that would be her mother's undoing.

Finally, she launched Cam's Instagram and had him reach out to Bee with the perfect bait—an Emily Dickinson poem. Whenever they DMed, she was careful to sound like a grown-up trying to sound like a teenager, when really, she was a teenager trying to sound like a grown-up who was trying to sound like a teenager.

Her original plan was to have Cam break up with Bee and that would be the end of it. But as she got deeper in, she realized it wasn't extreme enough. She had to make it look like her mother had done something horrendous, so taboo there'd be no coming back from it. And so she'd taken it one step further and posted the DMs of Bee trashing her friends.

Marley never imagined Bee would try to kill herself. Her intended prey was her mother, not Bee. She felt unbearably guilty; she tried to help Bee move on, but no amount of Atomic Fireballs or Netflix binges would make up for her betrayal. Marley hoped she and Bee would remain close, but she knew that was unlikely. She'd have to live with what she'd done.

When it was time to execute the final part of her plan, she'd gone back to Apps-R-Us one last time and purchased an invite to IN ONE EAR AND OUT YOUR MOTHER, Gemma's pod. Then came HappilyEverAfter's big reveal. She'd set her trap and she'd sprung it. It was a KO.

She doesn't think anybody else was suspicious of her, except maybe Mr. Nunez. She'd made the mistake of letting her mask slip a few times in front of him. The night of the talent show, when he'd warned Bee to stay away from Marley, he wasn't protecting Marley, he was trying to warn Bee. And the day Lewis Singleton fell on his face in the cafeteria? She'd asked him a simple question about VPNs that he couldn't answer. *Shouldn't a brogrammer know these kinds of basics?* So he'd gone to Mr. Nunez and asked the question on her behalf. He told her this at lunch, thinking she'd be pleased with his resourcefulness. Instead she was so furious, she tripped him. Mr. Nunez was skeptical when she'd told him Lewis had fallen, but he never connected the VPN question back to her mother or to her.

Marley returns to the Momonymous app and shuts down her pod. Her screen populates with a row of mailboxes. The doors open, the original invites fly out and flap away like birds, in search of the original invitees, with a new message.

We're sorry to tell you the MY MOTHER MADE ME DO IT pod has been deactivated. Please pod with us again!

Marley puts her laptop away and smiles. Luciana painted a mural of the night sky on her bedroom (formerly the office) ceiling. Oscar needs her help with his times tables. Her father had already filled the fridge with her favorite foods. Her heart skips. It jumps. It leaps.

"Excuse me, I need to use the bathroom," Marley says to her seatmate.

The woman moves her legs to the side and she squeezes past. Once freed, Marley dances down the aisle. She shimmies her hips. Runs her hand over the top of her head. Wipes her shoulders clean of imaginary dust. People look up and smile as she goes by.

For the first time in her life, all eyes on her.

ACKNOWLEDGMENTS

This book wouldn't exist if not for the brilliance of my agent, Elizabeth Sheinkman. You've been a true partner for over a dozen years. Simply put, I wouldn't be where I am without you.

My stellar editor, Marysue Rucci, who saw this book's potential and helped me realize it: thank you for making this book immeasurably better with your keen editorial insights, gentle nudging, and enthusiasm.

I want to thank everybody at Simon & Schuster, particularly Hana Park, Brittany Adames, Leila Siddiqui, and Heidi Meier, who shepherded this book into the world with great care. Thank you to copy editor Shelly Perron. Also thanks to Rex Bonomelli who designed the stunning cover.

Sylvie Rabineau—I'm beyond grateful to have you in my corner.

A huge thank you to Joanne Catz Hartman, Robin Heller, and Elizabeth Stix—my most trusted beta readers. You read draft after draft and offered invaluable observations, suggestions, and course corrections. I'm indebted to you all.

Also thanks to Dianne Click, Kathy Derby, Lisa Moscaret-Burr, Lisa Rubin, Vickie DeArmon, Graziella Louise Gulli, and Dawn Gideon who gave much needed feedback and encouragement.

Thank you to Amy Weston who years ago planted the seed for this novel by suggesting I write something entertaining and fun.

Benjamin Gideon Rewis—my "teen culture consultant"—

thank you for saving me from making myriad embarrassing mistakes.

And lastly, thanks to Benjamin Rewis, who has been on this journey with me for nearly thirty years. This is your book as well as mine.

ABOUT THE AUTHOR

Melanie Gideon is the bestselling author of the novels *Did I Say You Could Go, Valley of the Moon,* and *Wife 22,* as well as the memoir *The Slippery Year: A Meditation on Happily Ever After.* Her books have been translated into thirty languages. She was born and raised in Rhode Island and now lives in the Bay Area.